As above the fiddler played . . . .

The steerage passengers were not allowed on the decks of the *Lady Franklin*, so it was a matter of wonder for Liam O'Donnell when the ship's clerk appeared in the hatchway and shouted, "Pass the word for the fiddler and the whistle-player, they're wanted on deck!"

As Liam was launching into a jaunty version of "The Trip to Sligo," Mary O'Donnell lay listlessly on her bunk, her mind wandering the fields and hills of the land she'd left behind. Suddenly a sharp pain flared in her belly. She felt a sticky warmth on her thighs, and her face became ashen gray. "Jesus, Mary and Joseph," she whispered, "I'm losing the baby!"

Every fiber of her wanted to scream, but she pressed her lips together and struggled down from the bunk. She had to find Liam. Where was her husband when she needed him so?

She staggered to the stairway and up toward the open hatch. "What's this?" a voice growled. "No steerage scum on deck, that's the orders."

Trembling violently, Mary pushed herself up onto the open deck. Where was Liam?

"Oh no, you don't, you black Irish bitch!" Rough hands grabbed her and shoved her backwards, and she tumbled down the steep stairs to the deck below. Now, at last, she allowed herself to scream . . . .

from the Shamrock Shore

ian Kavanaugh

A DELL/JAMES A. BRYANS BOOK

Published by
Dell Publishing Co., Inc.
1 Dag Hammarskjold Plaza
New York, New York 10017

Dell ® TM 681510, Dell Publishing Co., Inc.

ISBN: 0-440-02798-5

Printed in the United States of America

First printing—October 1982

1

Farewell to old Ireland, the land of my childhood
That now and forever I'm bound for to leave
Farewell to the land where the Shamrock is growing
It's the bright spot of beauty and home of the brave.

It's hard to be forced from the land that we live in
Our houses and farms we're obliged for to sell
To wander alone among Indians and strangers
To seek some sweet spot where our children may dwell.

the day promised to be fine and mild. White drifts of mist still lingered in the dells, but already the August sun was drying the droplets of dew that bejeweled the heather. In the distance, beyond the roofs of the town, steep-sided Knocknarea loomed purple, its flat top crowned by the great cairn of rocks that marked the grave of Queen Maeve. Rain clouds were gathering over Sligo Bay, graying the waters beneath them, but farther out the broad Atlantic gleamed its brightest blue under a brilliant sky.

Liam O'Donnell was only twenty years old, but his neighbors accounted him a man of education and culture. From Sean McLynn, the hedge-schoolmaster, he had learned to read and write, in both English and Gaelic, and much besides. He could make his way through an ode of Horace in the original Latin. He knew the history of his race from the ancient sagas of Cuchullain and Fionn Mac Cumhaill and Brian Borumha. And from the English poets, from Wordsworth and Keats and Shelley, he had learned to look on Nature with an appreciative eye.

Another time he might have savored the landscape before him, taking delight in the play of light and shadow, the subtle contrasts of colors. Not this morning. Instead, he stood near the door of his cottage as if he had been turned into one of the stone dolmens that dotted the fields in that part of the West of Ireland. He was blind to the wide prospect of mountains and sea. For Liam O'Donnell was staring at the face of Death.

At evening the day before, returning home, he had seen the fields green and flourishing, the visible promise of a great harvest. Now every stalk was blackened, as if scorched by the flames of Hell. Breaking his immobility, Liam strode to the edge of the field and fell to his knees, scrabbling with his hands in the soft loam. Moments later he saw what he had known he would find. At the base of the blasted stalk, where a fine large potato should have been, was a black lump of putrifaction, soft with its own rottenness. He gagged as the odor of it rose to his nostrils.

"Jesus, Mary and Joseph!"

Liam's wife Mary, scarcely eighteen and heavy with her first child, stood in the doorway of the cottage staring at the blighted crop with wide, frightened eyes. Warned by her sudden pallor, Liam sprang up. He reached her just as her knees gave way and she started to slump to the ground. At his touch, she looked around and seemed to see him for the first time. She clutched at his supporting arm with both hands.

"Liam, what are we to do?" she cried. "God save us,

8

the Hunger is upon us again! Whatever are we to do?"

He stroked her thick black hair, smoothing it back from her white brow, but his eyes were still fixed on the ruined potato field. "I have no notion at all," he said quietly, "but you're not to be exciting yourself so in your condition."

"My condition! And am I to bear the child only to see him starve or be carried off by the fever as all those of our blood were two years since? I'll not do it, Liam! I'll throw myself in the Garavogue first!" Angry blotches of red flamed in her cheeks, and her eyes met his with a kind of defiance that faltered and faded under the steady pressure of his sympathy.

His arm tightened around her waist. "Rest easy, *a cuisle mo chroí*," he said. "You'll only upset yourself and frighten young Tom. Is there any tea in the house?"

"Devil a bit; no, nor sugar either. But who are we to be talking of sugar to our tea, when winter will find us starving altogether! Liam, what are we to do? How will we live?"

"However we can." He helped her inside, to the big room that served them as kitchen, parlor, and bedroom all in one, and lowered her to a chair near the hearth. "Do you rest here a while," he said gently. "I'll just be going down to town now, to seek for news and a bit of tea. It may be the rest of the country is not in so sorry a state as our own field. And we've still the oats and rye, after all. There are many folk in a worse plight."

Mary's eyes flashed. "Aye, and many more turning to dust! Will it keep me from feeling the hunger to know that others are dying in a ditch? But there," she

9

added in a softer tone, "you go on to town and see what you can learn. Tom will be back with the milk soon, poor motherless lad. Oh, Liam, I pray I am taken before him. I don't think I could bear to watch him starve; it would break my heart entirely."

"That's enough talk of dying, enough and more! Tom's a healthy boy and equal to his sad trials, and with the sister's care you give him, he is sure to thrive. Come, Máiread love, leave these dire thoughts behind you and look in the fire for the shape of our dream land, as we did when we were courting. I'll return as soon as ever I can."

"Yes, Liam," she answered submissively. Her arms, in her lap, seemed to close protectively around her swollen belly, and he saw a bleakness in her dark eyes. "But lately, when I look into the flames, I seem to see our country moving away from me. I try to draw it back, or move after it, but still it goes, away and ever away, like a swan on the lake in the evening mist. Then the peat blackens and crumbles as it burns, and falls in upon our world like a night that has no dawn. Liam, I'm frightened!"

He knelt before her and took her hands in his. "I am pledged to you, Mary, to you and our child, aye, and to your poor orphaned brother as well. Our fates are in God's keeping, but what I may do, I will. You have my oath on it. But you must save your strength, to give me the help I'll need if we are to come through this trial unharmed. You owe it to the babe. Now, rest you here, and I'll be away."

She clung to his hands for a few moments more, then he gently disengaged them, gave her an encouraging smile, and left. The smile vanished the instant he was out of her sight. He did not believe that he had deceived Mary, and he knew that he could not deceive himself. The potato crop was ruined entirely. No amount of oats and rye, or Indian corn from the tiny stocks, could make up for the loss. It was as Mary had said. The starving time was upon them once more, and this time it was striking at a country that had already used up all its reserves.

The Blight had first appeared in Ireland three years before, brought, so it was said, from England and before that from America. In a nation that depended entirely on the potato, even a partial failure brought hunger and suffering to many. Liam still recalled the morning he unearthed one of his father's storage pits, to find that three hundredweight of potatoes that they had counted on for the winter had become a stinking mass of liquid corruption. Still, they had survived.

The next summer, of 1846, was all a farmer could ask. The fields bloomed and flourished, and everyone nodded sagely; for was it not a law of nature that a good year followed a bad? But in a few days their hopes were as blighted as their fields. By the middle of August, not a potato plant blossomed in all of Erin. The Hunger was upon them in truth.

It was not a time Liam liked to recall. His father, Owen, was a man still in the prime of life, but a year of skimping on his own food to feed his wife and children had weakened him. In late November the cold descended to his lungs and carried him off. His sacrifices were not enough to save little Kathleen, who died two months short of her fifth birthday of brain fever, or seven-year-old Bobby, who followed her to the grave a month later. And with Spring, the typhus came, reaping a hideous harvest among a people already inches from death. One of the many thousands it took was Liam's mother Dierdre; Mary lost both parents and two sisters to it.

But more bitter still than the heaped dead and the mass graves was the memory of watching the provisions ships loading in Sligo harbor. English soldiers with loaded muskets had ringed the docks while thousands of bushels of grain and countless sides of Irish bacon and tubs of Irish butter were carried aboard for shipment to wealthy, overfed England, while Irishmen starved and died where they dropped by the roadside. The butter and pork and grain were the tribute demanded by the great English landlords whose great grandfathers had seized the land by force, but that did not stop the London newspapers from saying that the Famine was a myth, since Ireland exported food!

No one knew, no one would ever know, how many had died in that Famine year. A million perhaps? The number was too large for Liam to grasp; but he knew of parishes within a half-day's walk of Sligo that had once been home to five thousand souls but now stood deserted. Whoever had survived the hunger and the fever had fled, to the mines and mills of England or to the far fields of America. And as fast as they went, the bailiff's men pulled down the cottages and moved in sheep. The villagers in their despair had tried to live on grass and failed, but the sheep succeeded.

Not many had the strength or the heart to get in a new planting of potatoes in 1847. Liam did. The only one of all his kin to survive, he felt that he would betray their memory if he did not keep struggling to the last. And he had a new wife and a young brother-in-law to provide for as well. As if in reward of his determination, the weather was fine, with just the right balance of sun and light rain, and the blight did not reappear. Liam's crop was one of the best in his memory, and so too were those of his neighbors. But still the Hunger kept its grip on the country, for not one field in five had been planted. Too many farmers had in desperation eaten their seed potatoes and there was no money to buy more.

As the Spring of 1848 approached, a new fever had seized the stricken nation, a fever to plant as large a potato crop as possible. Men borrowed every penny they could, pawned their kettles and bedding and the very coats from their backs, to buy seed potatoes. Farmers who had survived two years before on their green crops now planted no cabbage or beans or kale, sowing the plots with potatoes instead. The survival of the country was wagered on the turn of a single card. The wager had been lost.

The fields on either side of the lane were as blighted as Liam's own. Here and there he saw a solitary figure standing between the rows of blackened stalks, but he called to no one and no one greeted him. From a windowless sod hut he heard a keening wail, a thin shrill cry that raised the hairs on the back of his neck. In the next field, Paddy Donovan was digging up the rows at a frantic pace, trying to find a single sound spud. He did not look up as Liam passed. A few yards along, Liam turned and saw that Donovan had fallen to the ground, his spade still clutched in his hands.

Moments later Liam had forgotten him. He was not callous—he grieved for all his hard-pressed countrymen—but Mary and their unborn child had first place

13

in his thoughts. He had decisions to make, and if they were all to survive, he must think quickly and choose correctly. Already the conviction was growing in his mind that only heroic measures would save them. But what would Mary say? How could he convince her that his plan was their only hope?

The sound of a horse's hooves roused him from his bleak thoughts. He looked up to see William Orne, the young solicitor who was the local factor for the Marquess of Sligo and for other important landowners, including the Ormsbys of Cummen from whom Liam held his farm. Orne was also, without the knowledge of his patrons, a figure of some importance in the Young Ireland movement. He and Liam had often discussed politics over a glass of porter. Orne was sure that the Irish people were ready to rise against their English rulers the moment the word was given. Liam was just as sure that people were too starved to think of rebellion—unless the rebel leaders could promise to feed them.

Orne's face was grim as he reined up beside Liam. "It's a sad, sad day for Ireland," he said.

"It is that."

"You've heard the news then?"

"Heard? What should I hear that my eyes do not tell me? I can see for meself that the crop is ruined entirely."

"Crop?" Orne seemed puzzled, then he looked around and his face cleared. "Oh, the potatoes! Yes, what a shame. But I was speaking of the news from the south."

"If it is so bad as to make you forget the return of

the blight, it must be terrible indeed. But I've heard nothing from the south at all. What is it then?"

"The worst news possible! The rising has failed completely. Habeas Corpus has been suspended, Meagher and Smith O'Brien are jailed, and there are warrants out for hundreds of Young Irelanders."

He glanced around, to be sure they were not overheard. "Man, it was pitiful! McManus and Smith O'Brien made a stand at Ballingarry, but no more than twenty men stood with them, and half of those armed with no more than rocks and sticks. What kind of people are these that will not strike a blow for their own liberty? That allow the tyrant to imprison their leaders? That meekly bend the neck to the conqueror's yoke?"

Liam took a deep breath and forced down the rage that had boiled up within him. He reminded himself that Orne was an honest man who was risking his career and reputation for the cause. It was not his fault that he had been born into the Protestant Ascendency and had never, even in the darkest days of the previous year, known want. But how could anyone be so blind!

"What kind of people?" Liam repeated, in a voice that shook with passion. "A defeated people; a starving people; a desperate people. Man, look at the fields! Let the English hang our leaders for treason, the blight has already passed a death sentence on the whole land! In six months the Irish Question will be solved, for there will be no Irish!"

Orne looked around again more slowly, as if waking from a deep sleep. When he spoke, his voice was low and uncertain. "It's '46 come again, isn't it? There will be great misery this winter, I fear."

"Nearer than that. Most folk are hungry already, and were looking for relief to the first of the new crop. I look to hear of deaths from starvation before the summer is out."

Orne nodded soberly and looked again at the blackened fields. "I fear this will leave Lord Sligo no choice but to go on with his plan."

"And that is?"

"To clear his estates of tenants and bring in sheep."

Liam's face hardened. "And will he make his name a curse and a hissing, like Lord Palmerston, who herded his tenants half-naked into coffin ships and set them adrift on the cruel ocean? I have heard it said that honest folk whose fathers paid him good rent for a hundred years are now begging in the streets of New Brunswick and Quebec, and count themselves blessed to have survived the journey at all."

"It doesn't have to be that way," Orne protested. "Look at Gore Booth: his tenants went well-supplied, in sound, well-founded ships, and write back to thank him for saving them from the fate of their countrymen."

"Aye, perhaps, but it's a dirty business, forcing people from their homes and tumbling whole parishes to rubble. I'd not thought Lord Sligo was one for such a game."

"What would you have him do? I waited on his lordship at Westport House four days since, and he is living upon coneys snared in his park. Think you, his estates are worth some seven thousand pounds in rents. A fortune, you say, but the Poor Rates alone are more than six thousand under the new Act, and it is three years since any rents have been collected. No one can pay. His lordship's steward told me in confidence that the only ready money in the place comes from renting the family box at the Covent Garden opera house! He must pay the Rates; but who would lend to an Irish landlord in these times? What is he to do then? He has always done his duty to the poor, but unless he clears the estate of paupers, he will become one of them himself. You'd not have him do that, I suppose?"

"I hardly know. Perhaps he has no choice. But I'll not wait for Charles Ormsby to reach the same conclusion and send the bailiffs to my door. I'm off to America."

"You, Liam!" Orne was aghast.

"Sure and why not? I've no heart to pass another winter in a charnel house, and that is what the blight and the landlords have made of ould Ireland. Mary and I are young and strong, maybe, but a few months of nettle soup and government corn would kill us both."

"But the baby! Surely you'll wait until after your wife's confinement!"

"I daren't, Willie!" His voice was anguished. "The babe is as safe where he is now as he would be at the breast, and the sailing season will end in a few weeks. A winter crossing is not to be thought of, and we cannot wait until spring. The Hunger would carry us off before then. No, we must away as soon as ever we can."

"This is sad news, and I know that Mister Ormsby will take it so as well. Did you not play at his son's coming of age?"

"I did that, and my da played after his christening. I'm told that six generations of O'Donnells have fiddled for the Ormsbys of Cummen House and held Ballynora Farm from them, and it is said that we were harpers to the Fitzgeralds and O'Rourkes before that. It is no light thing to bring that to an end, you may be sure, but *níl tuile ná trághann ach tuile na ngrás.*"

Orne looked blank. Liam remembered that the lawyer had no Gaelic and translated. "For every tide, an ebb. I never thought of leaving, nor wouldn't now, but death stares me in the face. I can stay in Erin no more."

Orne's horse, a handsome bay gelding, snorted impatiently and danced sideways a few steps. Orne patted his neck and asked, "Are you for town? Come take a drop with me and let us talk of this some more. I'd have you do nothing in haste."

Liam hesitated, but his regard for the young solicitor, and his sense that Orne was genuinely concerned for him, won out. "One dropeen then," he agreed, "but then I must go. I dare not leave Mary alone too long in her state."

McGowan's alehouse stood in the shadow of the ruins of the Whitefriars Abbey, sacked in 1642 by Cromwell's men under Sir Frederick Hamilton. The English soldiers had shot the monks as they prayed at the altar, set the Abbey afire, then ranged through the town killing every inhabitant they found, from grandmothers to babies still at the breast. No Irishman passed the ruins without recalling that night's dreadful deeds. And still the English could not understand why their Irish subjects did not forget ancient history, give up their outdated religion, and become good, sensible nineteenth-century Englishmen.

Even William Orne, for all his dedication to Irish freedom, was often impatient with his Irish comrades for being so . . . so *Irish*. He was bored by their florid, grandiloquent speeches and alarmed by the ease with which they swung between soaring optimism and a suicidal despair that was equally unjustified. He even suspected privately that the rising had failed so dismally because Young Ireland's leaders had started to believe their own boasts of their strength and acted without proper preparation, something he was sure no Englishman would do.

As he looked across the scarred table at Liam O'Donnell, it occurred to him that he liked the young fiddler in part because he was so level-headed. And yet he had a fanciful side to him as well, that showed most clearly when he lost himself in his music, in the wild abandon of a mountain reel or the melancholy of a slow air. At those times, watching him and his listeners, Orne could easily believe the legend of Orpheus and his power over all creatures, or those darker tales of musicians who had gained their uncanny talents from a Satanic bargain.

What would his life be like in America? Orne was too knowledgeable to believe stories about streets paved with gold, and was not quick to credit the accounts written home by earlier emigrants either. After all, he thought, who would be brave enough to write the relatives he had left behind and confess that he had failed miserably? Orne had also read Mrs. Trollope's book about her stay in America, and Dickens'

American Notes as well. The picture they presented did not attract him. From what they said, the United States was crude, uncultured, and devoted solely to sharp dealing. He imagined that Canada was much the same, only colder.

Here at home, Liam O'Donnell was known and respected by populace and gentry alike. Across the Atlantic, who would know or care that he was accounted one of the best fiddlers west of the Shannon? What use would he have for his Gaelic poetry and Latin oratory? He would be seen as one more dirty Irish pauper and set to building roads or tending a steam loom, when by rights he should be a great man in the Ireland to come!

Orne took a sip of his porter and mustered his arguments. "I fear you are right," he said finally. "A terrible time is upon us again. But to cross the ocean, with all its perils, to land penniless and friendless in a strange land—that too seems terrible to me."

"And to me," Liam retorted, "but I must."

"Ah, but that's the question. Must you? When I spoke of clearances, you must have known I didn't mean you. You'll have no bailiffs at your door. The Ormsbys hold you in respect and affection as a valued friend and faithful retainer. The rent will be freely forgiven you, I'll take my oath on it, and if the failure of the potato crop inconveniences you, you will have first call on the resources of Cummen House."

"I may lodge in the Folly and gaze out across the strand, you mean? No, William, I know you speak as a friend, and it's grateful I am for your offer, but I am not seeking the Ormsbys' charity, no, nor yours either. I see no future for me here, even if I might live through the dreadful time to come. The blight has killed more than praties; the old ways are dead as well. I want a different life for my child."

"And what if all chose your course? What of Ireland? Your country needs men like you; will you abandon her in her hour of need?"

Liam's jaw tightened and his nostrils flared at his companion's rebuke, but he answered him quietly. "If Ireland needs me, she needs me first alive. She has corpses aplenty already, and millions more to come before Spring. I do not mean to forget the suffering of my people when I am in a foreign land, and if I have any power to relieve them, I'll use it. But I'll not condemn my family to starvation. I'll not spend another summer fearing each morning to look at my fields and see that the blight has returned. I'll not pass another winter watching the typhus and the dysentery and the cholera strike down those the hunger has spared. I'll not live out the rest of my days in a graveyard!"

There was a long silence.

Finally Orne sighed and said, "You are resolved, then."

"I am that."

"Will you take ship here, for Quebec?"

Liam heard and understood the concern in Orne's voice. The emigrant ships that sailed from Sligo and the other ports in the west of Ireland were most of them old, ill-provisioned, unseaworthy, and overcrowded. They well deserved the name they had gained—*coffin ships*. The tale was told that one such had sailed from Westport and foundered within sight of land, taking eight hundred souls to their death while their helpless relatives watched from the shore.

Others reached the St. Lawrence having lost half their passengers to ship fever.

"Not that, no," he replied. "I suppose we must make our way to Dublin and take the steamboat to Liverpool. The American packet ships are said to be faster and more comfortable than those bound for Quebec, and I've a hankering for the States. It's not eager I am to go on living as a subject of the English Queen, either!"

"Hush, man! Such talk is dangerous these days! Do you want to bring the peelers down on us?"

"Not I, no, but you mind the saying, Willie: sooner the prison than the workhouse." Liam suddenly realized that the glass of ale, on an empty stomach, was making him talk daft, and that he was tarrying too long in town. He pushed his stool back. "I'm for home then. You'll tell Ormsby of my decision and give him my regrets?"

Orne nodded. "I will. But stay a moment. I recall that one of Pollexfen's ships will be sailing for Liverpool Monday next. If you are resolved, you could spare yourself a long tramp to Dublin and a crowded crossing, and be among folk who know you for a little longer. You'll be parted from your friends soon enough anyway."

"Thank you, William; I'll bear it in mind. Now I must get back to Mary. It'll be a long day and a hard one, telling her we must leave our home forever."

mary Flynn O'Donnell leaned back against the railing and turned her pale face gratefully to the summer sun. The schooner *Ben Bulben* rocked gently in the swell, with so lulling a motion that she almost forgot the terror of the night before. Almost, but not quite: she knew that the memory would be with her for the rest of her life.

The great wind had struck suddenly from the north, catching the sails and tipping the ship over until the railing on the right side was scarcely clear of the waves. The hundreds of passengers who were trying to sleep woke to find themselves sliding helplessly down the steeply slanting deck toward the water. The most of them were poor unsophisticated peasants who had hardly seen a ship before, let alone traveled in one, and their cries and prayers were pitiful to hear as they fetched up in a tangled heap against the bulkhead. Moments later their screams grew louder as their boxes and sacks careered across the deck into the mass of people. For a wonder, no one was killed or lost overboard, though a man from Donegal broke his arm and a child was knocked senseless.

Even after that first shock, the ship continued to pitch and toss unpredictably like a maddened stallion. Those who were not too sick to speak prayed or cursed aloud, and some did both, blending with the howl of the wind to make a wondrous noise. Liam wedged Mary and Tom between one of the masts and a lasheddown crate, and Tom clung to her the rest of the night like the baby he still was in truth, though he tried to pretend that he was protecting her.

In time the storm passed and she fell asleep, waking again in the first half-light of day. She carefully wriggled free of her little brother's clasp and stepped over Liam's legs to the railing. The sun was just beginning to peep over an irregular gray smudge of a horizon. One of the sailors, passing by, told her she was looking at Scotland. She looked again, both thrilled and uneasy at her first sight of a foreign land. It looked like nothing in particular—it could as easily have been a low bank of clouds—but it brought her closer to the realization that she had left Sligo behind forever.

How long had it taken her to understand what Liam was telling her, that day that the Blight had returned? And yet there was nothing strange about the idea of going to America. Thousands had done it every year, and with the Famine the steady stream of movers had become a flood. In '47 she had watched them trudging along the lanes, lugging their pitiful bundles and their babies with matchstick limbs and distended bellies, seeking passage on anything afloat that was leaving

Ireland. Some had collapsed in the hedgerows and ditches and died within sight of the harbor, to be hurried into a nameless grave. Others took ship and were heard from no more.

Yet she had never thought to be one of them. In good times she had imagined herself rearing a family and growing peacefully old at Ballynora, and in bad times she thought of being carried off by the hunger or the fever and being laid to rest next to her parents and sisters. She could not, try as she might, see herself in a far-off land, among Indians and strangers. Even when Liam took his spade to the midden and unearthed the clay pot that held their little store of precious gold sovereigns and told her to sew the coins into the hem of her underskirt, she didn't really believe him. What of the farm? Who would milk the cow and feed the pigs? And who would care for the family graves if they went away?

"We'll sell the stock," Liam had explained patiently, for the third time, "and the lease to Ballynora if anyone will buy it. If not, why, we'll walk away from it. And as for the dead, they must look after themselves. It'll do them no good for us to stay here and join them."

"But must we go so soon?" she protested.

"We must. We have food for a few days only; when that is gone, we must spend ready money if we are to eat, and we need every ha'penny for the trip to America. The Pollexfens' schooner sails for Liverpool on Monday. God knows when next we would find so direct a way to go. And we must think of the child. I'd not have him born on shipboard if I can help it."

Remembering the words, Mary shuddered and cupped her hands under the swell of her belly, and felt a small answering stir. Whatever would she do if her time came on in the midst of a gale at sea? She tried to push the thought away, but it would not stay banished, instead becoming more vivid. She had assisted at births before, and it seemed a terrible, bloody business at best. How then would it be if the floor was rocking and pitching and dropping from under you?

Liam woke, and Tom, and Mary went off to take her place in line for a turn at the galley fire. Then she would heat water for their morning bowl of Indian corn-meal and rice, or "stirabout." It was a poor enough way to start the day, to be sure, but there were plenty on board who lacked even that. She looked, with a mixture of compassion and horror, at one such huddle of misery. They were two women and a man, their faces so drawn with want that she could not guess if they were brother and sisters or mother, son, and wife. Their accent was so barbarous that Mary could scarcely say that they were speaking Gaelic and not Hindoo. They glanced around constantly like some shy creatures of the wild, and flinched each time someone moved in their direction. They were clad in filthy rags that hardly met the most basic demands of modesty.

Three children with thickly matted hair clustered near them. The oldest, a girl of perhaps nine, wore only a tattered shift that did not cover her, and the two babies, a boy and a girl, were bare of even the pretense of clothing. Marys' heart went out to the little ones. She longed to take them in her lap, to wash their faces and comb their hair and spoon stirabout into them. But she had her own baby to think of, and her husband and brother. The most she could spare the poor darlings was a smile. The older girl looked away quickly, but the little one beamed back and gave a tiny chuckle that made Mary catch her breath in sudden wonder.

The morning wore on, and Mary took her rest in the sunlight. She seemed so often tired these days, but perhaps it was the baby. Surely it was a draining thing to bring a new life into being. Hadn't God Himself needed to rest on the seventh day?

Tom and another lad darted by, intent on some game. Mary's eyes followed him fondly. The young met change with such ease! Who could look at Tom and think that scant days had passed since he was torn from the only home he could remember? That his few years were marred already by dire want and the deaths of so many close to him? But with the help of the blessed saints, he would grow up healthy and strong and make a way for himself in the New World.

Though some of the passengers still showed a greenish pallor, most had shaken off the worst effects of the gale and were beginning to take what pleasure they might from the voyage to England. Liam unpacked his fiddle and sat beside Mary to play one of her favorite airs, a wonderfully plaintive melody called "Eleanor Plunkett" by the blind harper O'Carolan. Soon a circle six-deep formed on the deck. The faces were intent on the music, taken away from the miseries of poverty and hunger and forced flight from their homeland. Mary thought once more what a great gift from God it was that Liam bore in his fingers and his mind.

The O'Carolan piece came to an end. Someone at the rear of the crowd started shouldering his way to the front, one Dugan from County Fermanagh. His fine frieze coat and sturdy brogues made him the best-dressed man on the ship, and it came to Mary that if a "strong" farmer, with acres to his name, was forced to emigrate, old Erin was in a sad state indeed. The others gave way to him, as if acknowledging his superiority.

"That was a darlin' air, Liam *a grá*," said Dugan, as if he had been elected as spokesman. "A darlin' air. But will you not give us a tune we can dance to? It's more than one I see with restless feet, and sure we all have that we'd as soon forget for a little while."

His words called forth a faint murmur of agreement from the crowd. For answer, Liam played a preliminary chord and launched into a lively, bouncing double jig. Mary smiled as she recognized it as "Out on the Ocean." The listeners backed off, to form a larger circle, and Kathleen Grady, from the wild Nephin Beg mountains in the west of County Mayo, stepped to the center. She stood as straight as the ship's mast and her face was still as she took in the rhythm of the tune. Suddenly she flashed into motion, her feet and legs stamping, kicking in intricate patterns with and against the music, carrying her in leaps and turns, even while her hands stayed motionless at her sides and her body was held so straight that it might have belonged to someone else. The watchers clapped and stamped their feet, and soon two more colleens ventured into the circle and burst out laughing as each tried to follow the steps of the other. A set of reels followed the jig, and the dancing became more general. Almost two hours passed before his fellow emigrants allowed Liam to stop playing.

Afterwards, as Liam stood near the bow watching the spreading wave made by the schooner's passage, a young man he had noticed in the crowd made his way over and leaned on the rail next to him. Liam nodded.

"You've a rare gift for playing," he said to Liam. "You'll not have many years on me, but I'll count myself fortunate if I can play so well before I die. Oh— me name is Sean McMahon, of Costelloe in County Galway."

"I'm Liam O'Donnell, from Sligo."

"O'Donnell . . . would you be related to Padraig O'Donnell, then?"

"My da, God rest his soul."

"Amen. I heard him once, at a fair in Galway City, then went home to Costelloe and tried to remember some of the tunes. Wonderful tunes they were, too, but the most of them escaped me. There was one reel he played . . ."

Soon the young musicians were deep in a discussion of the traditional music of Connacht, breaking off to hum or lilt examples of tunes to each other. Before long, Liam went to fetch his fiddle—Sean confessed shamefaced that he had sold his for passage money—so that they could compare different versions and elaborations of the same melodies. By the time evening came, they were fast friends.

"My tale is no different from many others," he said as he shared their meager supper. "My da holds a fine farm, if small, from the estate of a great lord. In good times, when the wind was right, we fished as well, though we had to take care not to run afoul of the Claddagh men."

"What's that?" Tom asked avidly. "Are they giants?"

Sean chuckled. "Not that, but they are right quare, to be sure. They are folk that live in quare huts like beehives, and speak their own tongue and have their own king, and consider that all the fish in Galway Bay belong to them alone. If they catch you at fishing, be you who you may, they lather you well and cut your nets. But there, the straits they are in are as sore as any in these dreadful times, for they've sold their own nets and gear to buy a bit food, and they'll fish no more 'til the times change round again." He fell silent for a moment, as if mourning the passing of another part of Old Ireland.

"Anyway," he continued, "when the Blight came, we suffered, but the oats and barley and greenstuffs carried us through the first year and even the second, but we'd nothing to pay the rent with. The Big Lord holds a hanging gale over my da, so it was no trifle to be behind as well."

Liam nodded. He knew that all too many Irish tenants were prisoners of the "hanging gale," the practice of letting the tenant leave his rent twelve months or more in arrears. Few ever had the ready money to pay the current rent and the hanging gale, so the tenant was always behind, always subject to immediate eviction.

Sean twisted a lock of his silky reddish hair around a finger. "Last year we did wondrous well with rye and kale and beans, but the most of it went toward the rent. We were looking to this year's potatoes to bring us even again, and when the Blight came back . . . I was no more than another hungry mouth to feed. I can help them more from Americay, and in time I hope to send the passage money to my sisters, too."

* * *

The passengers stared in silence as the *Ben Bulben* sailed up the Mersey. Most of them had never been much beyond their own parishes and townlands before they footed it to the nearest port and took passage to Liverpool. A steamboat passed, thick smoke belching from its tall sooty stack. It was greeted by a flurry of wondering comments from most, and by some astonishing explanations from the few who thought they understood the principle behind the infernal device. Then the first of the docks came into view. A stunned silence fell.

The Liverpool Docks were among the wonders of the century. The town had grown fat, first on the trade in slaves, then on American cotton for the mills of Manchester, and had poured a tithe of its riches into the construction of the largest, sturdiest, and costliest dock complex in the entire world. The great granite walls stretched for miles along both sides of the Mersey. Behind them, a thicket of masts hinted at the hundreds of ships that lined the protected quays and wharfs, and beyond the masts were solid blocks of stone-built warehouses, graving docks, shipbuilders' yards, and rope walks. As if to underline the source of all this magnificence, the river itself was a turbid brown, thick and foul with the refuse of England's second city. After two days on open water, the passengers found the stench unbearable. Two were sick over the side of the ship.

As the schooner drew nearer to the landing stage, a huge structure that floated on pontoons and rose and fell with the tide, a crowd started to gather. It seemed odd to Liam that so many would come to welcome just another shipload of poor Irish emigrants. The moment the first passenger stepped off the ship, however, he started to understand. Two ruffianly fellows dashed at the dazed man, grabbed his box, and slung it onto a barrow. Ignoring his protest, one of them started off with it. His only choice was to follow or to lose all his belongings. The same scene was being repeated all over the quayside. Liam saw one poor man's coat ripped from his back by two rival hooligans, while his wife and brood of children watched and screamed their fright and dismay.

"I was warned of this," said Sean. "They bear the name of *crimps* or *runners,* and they live on the flesh of the poor. Unless you know what you are about, they will beguile or drag you to a low boardinghouse and hold you there 'til your money is near gone, then take you to provision merchants and shipping agents that will pay them their Judas fees."

A fight broke out just below where they stood, between a red-faced Kerryman and a runt of a runner. The runner stood no chance, it seemed, against an Irish shellelagh, but then six of his fellows jumped on the Kerryman and bore him to the ground. Before he could regain his feet, his baggage was vanishing into the jeering crowd.

"To fight them seems unwise," observed Liam dryly, "though if I hadn't Mary and the boy to think of, I might hazard it still. Were you warned how to deal with them as well?"

Sean shrugged. "Never let them think you have money, for they'll not let you from their claws until they think they have it all. For the rest, you must sleep somewhere, and I hear each lodging house is as foul as the others. You're an educated man—you need not trust others to tell you what is the next packet to sail and where to buy passage in her."

Liam looked over sharply. "Do you not sail to New York as well though?"

"I do." Sean glanced away, as if suddenly interested in some happening on the far side of the landing stage.

"Then . . . ," he hesitated, then plunged ahead. "Won't you make party with us, then? We'll be all among strangers soon enough, when we reach the other shore. We can have a rare time of it, trading tunes."

"I will, then," Sean said simply. "And I take it as kindly of you." As he spoke Liam realized that the boy had been ready to walk away, to disappear from their lives, because he feared to intrude on them. What had the Hunger done to people! Before, the door of the meanest mud-walled hut was open always to the stranger, and there was generally a boiled lumper and a pinch of salt for his dinner as well. And even if food was short, there was room for him next to the turf fire.

The fever had changed that. Hospitality might be a sacred duty, but not if it meant inviting a terrible death into your family. And there was no way to know who might bring it down upon you, if not the typhus, then the dysentery or the cholera. So the stranger was turned away, directed to the Union poorhouse if well or the fever tents if sick. And if both were full, as so often they were, the stranger was at liberty to pick a handy ditch to sleep and maybe to die in. It was hard to call to mind that once Ireland had been a gay land, full of music and dancing and the laughter of children.

The crowd on the quay had thinned, as the triumphant runners carried off their prey. Liam gathered up Mary and Tom, hoisted their small box onto his shoulder, and started down the gangplank with Sean close behind them. A short, ragged man with sandy hair and a turned-up nose noticed them at once and came over, smiling broadly.

"*Arra* but it does my heart good to see two such sturdy lads and such a fine-looking family," he said in strong Cork accent. His manner was so confident and familiar that Liam wondered for a moment if he knew them from some other occasion, or thought he did. "It's for America you'll be, I doubt not," he continued, "and sure, isn't it the proper place for a young man with spirit to win his way in the world and all! Well, I'm the man to see you're done fairly by. Tom Regan's the name, late of Queenstown, and entirely at your service. You'll be Connachtmen, of course?"

Liam and Sean introduced themselves and exchanged a glance full of meaning. Regan was a runner, of course, but one who seemed to rely on flattery to draw in his prey. He might prove easier to deal with than one of the bullyboys.

"Thanks be to God," said Regan surprisingly, crossing himself, "but the blessed saints have an eye to your welfare. I'd have you know that the finest American packet, the *Rappahannock*, sails for New York in only two weeks' time. Sure, she's a palace of a ship, the pride of the Western Ocean, and it's not everybody can sail in her, for she's booked far ahead. By chance it is I have four tickets, though, booked for me own sister's family, and her not able to take them up because her husband's mother, the saints preserve her, has taken ill of a sudden. I've been hoping to spy some fine countrymen of mine to pass this blessing along to, and something in your air must have caught me eye."

Part of Liam wanted to laugh and applaud, as he would an entertainer at fair-time, and part of him wanted to wipe the lying smile from Regan's face with his fist. He set both parts aside and met the man's guile with his own. "What a pity, to be sure," he said sweetly. "We thank your honor, but I fear we cannot wait the two weeks. We've our passage money, but there's little enough to spare for such a long stay in this fine English city as well. No, I'll have to go in search of a ship that leaves tomorrow or Friday, and a place for us to stay until then. It's in my mind that we'll need to buy seastore as well, to carry us through the voyage."

Regan's eyes lit up at the thought of his percentage on Liam's tickets and purchases. "Friday, is it?" he cried. "Sure, I near forgot, but that's the very day the *Lady Franklin* sails. You'll have heard, surely, of the Black Star Line, that has the fastest packets and the very newest. The *Lady Franklin* is their finest ship, with spacious and airy accommodations for all and a captain and crew who are famous on both sides of the water for their tender concern for the passengers. I did hear that all the spaces were taken, but Captain Drummond is a good friend of mine. I'll try my luck to get

you aboard, and being you're such fine upstanding
folk, I'll try to persuade him to take you for only five
pounds, instead of the seven that is usual."

"That's good of you,' 'replied Liam, avoiding Sean's
outraged expression, "good of you indeed, but we were
told back home that the cost of passage was three
pounds tén, and we've not allowed for more. I'm afraid
we'll have to seek elsewhere for our passages after all,
with thanks to your honor."

Regan's gaze darted here and there, searching for a
way out of the trap his greed had dug for him, and
his eyes lighted on the case of Liam's fiddle. *"Arra,* is
it a musician you are then?" he exclaimed. "I'd have
you to know that Captain Drummond, him I just told
you of, is a famous lover of our music. When I tell
him I've a fiddler seeking passage to New York—"

"Two fiddlers," Sean muttered under his breath.

"I'm sure he'll agreed to take you for the price you
mentioned, though you'll do me the favor not to tell
anyone of this. As a general thing only the poorer
class of ship will give you passage for so little. As for
accommodations until you sail, I know of a fine lodging
house in Tithebarn Street, not so far from here, that's
clean and wholesome and ouly sixpence the night, half
for the child."

Sean had taken the trouble to ask his friend who
knew Liverpool about the price of lodgings as well.
"Say fourpence the night," he struck in, "and we'll cry
a bargain on it."

For a single moment, rapacity and rage blossomed
on the runner's face, then his broad smile returned and
he agreed.

Mary and Tom huddled close to Liam as they fol-

lowed Regan through the streets of the town. It wasn't
so much the crowds and the noise that frightened
them, though that was alarming enough in all truth,
but the dreadful faces of the people, the brutality and
hopelessness written here. Mary had thought that she
had seen despair, in the eyes of the starving, but these
people had been condemned, not to death, but to life.
Barefoot girls, no more than children, watched with
dead eyes for the approach of a sailor. Old crones,
scrawny mothers with unwashed babies at the breast,
the crippled and maimed lined the way, begging for
farthings. One man, whose legs ended at mid-thigh,
sat on a wheeled cart; on his lap was a painted board
that showed a figure falling into the gears of a gigantic
machine. Another pointed silently at a chalked in-
scription on the sidewalk: "I have not eaten for three
days. My wife and children are dying."

The street Regan led them to was mean and dirty
and reeked of concentrated sweat and sewage. Every
third cellar held a spirits vault, and every gutter held
their besotted customers. Mary shrank away as a
rough-looking man, unshaven and stinking of gin, staggered up some steps and across the pavement toward
her. Sean stepped between them. The man growled
incoherently and took a step toward the lad, but then
he folded at the knees and sank unconscious to the
ground. Liam took Mary's elbow and hurried her
along. When she looked back, the crowds were step-
ping over the man as though he were a stone or log.

Regan stopped in front of a three-story house in the
middle of the block. All that distinguished it from the
neighboring tenements was a crude sign over the
door: GRAND HOTEL D'ALTON. As she climbed the dark,

narrow stairs, Mary was acutely aware of the nauseating smells and of the pains in her lower back and swollen feet. Their room was small, and they would be sharing it with a family of five from Derry, but at least she would not have to sleep on the filthy floor. She set her bundle of bedding on the rough boards of the bunk and stood for a moment with her eyes closed. Suddenly she gasped as a pain pierced her side. She distantly felt Liam's arms around her, heard his voice from across a great gulf.

She opened her eyes to see his dear face, so troubled with worry for her as he brushed the tears from her cheeks. "What is it, *Máire arún?*" he whispered.

She shook her head and did not reply. It was only a moment's weakness, this sudden conviction that she and her baby were doomed. But why did the tears continue to stream from her eyes?

3

Papers. Show me your tongue. Are you quite well? Passed; next!"

The stamped paper, proof that Sean had been given a medical examination, was thrust into his hand. In the seconds he took to collect himself, the government doctor had examined three more emigrants and stamped their papers. "Move on, there!" he called. "You are blocking the queue!"

Sean moved on, looking around the crowded quay for Liam and his family. There seemed to be hundreds of tattered souls standing passively near the side of the *Lady Franklin*. Stevedores, bent nearly double under their burdens of bags and boxes, shouldered their way roughly through the crowd, which swayed to make a passage, then closed again like a field of grain behind a mounted man.

"Make way there!"

Sean stumbled aside as a heavy dray thundered

across the quay with a load of huge oaken barrels that dripped a trail of water on the granite paving stones. The driver ploughed straight for the side of the ship, trusting the agility of the waiting emigrants to keep them from under his iron-bound wheels. Curses and screams filled the air.

A woman in a gray Connemara shawl, with three small children clinging to her skirts and a fourth in her arms, tripped and fell to her knees directly in the path of the horses. Instantly a man in a ragged frieze coat dashed from the crowd and leapt up to grab the bridle of the nearside horse. The team swerved and stopped, their eyes rolling nervously.

"Damn 'ee!" the teamster shouted. "Damn 'ee to hell! Unhand my nag, Paddy, or it'll go the worse for you, by God!"

He flourished his whip. The man in the frieze coat looked at him coolly and waited while the woman who had tripped was helped to her feet, then he faded into the crowd.

"Ye dirty bogtrotter!" the driver screamed after him. "Ye'd best learn to keep yer filthy hands off an honest Englishman's team from now on!"

A low, almost animal growl arose from the crowd. The driver, suddenly alert, glanced around nervously and hastily flicked the reins. For a moment it seemed that the crowd was going to keep him surrounded; then a narrow path opened up ahead of him and the dray rattled toward the gangplank.

Sean followed in the wake of the dray and scanned the faces to right and left. He should have felt easy, he knew, for Liam and Mary and Tom were bound to be somewhere in the crowd. If he missed them on the quay, he would find them once they were aboard the ship. He knew that very well. Even so, he began to feel abandoned. What if the O'Donnells somehow missed the sailing and he had to go on to America without a single familiar face or friendly smile to keep him in spirits?

He was one of seven surviving children, all but his oldest sister Alice still at home. Until the day he hiked to Galway city to take ship to Liverpool, he had never known what it was to be alone. At first he was proud of the independence and sure that he had passed an important test of his adulthood. A day later he admitted to himself that he was miserably lonely. Between bouts of seasickness, he tried to calculate how long he would have to work in New York to save enough to bring over a brother or sister to keep him company. However, he figured it, the answer was far too long. The chance meeting with Liam O'Donnell, and the warm welcome his wife had extended, had rescued him from his black mood of desolation, but he sensed that it lurked somewhere just out of sight, ready to leap upon him again at the first opportunity.

Another commotion erupted near the head of the quay. Sean stretched to look over the heads of the crowd. Two matched grays were pulling a handsome open landau toward the *Lady Franklin*. Its passengers were a red-faced man of forty with thin sandy hair and thick sandy sidewhiskers, and a pretty blonde girl of twelve or fourteen. The man stared straight ahead, as if unaware that hundreds of people surrounded his carriage, but the girl darted glances in every direction with a lively interest in a scene so apparently new to her.

As the landau drew near the ship, Sean heard shouts on board. Half a dozen sailors ran over to clear a space at the foot of the gangplank, to hold the horses, and to start unloading the trunks of gleaming leather from the rear of the carriage. Moments later an officer appeared, still buttoning his blue uniform coat, and saluted the red-faced man, then offered his arm to the girl. She seemed surprised, almost alarmed, by the attention, and glanced toward her father (as Sean had decided he must be) for guidance. He nodded, and the little procession made its way onto the ship.

"Have you set your heart on marrying into the Quality, then, Sean *a grá?*"

He turned. Liam was looking at him with a bitter half-smile. "Those two," Liam continued, "they haven't the look of those who have known hunger. Nor would they look twice at those who have. We're no more than dirt under their feet."

Sean protested. "The child was pretty, and too young to be held to blame. As for the man, what do you know against him beyond his carriage? Must everyone take vows of poverty to win your favor?"

"That, no. I mean to win wealth for myself one day, God willing, but I swear I won't think less of those who don't, or take mean privilege from it. Here's Mary, not far from her time, as anyone can see, and tired to near fainting, but she's forced to stand for hours on the hard stones while yon mightiness and his yellow-haired brat are escorted aboard and given tea and cakes in the captain's cabin. Is that as it ought to be, now?"

Sean looked over in the direction of Liam's gesture. Mary's face was very pale and drawn, and there were crescents of a delicate purple hue under her eyes, but when she caught Sean's glance she managed to smile. Sean smiled back and turned to Liam.

"Why don't we go on the ship then?" he asked. "We were told that she sails at eleven, and isn't it nearly that now?"

"It is. But we're not permitted. No steerage passengers to board until they're done stowing cargo, and four men with batons at the foot of the gangway to be sure no one disobeys. One lad tried to climb over the railing and they pushed him into the water with all his belongings, then laughed when he cried that he couldn't swim."

As Sean opened his mouth to comment, a murmur sprang up from those nearest the ship. The crowd swayed, and began to flow toward the gangway. The murmur swelled as children cried out in fright and separated companions shouted to each other, then grew quickly to a tumult as those toward the front were crushed against the gangway railings or carried toward the edge of the quay.

By chance, Sean was carried along by the force of the crowd up the gangway and onto the deck. As he turned to avoid falling over a pile of grain sacks, he saw that Liam had somehow gathered Mary and Tom in his arms and brought them on board. He struggled through the stream of people to their side and was opening his mouth to speak when the shouting around him changed its timbre to a wail of dismay. Alarmed, he looked around.

At first he could not make out the cause of the new uproar. Then he realized that the sailors had cast off the mooring lines and were scrambling aloft to set the sails. Already a foot or more divided wooden hull and granite quay, and the gap was widening rapidly, stranding a hundred or more passengers on land. Some, more daring or more desperate than the rest, jumped for the side of the ship and were hauled on board by eager hands, but the others seemed unable to move, as if this last blow from Fate had finished them.

Liam brushed past Sean and clambered up onto the bulwark. "The entrance!" he shouted in a thunderous voice. "Run to the entrance!" His arm swept around in a commanding gesture. Sean looked ahead and understood at once. The docking basin was a long rectangle, with quays on three sides. On the fourth side was the narrow channel to the open river, with its drawbridge and tidegates. The channel was not much wider than the *Lady Franklin;* the captain would be forced to take it slowly and to pass very close to the edge of the quay.

Others on board saw it now, and joined Liam's shouts. The stranded emigrants ignored them at first, or didn't understand, but at the last moment their immobility broke and they dashed for the entrance to the basin. Those who had managed to get aboard rushed to line the railing, ready to help. As the bowsprit of the *Lady Franklin* neared the entrance to the channel, a silence fell broken only by the frantic wails of a baby. Then the man at the extreme corner of the quay threw his bag aboard and leapt for the rigging, and the clamor rose once more. Those ashore cried out for help, while those aboard shouted encouragement and instructions, and leaned down to catch them by what-

ever part of body or clothing they could reach. Women
and children were jerked aboard and tumbled helter-
skelter on the planks; poor threadbare coats were
ruined beyond the hope of repair; boxes split open
and spilled their stores on the deck or into the scummy
water; but by the time the ship cleared the entrance
and started downriver, not one of her passengers was
still stranded on the quay.

"Look at them!" said Liam in a bitter undertone.
He jerked his chin toward the rear of the ship. Sean
turned and saw a dozen or more well-dressed men
and women at the railing of the bridge, laughing and
pointing. One of them, by his uniform and appearance,
seemed to be the captain.

"We're no more than performing animals to them,"
Liam continued, "a spectacle to keep them amused
during the long voyage! There was no need to leave
like that, with so many not yet on the ship, but they
don't care as long as they've our three pound ten in
hand. It's the landlords all over again, taking all the
silver they can wring from us and giving as little as
they can back again."

"Hush, Liam," said Sean, glancing around to see who
might be listening. "Do you want to be taken up as a
Whiteboy or a Red Republican from France?"

Liam gave him a wry half-smile. "Ah, lad, but there's
the secret the agents and bailiffs and gombeen men
will never learn: once rob the poor of all they possess,
and they'll have nothing left to lose. And a man with
nothing to lose is a fearsome creature, Sean *a grá*."

"You've a wife, and a child in your care, and a child
of your own to come—you'd not be calling that nothing?"

"That I wouldn't, and me jabbering away here with you, filling you with my nonsense while I should be after finding Mary a spot to rest herself." He moved in her direction. Sean was on the point of following, when a new commotion started. Half a dozen burly sailors were pushing all the confused, frightened steerage passengers toward the front of the ship, ignoring their questions and protests.

A member of the crew stepped into the cleared space and shouted in a strange, flat accent that Liam realized with a thrill must be American. "All right, shut up, all of yez! Listen for your name, and when you hear it, come over to this side with your tickets ready. Paddy Murphy! . . . John Connolly! . . . Bridget O'Neill! . . . Alistair Anderson! . . ."

After each name, there was a stir somewhere in the packed mass as its owner struggled to make his way to the clearing. As the list droned on, Liam saw a small group of sailors going below. Each of them carried a long pole like a pike, with a slender point on the end. He puzzled over their purpose for several minutes before he realized that they were searching for stowaways, poking into all the dark corners of the ship.

". . . Lime O'Donnell! . . . Tom Flynn! . . . Seen Mac-Man! . . ." The combination of last names, and an anxious nudge from Mary, woke Liam to the fact that the American had just called them. Shouldering their box of provisions, he led them through the thinning crowd and presented their tickets to the bored ship's clerk, who glanced at them and said, "Right. Over there."

Liam waited until the clerk looked up again. "When are we to be allowed to go to our berths?" he asked softly. "My wife's been standing since the break of day, and you can see her condition for yourself."

The clerk refused to look at Mary. "Do as you're told," he said. "Over there. Next!"

"I'll go over there, and gladly, when you've answered a civil question." Mary was tugging at his elbow, urging him to let the matter go, but he disregarded her. "When may we go below to rest?"

"This fellow giving you trouble, Asa?" a new voice asked. The speaker was heavy-set, with a low, brutal forehead and tiny piggy eyes. He wore ragged jeans, like the other sailors, but topped with a jacket that seemed a shoddy imitation of those the officers wore. He bounced a short wooden club against his open left palm and eyed Liam appraisingly.

"He won't go over with the rest. Says he wants to know when he can go to his berth. You tell him, Bo'sun."

"When we say so, that's when," the bo'sun growled. "Now git!" When Liam still hesitated, the veins in his neck swelled. "Move it, damn your eyes, you and your doxy! Or by God I'll tear a strip off your ass and have it for lunch!"

Liam's hands knotted into fists and he started to take a step toward the foulmouthed sailor, but Sean caught his right arm and helped Mary pull him back into the watching crowd. The bo'sun stared at him for a moment longer, as if memorizing his features, then turned away, satisfied with the success of his efforts.

"Why did you stop me?" Liam fumed. "Did you mark his words? I'd have flattened him, I would, by Jesus!"

"Aye, and left your teeth in his club and traveled to New York in chains," said Sean. "Little enough help you'd be to Mary in that state, I'm thinking."

"Liam, please," Mary added. "I don't mind what he said. He's only a low, ignorant man when all's said and done. You mustn't take any notice of his sort."

"I mustn't take notice, but I must do as he says, is that the way of it then? I thought we were done with that when we left ould Ireland for the land of sweet liberty!"

"We're not there yet," said Mary tartly.

Surprisingly, Liam burst out laughing. "No, *mo cuisle*, you've the right of it there! So until we touch the land again, I'll put all notions of freedom away from me. And if they have such a thing as a hedge in New York, I'll wait for that boyo behind one and teach him to put a disrespectful name to the wife of Liam O'Donnell!"

He distorted his face into an expression so comically belligerent that young Tom, who had been in a state of constant alarm all day, crowed with delight and pretended to attack him with his fists. Liam caught them in one hand and wrapped the other arm around the boy's waist, lifting him from the deck and holding him upside down. Tom's face turned red and he giggled helplessly.

Mary finally protested. "Liam, don't! You'll make him sick!"

Liam sheepishly flipped Tom over and set him on his feet. A few of their fellow passengers were watching and smiling, but most stood or sat listlessly, too sunk in their misery to take notice of anything.

The *Lady Franklin* was leaving the shelter of the

Mersey and beginning to nose into the waves of the Irish Sea when the captain at last took notice of the huddled steerage passengers and shouted, "Mr. Thatcher, get those damned emigrants below and close the hatches! There's rough seas ahead of us!"

A moan went through the mass at the thought of a storm, but they moaned even more loudly when they saw the quarters they would occupy for the next six weeks or more. Their ship was no hastily converted timber ship—she had been built, and quite recently, specifically for the emigrant trade—but her designer had cared for nothing but cramming as many passengers aboard as possible. The steerage deck was just six feet high, less where the thick beams crossed it, and ran nearly the full length of the ship. Along both sides and down the center were wooden platforms suspended, three high, from iron rods and separated by two-foot-wide aisles. Each platform was six feet by six feet, and each had four people assigned to it, which gave every adult passenger slightly less room than he could reasonably expect to have in his coffin. And these were the "spacious and comfortable accommodations" the Black Star Line spoke of in their posters and handbills!

Because Sean had bought his passage at the same time, he found himself assigned to the same berth as Liam, Mary, and Tom, a top bunk in the center row, not very far from the pale light of a ventilator. The aisle was too narrow for hesitation. He climbed up onto the bunk and sat in the corner, his legs drawn up, wondering what he should do. As far as he could judge in the gloom, every berth was full, so it wasn't likely that he could move to another spot. The aisle was already nearly blocked by the bags and boxes of the passengers, and anyway he could hardly hope to stand all the way to New York!

Liam noticed his disquiet and somehow divined its cause. He edged over, nearly bumping his head on the rough ceiling, and said, "You're welcome here, lad. If it weren't you, we'd have a stranger put in with us from God knows where, so you're doing us a service by sharing the bunk. If you take the outside, you can save the boy from falling out when the boat commences to roll."

As if in response, the bow of the ship rose, then fell twisting to the left. For a long moment the ship held the slant, then rolled back to the right as the bow rose once more. Sean grabbed the edge of the berth and held on, grunting when Tom's head cannoned into his abdomen. Liam was holding his wife, helping her to fight the unpredictable lurches. All around them, people were screaming, cursing, praying. The granny in the berth across the aisle started a Hail Mary, then broke off when one of her bunkmates, a middle-aged man in the rags of a tinker, lunged past her to the edge of the bunk and was violently ill.

He was only the first. Soon the steerage deck was filled with the unmistakable sounds of seasickness. The terrified victims writhed helplessly on their bunks, too weakened by the constant spasms to venture into the choked and filthy aisles, even if they had known where to go. The air in the badly ventilated compartment quickly turned fetid. By the time nightfall came, marked only by a deepening of the gloom from murky to pitch-black, almost everyone had succumbed either to the continual random tossing of the ship or to the nauseating miasma that had built up.

Liam was lucky. For some reason, the motion did not bother him. As for the stench, it was not much worse than the well-rotted seaweed he used to spread on his potato fields to enrich the soil, and a good deal more tolerable than the noisome reek of a pit full of blighted potatoes. He stayed next to Mary, holding her steady against the pitching of the ship. When necessary, he fetched the pail, held her head, and wiped the cold sweat from her pale brow. Meanwhile Sean, who had ridden out seas as rough as this in his father's tarred-canvas curragh, took Tom onto his lap and stroked the frightened child until he fell into an exhausted sleep.

Around midnight the tossing eased. The ship still rocked in a gentle seesawing motion, but the deck slanted only slightly to the right rather than rolling violently from side to side. Liam made Mary as comfortable as he could, wedging the bedding around her, then turned onto his side to try to sleep. As he drifted off, he was grimly thankful for the chance that had allotted them a bunk on the top level. He did not like to think on the plight of those in the lower berths.

At dawn the hatches opened with a crash. Light and air seeped into the fuggy space. A sailor stepped halfway down the stairway, his face twisted with distaste. "Water ration!" he cried. "On deck for water ration. Bring your cans, fifty at a time."

The emigrants, most of them still half-asleep, pushed toward the stairs, shrugging on their clothes as they went. No one wanted to give way to another, for fear that the supply would give out before he had his turn. Liam, carried along in the rush, thought to himself that their urgency was ridiculous. If the ship's supply of drinking water gave out this soon, they would find themselves back in Liverpool by the next day, so why crowd and shove each other like dumb brutes?

On deck, even the pretense of an orderly line disappeared. The passengers crowded around a huge cask, holding their containers out and pleading with a tall, hollow-cheeked sailor who directed the stream from his hose now to one side, now to the other. Those at the back pressed forward even as those who had gotten their ration struggled to win free of the mob without spilling the water.

Liam hovered on the edge of the crowd. He could not decide whether he should plunge into it or wait until it thinned out. Suddenly he felt a sharp blow on his backside. He staggered and whirled around.

"Clear out, there, damn your eyes!" The bo'sun waded into the crowd, swinging a length of heavy rope at everyone in reach. "Blast your souls to Hell, line up and wait your turn or there'll be no more water today!"

Stirred to panic by the threat, the mob pressed in closer, swallowing up the bo'sun and drowning his curses in its din. Liam backed away, positive that the uproar would soon become a brawl. Already several eddies swirled in the mass where fights were breaking out. Liam remembered the last faction fight he had seen, in Sligo on fair-day, the Spring of the year the Blight had first appeared. The peelers had stood aside, content to let the drunken peasants break each other's heads as long as no property was damaged.

Perhaps the captain of the *Lady Franklin* felt the same. The fighting spread until it threatened to involve all the male passengers on deck, but the crew made no real attempt to control it until the water cask started to rock back and forth. The sailor who had been giving out the ration played the hose on those closest to him, with no effect that Liam could detect. Just as it seemed that the giant cask must overturn, six or seven sailors charged the crowd. Their long wooden batons rose and fell repeatedly, and the mob recoiled. The bo'sun reappeared, standing up from a protective crouch, and directed the sailors in herding the crowd toward the open hatch. In minutes, only a handful of steerage passengers were still on deck. Liam was one of them.

The bo'sun stalked over to him, twitching his rope from side to side. Recognition, and something more menacing, lit up his eyes. "Get below," he said shortly.

"Yes, sir. May I have my ration of water first?"

The bo'sun scowled. "Don't sir me, I'm no pox-rotted officer! Get below with the rest of 'em or you'll feel the end of my rope on your arse. Jump!"

"I'll go below, but my wife needs water. It's little enough time it'll take to put a dropeen in my can for her."

The bo'sun's face turned the color of well-fired brick. His right arm drew back to slash Liam with the tarred rope. Instantly Liam caught his wrist and held it frozen in place. The bo'sun, taken by surprise, hesitated a moment before jerking his knee toward Liam's crotch. That moment was time enough for Liam to step to the side and let the blow brush by him. He raised his fist, ready to drive it at the base of the bo'sun's skull, but then he remembered Sean's warning the day before. Whatever the penalty might be for striking a member of the crew, it would not be light. Mary needed *him* far more than she needed the water he was fighting over.

"Stockman!" Involuntarily the bo'sun turned his head toward the bridge, where the captain stood watching the commotion. Liam seized that moment to release his arm and dash for the open hatch. As he ran, he heard the captain continue. "Damn it, Stockman, keep those animals under control, or it'll go the worse for you! And stand to attention when I speak to you! I'll have discipline on this ship if I have to have every man-jack of you at the gratings with his back flayed to ribbons!"

Safely below, Liam found that he could not stop himself from shivering. He was starting to understand what to expect on this voyage. He, and the other passengers in steerage, were nothing, or less than nothing; subject at every turn to the whims of willful men who, from the little he had seen and heard, were as sensitive to justice and mercy as the most infamous landlord in Ireland!

After a few moments, he regained control of his body and worked to put on a cheerful face. The voyage would be long, and Mary had enough to trouble her without giving a share of his own dark thoughts.

4

God save us, whatever are we to do?" Mary knelt by the open provision box, staring up at him with stricken eyes. "Liam, however could such a thing come to pass? I do believe some devil wants the lives out of us!"

"Far worse than a devil," replied Liam bleakly. "Greedy, soulless, godless men, and the names of the chief among them are Pedlock and Holmes, aye, and you may add their agent Regan to the list. If we die of this, starved altogether, our deaths will be on their heads, though I'll wager a bright john o'goblin to a groat they'll lose no sleep over it."

He stooped down by Mary's side and looked at the contents of the box again. Passengers, whether steerage or cabin, were expected to supply their own food for the voyage. By Act of Parliament, the captain was required to provide each passenger with seven pounds of bread, flour, oatmeal, or wheat per week, but that was never meant to do more than insure against starvation. Nor was the law always obeyed; the Houses of Parliament at Westminster were very far away from an emigrant ship in the middle of the North Atlantic.

Knowing this, Liam and Mary had taken almost every penny that remained after paying their passages and laid it out for sea-store: hard biscuit, bacon, vinegar, rice, smoked fish, a ham, and even a tiny packet of tea. They had been careful to check the prices at several provision merchants. To their surprise, the firm Regan had directed them to, Pedlock & Holmes—London, Liverpool, New York, was the most reasonable. Liam began to wonder if he had been unfairly suspicious of Regan.

Now, three days at sea, he knew the answer. Somehow their sea-store had been stolen, switched for provisions that were much worse than useless. The biscuit was more weevils than flour, the ham was full of maggots, and the fish was good only to be buried deep in a garden. There was no trace at all of the bacon, rice, or tea. "Of course," he muttered to himself. "They could well afford to sell that ham for less, being that they meant to sell it half a dozen times over. I do wonder how many others on this ship paid for a slice of it!"

Mary was still staring at him, as if she expected him somehow to make the situation come right. He felt a spasm of impatience with her that surprised him by its unfairness. He was her husband, the father of her unborn child, under holy vows to keep and protect her. Of course she looked to him. Who else could she look to? But what in the name of all the saints was he to do? He could not make maggots and weevils disappear by waving his hand!

"Liam?" she said tentatively.

"I don't know, *a grá mo chroí*. I don't know at all." He reached for the lid of the provision box and shut it carefully; not to protect its contents, which were worth no care, but to hide them from his sight. "I suppose we must try to live on the ration they give us. It is more than many of our old neighbors will be having by now."

"And what of the cook? We'll have nothing to give him now." Three cookstoves had to serve for over six hundred passengers. Though they were in constant use from before dawn until well after dark, only those who could fight for a place at the ranges managed to heat their food. Mary was willing to fight, but her condition disqualified her. The only other choice was to bribe the ship's cook, a half-breed Indian from Spanish America who understood English only when he chose to. For money or a portion of the food, he found space to cook on the range that was reserved for him and the cabin passengers' servants.

"Faith, then," Liam said stoutly, "we'll eat our victuals cold. The summer's hardly over; we'll not take sick from it." But he knew, and knew that Mary knew, that that was no answer at all. Rice, or flour, or oatmeal was no use to them uncooked. Unless he found a way, they would starve as surely on the *Lady Franklin* as they would have back at Ballynora.

Tom came skipping along the narrow path that twisted among the boxes and baggage. "Please, Liam," he said in a rush, "please say you'll come. The gentry are there, and there are dancers *go leór,* and when I said you were the best in all Erin they laughed at me! You'll come and show them, won't you?"

"To dance, is it?" said Liam, reaching over to rumple the boy's hair.

Tom retreated indignantly. "No! To play! Anybody can dance, but nobody plays fiddle the way you do."

Liam was both diverted and touched by the boy's declaration. He glanced over at Mary.

"Do," she said with abrupt decision. "You've not played for days now, and maybe it will take your mind from our troubles for a little while." Without meaning to, her eyes moved to the provision box.

"Will you be coming?"

She shook her head slowly. "No, I feel the need to rest. I tire easily." She sighed. "I wish this journey were over, *mo cuisle.* I feel sometimes that it will never end."

Liam helped her climb up to the bunk. "Rest now. It will be over soon." He grabbed his fiddle case and followed Tom to the open deck.

A crowd had gathered to the number of a hundred or more, but only a dozen were in the cleared center, dancing to the shrill sound of a tinwhistle played Kerry-style. As Tom had said, several of the cabin passengers were watching from the quarterdeck. When Liam started to tune his instrument, one of them pointed to him and made some comment that greatly amused his neighbor. Liam tried not to notice. but he knew that the back of his neck was turning pink.

Those nearest him in the crowd noticed him tuning and stood aside to let him through to the front, where the tinwhistler nodded a greeting without miss-

ing a note of the fast polka he was playing. He had a
cunning hand with his ornaments and grace notes,
Liam, thought, but he was not in condition. His face
was an alarming shade of red, and he gulped for air
at every rest. Sure enough, at the end of the next
repetition of the tune, he finished off and stood panting, deaf to the shouts for more.

"Yours, lad," he said when he caught his breath.
"I hope your arm is better than my wind. I'll just keep
my hand in with these." He pulled a set of bones from
his pocket and gave them a few tentative clacks.

Liam glanced around. Most of the people in the circle and in the front row looked young and full of
energy. "Form sets," he called out. "Form your sets for
a reel!" Two sets of four couples took their places. The
crowd moved back to make room, and he saw from
the corner of his eye that there were two or three
more couples too shy to step forward. Too bad; it
wasn't his place to coax them. He scraped a few preliminary notes and launched into an old Sligo tune
called "The Bird in the Bush."

There was a lot of confusion at first, and more than
one collision. The dancers came from every county
of Ireland, each with its own firm ideas about how a
reel should be danced. But patience, good humor,
and ingenuity carried them through. By the time the
first couples had reached bottom place in their sets,
an onlooker would have thought that they had been
dancing together since they were old enough to walk.

A stir off to the left caught Liam's eye. Sean was
clasping the hand of a colleen with bright eyes and
dark red hair, and urging the young people around
him to help him form a third set. By the time he

found three more couples, Liam was nearing the end of the tune again. Tipping a wink to the Kerryman, he fell silent for one beat, changed keys, and charged ahead with "MacMahon's Reel." The dancers, and some of the watchers, whooped with excitement, and Sean, who recognized the tune, grinned delightedly at Liam's little joke on his name.

The fourth time through brought the couples back to their original positions, flushed with the exercise and thoroughly winded. Liam gave a concluding flourish and lowered the fiddle. The Kerryman started a slow air on the whistle, and Liam closed his eyes to listen. It put him in mind of the wail of a heartsick girl, far off across the valley. Would he find such valleys and hills in America? Or would he pass the rest of his days in vain regret that he had left the shamrock shore? As nothing else had done, the music recalled to him all that he had lost when he quit his native land—the smell of a turf fire, the look of the rain clouds as they rolled in over the bay, the sound of thunder echoing off the slopes of Ben Bulben and Knocknarea. His eyes stung, and he squeezed them tightly against the shame of it. A moment more, and he would have himself bawling like a great girl!

He opened his eyes as the air came to an end. For some time he had been hearing, without taking any notice, an odd pattering sound on the deck nearby. Now he saw scores of coins winking at him from the planks at his feet. Most were copper pence and ha'penny bits, but he saw three or four sixpences and even a silver shilling.

"Something lively, maestro!" The accent was English, and so was the shilling that flew toward him from the quarterdeck. "That last was too doleful by half!" The comment evoked a burst of laughter from the other cabin passengers.

Liam struck up "The Rocky Road to Dublin" and was joined by the whistle player. Across the way, an old man with an old wooden flute made two false starts, then found the tune. Half a dozen boys and girls danced into the circle, grinning with exhilaration and clenching their teeth in concentration. The crowd clapped and stamped and whooped their enjoyment. But for Liam the pleasure had gone out of the moment.

His fingers flashed automatically through the evolutions of the rollicking slip-jig while he searched his mind to understand his abrupt change in mood. Was it the money? He should be glad, and more than glad, for that. There must be ten shillings or more on the deck, and even after he divided it with the Kerryman, it would be enough to feed them all for several days. He had prayed for a way to make up the loss of the rotten sea-store, and his prayer had been granted. Why then did he not rejoice?

Of course he knew the answer. The Englishman's remark and his casual alms were responsible. For centuries the Saxons had tried to destroy the wealth and culture of their sullen Irish subjects, and they had nearly succeeded. Even before the potato crop failed, Ireland was the most wretchedly poor country in Europe, and now the English policies and English landlords presented her people with a single choice: flee, or starve. But through it all, through massacre and famine and Penal Codes, the music had lived on. It was all the inheritance the people had, and it was all they were carrying with them to the New World.

But the Englishman understood none of that. For him, this was nothing more than a quaint entertainment, an exhibit from a fair or raree show, on a level with a gipsy and his dancing bear. Yet though he understood nothing, appreciated nothing, his silver shilling gave him the power to buy the fruit of three thousand years of culture for a moment's diversion. Only a matter of scale separated him from the English lord who took the great cross of carved stone, many centuries old, from a ruined monastery to use it for a garden ornament!

The tune ended. Liam handed the fiddle to Sean and knelt on the deck to gather the coins as the Kerryman started to play an unfamiliar reel. There were still dancers enough to make two sets, and more spectators than before, but Liam had no more heart for it. He carefully divided the money, left his fiddle in Sean's care, and went down to the stinking steerage deck once more. He averted his eyes as he passed a man and woman taking their pleasure—and in broad daylight!—and thought how greatly the conditions on shipboard had remade the customs and habits of them all. The way they were jammed together, quite literally on top of one another, made modesty a joke. And who could stay at all clean when there was barely water enough for cooking and drinking, and not always that? When six indescribably filthy privvies had to serve the needs of six hundred passengers, many of them ill? When they were not even allowed to take their bedding on deck to air it?

And then to have the shipowners, the very men who created these conditions and profited from them, blame them on the dirty habits of Irish savages! Liam had no illusions about his countrymen. Many of the emigrants were the poorest of the poor, landless farm laborers who had lived in mud hovels, sharing the single windowless room with the family pig and piling the manure next to the door. But they had not lived that way by choice, any more than they now slept four to a bunk by choice. They simply made the best of the situation they found themselves in and hoped that in time it would improve.

He leaned his shoulders against an empty berth and pursued his musing further. Had the English ever, for a moment, stopped to think what effects their laws were having on the Irish? Take the question of tenant-right: according to the English (and the Anglo-Irish who aped them), the Irish tenant farmer was a shiftless, happy-go-lucky fellow who, like the grasshopper in the fable, never gave a thought to the morrow. He never improved his land, never even whitewashed his cottage or planted a flower by the door, because he liked squalor. But according to English law (for Ireland; the law as it applied to England itself was very different), any improvement to a property was grounds for raising the rent.

A few years before the Blight, a hardworking Scotsman named Grant had leased a farm not far from Ballynora. He had labored mightily, turning and feeding the soil, rethatching the house, ditching and fencing and building a dairy and a piggery. When the agent saw what he had done, he doubled the rent. Grant worked all the harder, determined to make the place pay. He improved it to such an extent that the agent called in the hanging-gale, evicted him, and turned the farm over to his own wife's cousin. Grant left Ireland, determined, as he said, to find a country where the rewards of a man's labor were his own. Liam had often heard the story from his father, who believed to the day he died that Daniel O'Connell and Repeal were the answer to the problem of tenant-right and all else that plagued Ireland. Now O'Connell was dead in far-off Italy and all that he had worked for lay in ruins.

"Liam? Is it you?" His wife's voice broke the chain of bitter thoughts. He went to her and saw that her face was very pale.

"Here am I. How is it with you?"

"Well," she sighed. "And the music? How was that?"

"Oh, it was grand. And look!" He pulled the handful of coins from his pocket and held it out to her.

"Oh, Liam! There's enough there for a bit of food!"

"Aye, and for bribing the cook as well," he said sourly. "Folk are generous, even when it's little they can spare themselves. We'll not starve, *Maire arún.* Now, what can we do to make your rest more comfortable here? You're sure that you will not take a turn on the deck now? The fresh air would be good for you."

She sighed again. "Tomorrow, maybe. For now, I believe I'll sleep again if the babe will let me."

But Mary could not go up on deck the next day. That night the *Lady Franklin* met rough seas, the product of a hurricane off Bermuda, and Captain Drummond ordered the steerage passengers below and the hatches battened down. Eight days were to pass before they were opened again. For eight days, the six hundred emigrants were prisoners in the reeking hold.

They had no light or fresh air, no ration of food or water, no fire to cook the pitiful supplies in their boxes, no path to the befouled privvies. The wild gyrations of the ship threw them from their bunks and gave them the dry heaves. Cold seawater poured through the overhead ventilators and sloshed ankle-deep on the deck. Worst of all, there was no one to tell them if this was the usual way of a ship in high seas, or if they were on the edge of doom. With every roll, they expected the ship to founder, to take them to the bottom with no hope of escape or rescue. Shrieked prayers and curses fought to be heard over the crash of waves and the squeal of the ship's timbers working against each other.

On the fifth day, Sean took Liam aside. "There's a child a few bunks ahead fallen ill," he said in an undertone.

Liam looked at him narrowly. There were bloody few in steerage who weren't ill; why was this child so remarkable?

"Her forehead is very hot to the touch," Sean continued, "and her face is very dark."

"Sweet Christ!" Liam knew what that meant. No one who had lived through 1847 in Ireland could mistake those symptoms. Call it black fever or ship fever, famine fever or typhus, it was deadly and it went through a crowd like fire through dry brush. "And us shut in together like pigs for slaughter!"

Sean chewed on his upper lip for a few moments, then said, "If I were to knock on the hatch and ask the surgeon to come?"

"Don't think of it. He's nought but a drink-besotted fool, and would want a full bottle of poteen to look at her from across the room. There's more, too: Once let the captain learn of this, and he'll likely keep us locked in here all the way to New York. Who is the child? Has she people to care for her?"

"A sister," Sean stammered, "no one else. They're going out to an uncle in New York. Their father was sent to Van Dieman's Land years ago for poaching, and they lost their mother this spring to the dysentery."

It crossed Liam's mind that Sean knew a good deal about the two sisters, but he set the idea aside for a time. More urgent matters came first. "Have you had the fever?" he asked.

"No."

"Then you must stay as much away as you can. Mary and I both took it last year and lived, but I'd not put her in danger so near her time. Take me to the child."

She lay shivering and twitching on the hard bunk. She looked to be no more than seven, and Liam thought that she might have been a pretty child before the *fiabhras dubh* congested her face and stupified her gaze. He lifted the filthy blanket that was her only covering. No rash yet on her chest and stomach, so the crisis was still ahead.

Sheila, the older sister, stood watching, twisting her hands nervously in her skirt. He recognized her as the red-haired girl Sean had danced with that day on deck. He stepped over to her. "You know what this is," he said. She nodded quickly. "The fever must take its course. I have never yet heard of a way to cut it short. What you must do is try to help the child through it. Have you had it yourself?"

"I . . . I think so, sir. I was very sick with a fever

last year, which might have been the *fiabhras dubh*."

"And sea-store—can you feed the girl if she'll eat? She'll need the strength."

"We've little enough, I fear. Our uncle in America paid our passages, you see. I—" Two tracks glistened on her cheeks as she broke off, unable to go on.

"Never mind, *mo grá*," said Liam gently, "no doubt we can spare a little trifle, and there's more will step forward when your need is seen."

Liam's prediction about the kindness of the other passengers was both right and wrong. Food there was, more than little Maura could take in, in her delirium; but as the fever spread, the shortage of water grew desperate. Those who had any at all began to hoard it against the day when one of their own fell ill. Pounding on the closed hatches brought no response, and the rumor spread that the sailors had sealed them in to die.

At last the seas grew calmer. The hatches were thrown back. Blinding sunlight and sweet breezes poured through the openings, but even that relief was limited. The vile effluvium that was such a distressing symptom of the typhus alerted the crew at once. The ship's surgeon staggered over to one of the hatches, sniffed the noxious fumes, and put the entire steerage deck under quarantine. The captain immediately posted sailors at the head of each stairway to enforce the order, though he did consent to lower casks of water and barrels of ship's biscuit to the parched, hungry passengers.

Perhaps the fever was a milder strain than most, or perhaps the plague the year before had already carried off those most likely to die, for when two weeks had passed, only twenty-three passengers were dead. Little Maura, nursed faithfully by her sister, passed the crisis successfully and looked likely to live, to Liam's great joy. In helping Sheila to care for the child, he had become attached to her. She came to have some connection in his mind with his own unborn child, so much so that he was sure his child was a girl. He gave Mary a great fright by saying as much and calling her Dierdre by name. Mary had always heard that naming an unborn child brought the worst sort of luck to mother and child both. And at the moment Liam spoke the name, the child in her belly stirred and kicked. Mary furtively crossed herself but said nothing to Liam for fear he would laugh and mock her. She could not stand it when he laughed at her, though she knew he never meant it cruelly.

The few shillings that Liam had gained with his playing were soon spent, and their hunger grew sharp again. Liam grew gaunt on his diet of biscuit and found that his gums bled easily, but it was worse for Mary. It seemed to him that all the goodness of the little she ate passed her up and went directly to the baby. Her cheeks became hollow and her eyes sank deep into her head until, barely eighteen, she had the look of a care-worn woman of forty. Her black hair, once so thick and lustrous, hung limply about her wan face. Liam did all he could think of, even pretending to have eaten already and adding his meager portion to hers, but it was not enough. She needed beef-tea and custards and arrowroot, foods that would build up her strength. A pound of hardtack a day did nothing but keep her from dying of starvation, and it would not do even that for much longer.

Captain Drummond still refused to have the steerage passengers on deck, so it was a matter of wonder when the ship's clerk appeared in the hatchway one afternoon and shouted, "Pass the word for the fiddler and the whistle-player!" Minutes later Liam and the Kerryman were standing at the foot of the stairs. "You're wanted on deck," the clerk said sharply. "Look alive!"

"And who might be wanting us," asked Liam, "and for what?"

The clerk studied his face. "I've seen you before, fellow," he said. "You'd better watch your step if you know what's good for you. You're wanted to make music. There's money in it for you. Now get moving!"

Liam stayed where he was, though the thought of silver, and of the food it would buy for Mary, threatened to drive everything else from his mind. "Jaysus, it's a quare thing," he said in a thick brogue, "but hearin' orders cramps me poor fingers something terrible! Divvil if I can play a note till I know who my generous patron might be!"

"Goddam stubborn Micks! It's Mr. Holmes of Goree Piazza, the ship broker." His tone was that another man might have saved for talking of God Himself. "It's his daughter's birthday, and she asked for music."

"Mr. Holmes of Pedlock & Holmes? He sails in this ship?"

The clerk snorted. "Sails in it? He chartered it! Until we get to New York Bay, the *Lady Franklin* is his ship. Now, will your highness deign to play or do I have to send someone down there to kick your royal arse?"

Liam hurried to get his fiddle. He badly wanted the money, but worse than that he wanted to see the face of the man who sold rotten provisions to poor emigrants, then shipped them off in conditions that would make the captain of a slaveship blush with shame.

Holmes did not look at him once. He sat to one side of the quarterdeck with a cigar in his mouth, tapping his foot in a rhythm that had no relation at all to the music. But his daughter leaned over the railing, her blonde curls falling forward and shadowing her intent face. Liam recalled her at once; he had seen her and her father board the ship at Liverpool and remarked bitterly on them to Sean. Now, knowing her father's identity, his bitterness multiplied twenty-fold; yet still he played as well as he could, airs, and set dances, and lively jigs, and after each tune she clapped with real delight and looked at him with glowing eyes, and he softened toward her.

Belowdecks, Mary lay listlessly on the bunk. She had done little else for three weeks. Moving about made the hunger worse. Though her eyes looked at rough-hewn planks scant inches above her head, in her mind she saw the fields and hills and beaches of Sligo, and the hedge-flanked lane that led to the cottage where she was born. It was gone now, tumbled by the landlord after her parents died. Lulled by the memories, she closed her eyes and drifted off.

Suddenly she gasped as a sharp pang flared in her belly. Her eyes grew round with fear and she clasped her hands over the place where the pain ebbed, then returned fiercer. She felt a sticky warmth on her thighs, and her face became ashen gray. "Jesus, Mary, and Joseph," she whispered, "the baby. I'm losing the baby!"

Every fiber of her wanted to scream, to hurl her terror and rage to the very gates of heaven, but she pressed her lips together and struggled down from the bunk. Liam; she must stay calm and find Liam. He would make it all right again, but where was he? Where was he when she needed him so badly? God in Heaven, where was her husband!

Dazed with fear and pain, she staggered to the stairway and up toward the open hatch. The sailor at the top stopped her. "Now, now, you know you're not allowed," he said.

"Liam. I need Liam. Please, I—"

"What's this, Taylor?" a new voice growled. "No steerage scum on deck, that's the orders."

"Sorry, bo'sun, she won't go back."

Hysteria welled up in Mary even as she felt her strength drain away. Trembling violently, she pushed past the sailor and crawled onto the open deck. Where was Liam?

"Oh no, you don't, you black Irish bitch! Get back down in the kennel where you belong!" Rough hands grabbed her shoulders and shoved her backwards. The coaming around the hatch caught her behind the knees and she tumbled helplessly down the steep stairs to the deck below. Now, at last, she allowed herself to scream.

Liam was finishing a jaunty version of "The Trip to Sligo," one of his father's favorite jigs, when he heard a commotion behind him. He concluded the tune and turned just in time to see Tom wriggle past two sailors and run toward him. One of the sailors grabbed the boy's shirt as he went by, but it came away in his hand.

"Liam!" Tom cried. "LIAM!" He ran up and threw

his arms around Liam's waist. His emaciated body shook uncontrollably.

"What is it, Thomas *a grá*? What's the matter then?" He stooped down to bring his face level with the boy's.

"It's Mary, she's hurt. She's hurt bad. She's all bloody. She wants you. I'm scared, Liam. Is she going to die?"

Liam's heart seemed to freeze. He picked Tom up in one arm and strode toward the hatch. As he started down the stairs, a voice behind him said, "Here, Stockman, we're not done with him yet. We want more music!"

They had carried Mary to a bunk near the foot of the stairs. Sean, and his friend Sheila, and the Widow Gorman, who knew something of midwifery, stood near. Liam fell to his knees beside the bunk and looked deep into his young wife's eyes. At least she knew him; she tried to raise her head and speak, but he pressed her head back down. She clutched at his hand, and her eyes narrowed, then widened, as though she was trying to ask a question of overwhelming importance. Her breath caught in her throat and rattled noisily.

Liam stroked her hand. "Rest now, Máire," he crooned, "rest now, *a stóirín óg mo chróí.*" He refused to see the spreading pool of blood under her body. "You must save your strength. In but a few days more, we will reach the New World. We can be happy there, *mo cuisle.* Only a few days more!"

Her body arched convulsively up from the bunk, then fell back limply. The Widow Gorman crossed herself quickly, then stepped forward to press the lids down over the staring eyes. Liam watched her uncomprehendingly, then looked from the face to the hand he was still stroking. "Máire?" he said, in the voice of a child who wakes from a nightmare to find himself in darkness. *"Máire arún?"*

Sean put his hands on Liam's shoulders. He shrugged them off and struggled to his feet. As he looked around, understanding grew on him. He pressed his palms to his eyes, wiped them down over his face to clasp his neck. "How came this?" he said finally.

No one spoke.

"I'll know, by Jesus, whatever I must do! I say again, how came this to be?"

An old man at the back of the crowd told him. Liam stood stock-still for a moment, then in a movement too swift to follow, he knelt, dipped his fingertips in the pool of blood, and smeared it across his forehead.

"Now by all the saints," he said, in a voice that shook with passion, "I vow that I'll have vengeance for this deed! Hear me, all of you, and witness it!" His eyes rolled up in his head, and Sean caught him just as he slumped to the floor. Two strangers helped him carry Liam to the bunk, while Sheila led a sobbing Tom away from the corpse of his last relation.

Captain Drummond allowed Liam, Tom, Sean, and Sheila to come on deck for Mary's burial. The canvas bundle, achingly small, rested on a plank that protruded over the side of the ship. Four sailors held ropes that reached, over a pulley, to the other end of the plank. At a nod, they started to sing:

"Haul on the bowline,
  The Black Star bowline,
  Haul on the bowline,
  The bowline haul!"

On the last word, they tugged at the ropes, the plank
tilted upward, and the canvas bundle slid into the
ocean. Liam murmured something under his breath,
then turned away. As they returned to the steerage
deck, he didn't speak, nor did he seem to hear the
mutters of "Sorry for your trouble" from everyone they
passed.

When they reached the bunk, he stopped and stood
aimlessly, not looking at anyone. The silence stretched
out. Then Tom flung himself at Liam, shaking and
sobbing. Slowly, carefully, Liam reached down to
stroke the boy's head. "Don't cry, *mo stóirín,*" he said
softly, "your sister is in Heaven, praying for you.
Praying for us all, God rest her soul." He bent his
head over the child, but not before Sean had seen the
glint of tears on his cheeks.

5

at dawn on the thirty-eighth day, the masthead lookout spied the coast of Long Island. During the course of the morning, the steerage passengers were permitted to come on deck, a hundred at a time, to crowd the right-hand rail and stare out across the water at the featureless gray line on the horizon. Then they had to go to work, scouring the steerage deck with sand, sluicing it down with seawater, and drying the timbers with pans of hot coals from the galley. By late afternoon the hold was cleaner than it had been during the whole voyage, and the third mate threatened them with a month in the pesthouse if they failed to keep it that way.

The next morning found the *Lady Franklin* anchored in New York Bay, off the northern end of Staten Island. This time all were allowed on deck, to exclaim over the thickly forested hills, the many windows in the houses along the shore, and the number of steamboats crisscrossing the sparkling waters of the huge bay. One of the steamboats drew alongside the ship, bringing three bewhiskered gentlemen in black frock coats and white cravats who scampered up the rope ladder with a skill born of much practice. One was from the Customs; the other two were quarantine officers.

"Well, Cap'n Drummond," one of them drawled, "did ye have a good v'yage?"

"I'll tell you, Doctor, it was a spanker! An out and out spanker!"

"Not troubled with sickness, were ye?"

"Healthiest trip I can recall! Will you gents come down to my cabin? I picked up some wine in France I'd like your opinions on."

They hesitated, then the older officer said, "Delighted, Captain, after we've looked at your passengers. Have the clerk read the manifest, will you?" Each passenger, as his name was called, walked between the two doctors to the other end of the deck. All were passed as healthy, which was not surprising since seven bedridden emigrants were hidden away in the crew's quarters for'rard. Next the two officers climbed down to the steerage deck, then up again.

Finally, the younger one raised his voice to say, "Do any of you mean to complain about your treatment on this voyage, or the provisions you received, or anything else about the conduct of the ship? If so, please speak now, so that we can include it in our report."

The only sound was the sighing of the breeze in the rigging. Everyone knew that a complaint might mean weeks of confinement on the ship or at the quarantine station on Staten Island. Just in case someone was still mad enough to speak up, the bo'sun had spread his men through the crowd, ready to suppress the protester. But they were wasted.

"Good!" the quarantine officer said after a minute or so. "Well, Cap'n Drummond, you've a sound, healthy ship, as always. I think a glass of that wine you spoke of would not be unwelcome, then we'll leave you to take these people across to New York. They'll be glad to land, I suppose!"

Sean McMahon and Sheila Malone were among the passengers who thronged the sides to gaze out at the busy waterfront of the Jerseys and the green slopes of Brooklyn. Though they looked at the scenery, and Sheila kept one eye on the children, their talk was of Liam.

"What will he do?" Sheila demanded. "What of wee Tom? It's not fair to the boy, him going on this way, shutting off his grieving like a jar of fermenting fruit. That way lies destruction, I'm telling you." Her little chin looked very determined as she spoke.

Sean looked away. "It's little I can do," he said broodingly. "Losing your wife and child at one stroke is no light thing, and her so young, too. And he wouldn't hear of a wake, either. I think he wants to save up his anger. He's not been easy on the whole voyage, for he's not a man to let ill treatment go by, and Christ knows we've had ill treatment enough. I know he feels for the boy."

"Och, I'm not denying that! But feeling for him, and doing right by him, may not be the same. A young man, with his way to make in the world, can't always afford to be tied down." After a moment, her cheeks reddened as she remembered that Liam wasn't the only young man with his way to make. "I've an idea," she continued bravely, "but I'll not breathe it until we've met me Uncle Pat. I've not seen him since I was the age of Maura, when he went off to America. I wonder if he'll know we're due to come today. I hope so; New York looks to me like a bigger place even than Dublin, and I had the terror of a time finding me way to the Liverpool steamboat, dodging the waggons and all."

As the *Lady Franklin* drew closer to the great circular fort of Castle Garden, at the southern tip of New York, she altered course to enter the East River. Twenty minutes later she was tying up to a wharf in Coenties' Slip. The slip was lined on all three sides with substantial brick houses of three and four stories. The signs on their fronts proclaimed them to be the premises of chandlers, India merchants, fur dealers, coffee traders, and forwarders, whatever they might be.

Of more immediate concern to Sean was the mob that waited on the muddy wharfside. They were strangers, of course, but he knew from his stay in Liverpool who they were. They were runners, and an unsavory lot they looked, too, even if half of them seemed to sport cravats of the very loudest shade of green and speak in brogues so thick that Sean could hardly decide if it was meant for English or Chinese.

"Stay back when folk start to leave the ship," he warned Sheila, "and keep a firm watch on Maura and Tom. I'll mind your trunk; it's little enough of me own I have to be concerned over. Where's Liam?"

"Here," said a colorless voice from behind him. Sean turned. Liam's blue eyes seemed paler somehow, perhaps from the dark shadows under them, and he looked like a man who had not slept for days. He carried his fiddle under his arm, and the bundle of bedding lay at his feet.

"I was after telling Sheila that we'll guard her and the children from the runners," said Sean, "until she can meet up with her Uncle Pat. What will you do then, Liam *a grá*, you and the lad?"

"There's that I must take care of here, but I suppose after that we'll go west until I find work to earn our bread. And you?"

Sean glanced quickly at Sheila and blushed. "I'll stay here if there's work to be found. Sheila thinks her uncle may be of help—from what he writes, he's a well-respected man in the city. Perhaps he could help you too. I'm loath to see you go from everyone you know."

Liam agreed, but Sean sensed that it was more to close the subject than said in earnest. *Arra*, he would broach it again when they were well on land, over a glass of something warming to the soul.

The mayhem on the dock below them was far worse than they had seen in Liverpool. The English runners had carried off the emigrants' luggage as a way of forcing them to come to the right boarding-house, but the American runners were simply thieves who well deserved the name they were given of landsharks. The worst of it, to Sean's mind, was that their Irish accents sounded authentic. What a terrible fate, to flee oppression, famine, and pestilence, only to fall prey to one's own countrymen, who ought, if anyone was, to be sympathetic!

Through the din of shouts and cries, he suddenly thought he heard a bellowed "Sheila Malone!" He listened intently and scanned the faces on the wharf. There it came again, from a square-faced man with bushy eyebrows, on the outskirts of the crowd. He stood out from the ragged emigrants and the hardly less ragged runners, with his check pantaloons and skyblue swallowtail coat and general air of being well-fed. Sean nudged Sheila and directed her attention to him.

She hesitated, then, "Yes, it's him! It must be!" She waved excitedly. "Doesn't he look well!" she said to Sean between shouts of Uncle Pat. "My father was a fine-looking man, too, for all that he seldom got enough to eat with so many of us to provide for. Oh, why don't he look this way! UNCLE PAT!"

Her last shout did it. The square-faced man stared for a moment, then started toward the gangway. He ploughed through the tightly packed throng as if it weren't there, and Sean noticed that the runners pulled themselves, and their victims, out of his path. Pat Malone, it seemed, was someone to reckon with in New York!

Moments later he was clasping Sheila in a bear hug. "Och, *mhuirnín*," he exclaimed, "I'd have known you in a thousand. You're the very image of your mother, God rest her soul, when Rob brought her home as his wife." He spotted Maura hanging back shyly and reached a hand to her. "Come here, *mo cuisle*, and give your old Uncle Pat a kiss. Oh but it's fine to see you both, my word it is!"

He started to ask Sheila about the voyage, but she interrupted to call Sean over and introduce him. Malone took the situation in with a shrewd eye. "From Galway, is it?" he said genially. "Welcome to Amerikay, Sean McMahon. You'll find plenty of fine Galway lads here in New York, so many I wonder there's anyone left in poor old Ireland. And is it as distressful as they say?"

"Worse," replied Sean. "The praties are gone altogether, and no one has anything left to sell for oats or corn. There'll be corpses along the roads again before winter, and coffin ships sailing from every port in the West."

"Sad times," Malone said with a sigh, "sad times indeed. Is this all the baggage you have, Sheila *a grá?*"

She spoke briefly in his ear, and Sean knew by the movement of his eyes that it was of Liam she spoke. When she finished, he squeezed her shoulder and stepped over to where Liam stood gazing out over the city. "Mr. O'Donnell? I hope you and your young relation will join us for a bite of dinner, for friendship's sake. I'm sorry to hear of your trouble."

Liam looked as if he had been summoned from a great distance. He glanced around at Sean, and Sheila, and then to where Tom and Maura were seated on the deck playing some game, before saying, "Thank you, sir. I'd be honored."

"Good. Come along then, the lot of you. It's not a long walk."

Sheila had lived almost the whole of her seventeen years in a market town in County Clare. Since the day she and her little sister had climbed up onto the

Bianconi car for the trip to Dublin, her ideas of the world had undergone one shock after another. First Dublin's parks and palaces, then Liverpool, second city of the British Empire, with its grand public buildings and noisome slums, had shown her much that she had never dreamt of back in County Clare. Now, as she followed her uncle along Broadway, she realized that even Dublin and Liverpool were provincial compared to the Metropolis of the World.

She dodged back as an omnibus veered toward the curb, but even so the muck spattered her skirt. No great loss, she thought; for she had had no means to wash it on the ship. But what did fine ladies do when a dray or one of the horse-drawn railcars passed too close? A glossy black barouche approached carrying just such a lady, in a handsome violet dress trimmed with black feathers and holding a silk parasol to match. She lounged back against the cushions, gazing out at the street just above the heads of the pedestrians. By some chance her eyes fell just in time to meet Sheila's. An expression of vivid disgust flashed across her face, then gave way to practiced indifference as the carriage whirled past.

Sheila's face flamed nearly the shade of her hair. She had made a great effort to keep herself and Maura neat and clean throughout the voyage, but she knew now that here on the streets of New York she looked as dirty and ragged as a tinker. She hurried her pace and took her uncle's arm. "Uncle," she said firmly, "I'll not be disgracing you before your friends by appearing this way. Is there a back gate to where you live? Do point it out, and then walk ahead and meet us where none may see."

He looked at her amazed, then roared with laughter. "Lassie," he said finally, "when I came to this town, I'd hardly the means to keep me backside covered, and I was well-dressed compared to many and many! No friend of mine will think the less of you for a dress that is not over-clean, for they have all made the crossing too, and have sent for wives and sisters and old mothers to come out. Sure, and no man who sees your handsome face and bright eye will notice what you wear anyway! Ye'll have gowns enough, now you're here, don't worry about that. Pat Malone is not one to let his brother's orphaned children go in tatters! Now hush, for we're nearly there."

He led the small group off Broadway into a warren of narrow, twisting streets. Sheila lost her bearings immediately, but she was oddly comforted by the sight of pigs rooting contentedly in the muddy streets and of pale, thin children dashing and splashing past. New York was not all palaces, then! Her uncle, perhaps sensing her reaction, stopped and turned to them.

"There are three things you must learn about Amerikay," he said. His manner suggested that he had spoken these lines many times. "The first is that the streets are not paved with gold. The second is that the streets are not paved at all. And the third is that we're the lads who are expected to pave them!" He waited out their chuckles, then added, "And there's my shebeen, on the opposite corner."

The building across the way had the look of a rich merchant's house from a hundred years before, three stories, a basement, and a garrett, of rose-red brick with cut-stone lintels. A stone staircase led from the pavement to double doors flanked by narrow windows and topped by a graceful fanlight. A doorway at the side of the stairs led to the basement, which was little lower than the level of the street. Over this doorway a crudely-lettered sign proclaimed, "GROG. P. J. Malone, Prop."

"I let the house out in rooms," he explained as they followed him through the grog-shop, "but I've saved the three at the back for meself."

Pat Malone had decided even before he left County Longford that he meant to be a wealthy publican in America. Crops often failed, and stocks were subject to Panics, but he had never known a man's thirst to disappear. At Liverpool, while the others were buying sea-store, he filled his box with stone jars of poteen and sold it by the dram during the tedious voyage. By the time they reached New York, he had a small supply of gold sovereigns, tied carefully in his shirt-tail, enough to rent a ground-floor room in the notorious Five Points district and buy an initial stock of liquor.

Ten years later, he owned three houses that he rented out, a room to a family. There was no running water or indoor plumbing, but even the wealthy in New York went without those luxuries. The rents he charged were high, but they were not as high as many, and New York was a notoriously expensive place to live. There was overcrowding, with as many as eight people living in a room ten by ten, but people had to live somewhere, and the flood of refugees from the Hunger had strained the city far beyond its limits. All in all, Pat Malone felt that he was doing a service for his countrymen, providing them with homes, even while they were enriching him in return.

What was more, they, and many others in the neighborhood, agreed. They brought their troubles to his sympathetic ear, and he helped in any way he could. He sent those with citizenship problems to a friendly magistrate, introduced men who needed work to men who needed laborers, took up collections for widows and orphans, contributed generously to the parish building fund, put relatives and former neighbors in touch with each other. . . . And if he could help in no other way, he was always good for a small loan and a 'drop of the craitur' on the house. His grogshop flourished, and his customers and friends earnestly sought his advice on such weighty matters as who to vote for in local and national elections. It was a tribute to the respect they held him in that the man he backed always carried his district handsomely. He was still far from being a wealthy man, but he was content to know that he had placed his feet firmly upon the ladder that led to wealth, and to a kind of fame as well.

He put a platter of boiled potatoes, a bowl of buttermilk, and a dish of salt on the big table in the back room, then watched covertly as his guests dug into them, expertly peeling them with a thumbnail, then dipping into buttermilk and salt. Sheila was a fine, healthy looking girl, with eyes that would tear the heart from you. As for her sweetheart—for it was clear which way the wind set—he seemed a likely lad, not afraid of hard work but able to come through it with a smile. If he'd a mind to it, there was a place for him in the grog-shop.

His friend, though, had the look of one who thought too much. In Malone's experience, such men were dangerous, visionaries and fanatics who would set fire to a house to rid it of rats. Allowances must be made for one so recently widowed, and him so young too. Still, he would feel more at ease if O'Donnell moved on, the sooner the better.

Made uncomfortable by his own uncharitable thoughts, Malone brought a flask of poteen and three glasses to the table and filled each to the brim. "*Slainte,*" he said. Sean and Liam echoed the toast and drank down the fiery spirits. Both had fits of choking and tried to hide the tears that sprung to their eyes, but when Malone offered the flask again, they held out their glasses. Sheila discreetly left the table to play a game with the two children.

Some time later, Sean's eyelids were drooping uncontrollably, but Liam was as alert, and as moody, as ever. Malone had hoped that drink would lead him to talk of his dead wife, perhaps to turn maudlin and burst into tears before slipping under the table. The saloon-keeper had seen that happen often enough at wakes, and had seen that the bereaved generally felt the better for it the next day. But Liam, it seemed, was not the sort to take that path.

He was also, it seemed, a man of some pride. When Malone offered to fill his glass yet again, he held up his hand, palm outward, and said, "No, sir. I thank you for it, but you cannot live by giving away your fine whisky, and you must know that I am next to penniless. There is nothing I can do to repay your kindliness."

"There is, too," replied Malone as his eye fell on Liam's fiddle-case. "Give us a tune or two, and I'll call us even."

He knew from Liam's face that the request was not welcome, but there was no way the young musician could refuse it. He took out the fiddle and held it in his hands for a long moment with his head bowed, then tucked it under his chin and began to play the "Lament for Owen Roe," a slow air that swept upward like a cry, then fell sobbing into silence, not once, but again and again. Just when Malone was beginning to feel that he could take no more, Liam moved into a reel, gradually increasing the tempo until his fingers were scampering over the neck of the fiddle.

Months before a Leitrim man had borrowed two dollars from Malone and left as a pledge his bodhrán, the wide, shallow goatskin drum of the West of Ireland. Now Malone fetched it from its place over the bar and gave it a few tentative taps with the short double-ended beater. Sean blinked and pushed himself upright, then held out his hands for the drum. Malone passed it over. Sean held it upright in his left hand, the rim resting on his thigh, and shook the beater a few times in his right hand while he listened intently to the tune Liam was playing.

Liam did not seem to take notice of any of this, but suddenly he threw his head back and nodded. Sean flashed into action just as the fiddle soared into a new tune at an even faster tempo. The tabletop vibrated under Malone's fingertips; it was no accident that the drum's Gaelic name meant "The Thunderer." The doorway to the grog-shop was jammed with eager listeners, brought in from the street by the music, and Malone calculated that most who had the price in their pockets would take a drop of something before leaving. Music was no bad investment, it seemed!

When the reel ended, to cheers and shouts of encouragement, Liam struck up a hornpipe and little Maura in her bare feet and ragged dress skipped and danced across the floor until her face was flushed and she could scarcely breathe for the exertion and excitement of it. She finally collapsed laughing across her Uncle Pat's lap. Malone called for Sheila to dance, but she wouldn't before so many men, and her the only woman.

After the hornpipe, Liam passed his fiddle across to Sean and took up the bodhrán. Sean chose to play a set of jigs, beginning with "The Gander in the Pratie Hole" and moving into "The Mooncoin." He knew he was not the player Liam was, but the fiddle felt good in his hands and the music played so grand. He decided that once he found work, he was going to put a few pennies aside every week toward buying a fiddle of his own. Until then, perhaps Liam would let him play his now and again.

Perhaps it was ill chance, or perhaps Sean recalled the time on shipboard when Liam had played "MacMahon's Reel" as a compliment to him and wanted to return it. Whatever the reason, he decided to finish the set of jigs with "The Trip to Sligo." At the first notes of the tune, Liam abruptly put the bodhrán on the table and stood up. Sean stopped playing in surprise.

"I'm sorry," Liam said to Malone, "but I've just brought to mind something I must do. Sean, keep the fiddle for me, won't you? These kind people will relish another tune or two, I believe."

The nearest onlookers cheered their agreement.

Liam went over to where Tom was sitting on the floor and stooped beside him. "You'll be good and mind Sean and Sheila while I'm gone, won't you, *mo grá*?"

"Yes, Liam." The boy sounded frightened.

Liam patted his shoulder and stood up to go. "Is there no way I can help you?" Malone demanded. "You're a stranger still in town, after all. Do you need directions?"

Liam hesitated. "No, thank you," he said slowly, "but there is a thing. Me leg has been bothering me today. Could you give me the loan of a stick?"

"Whichever you fancy," said Malone, gesturing toward the umbrella stand by the door.

Liam looked the walking-sticks over carefully, finally selecting a heavy blackthorn stick. He hefted it thoughtfully in his hand, then seemed to come to some decision. "This one, then, and I thank you for it, Mr. Malone. I'll just be away then." He slipped through the crowd and disappeared.

"Your friend is a fey man," Malone said. "And divvil a sign of a limp I saw on him either. Why should he be wanting a stick?"

A sense of foreboding seized Sean. Now that he gave it thought, it seemed to him that Liam had seldom let his fiddle out of his sight. What was urgent enough to make him go like that, leaving it in another's hands? And why had his few words to Tom sounded so much like a good-bye?

He lifted the fiddle and played the first notes of another hornpipe, but his mind was not in his playing and he soon put the fiddle away.

6

the streets of the city were dark. The pools of dim light from the widely-spaced oil lamps served only to make the darkness beyond thicker. From time to time, a distant *clop-clop* echoed from the houses and the faint lamps of a carriage or the lit windows of an omnibus crossed an intersection ahead. From time to time, the opening of a door spilled a fan of light and a babble of drunken voices onto the street. Once the glowing tip of a cigar glided past on the opposite pavement.

Shapes loomed and vanished in the darkness—a barrow left carelessly by the curb; a pig returning home from a late excursion. Several times he sensed the near approach of other men, but whether they saw his clothes and dismissed him as a worthwhile target or saw his firm grip on the stick and decided he would be too much trouble, they sheared away again. It occurred to him that they might well have thought him a robber and been frightened of *him*!

Finding his way at night in a strange city was not easy. At one point he was sure that he had made a complete circle, and took to memorizing the twists of the street. Once he stumbled onto Broadway, though, the task was simpler. The railcars ran often, shedding light on the street from the huge oil lamps that swung from their ceilings, and the several large, luxurious hotels along the avenue were brightly lit. He strode confidently along the raised sidewalk, swinging the blackthorn with an air almost jaunty. After a few blocks he stopped, considered, and took the next turning to the left, toward the East River.

"I have a message for the boatswain."

The watchman at the foot of the gangway tipped his chair forward. "What, Stockman? He's not aboard. They're all gone. First night ashore. Leave it if you want."

"I was told to give it to him personally. Where would I find him?"

The old man pursed his lips and propelled a dark stream of tobacco juice toward the edge of the wharf. "Beats me, mister. Try the nearest bar—or the nearest whorehouse. He's not so particular he'd go farther'n he has to."

"Thank you."

"Sure." After a moment, he called, "Mister? Keep an eye out. He gets awful mean when he's had a few."

New York was one of the busiest ports in the world, perhaps *the* busiest, and the hundreds of ships that arrived put thousands of sailors on the streets with pay in their pockets every week. The businessmen in the

area around South Street were dedicated to reliev-
ing them of their pay and sending them back to sea
with pleasant, if fuzzy, memories. The saloons and
cribs stayed open day and night, though they were at
their most frantic in the hours after midnight.

He gave up after the fourth saloon. He might have
have passed within six feet of Stockman and not
known it, so jammed were the gin-mills with noisy,
drunken sailors and their slatterns. Or the bo'sun could
be upstairs in one of the brothels, or in a back alley
pissing against a wall. The one thing he knew for certain was that Stockman would return to the *Lady
Franklin* sooner or later. Returning to the wharf, he
slipped into a darkened doorway and prepared himself for a long wait.

The moon rose late in the partly cloudy sky, and
had already passed the zenith when he finally heard
uncertain steps approaching the wharf. Keeping to
the shadows, he looked out. The size was right, and
the muttering voice rang familiarly in his ears. The
edge of the moonlight crossed the river and sped along
the dock, revealing to his dark-adapted eyes the face
he was seeking. He gripped the walking stick and
stepped from his hiding place.

"Stockman!" he called softly.

The bo'sun stopped and swiveled his head. "What is
it, you poxy bastard? Who are you? How do you know
my name?"

"You killed my wife, Stockman! I'm here to pay you
back!" He stepped closer and shifted his grip to the
middle of the blackthorn.

Stockman seemed confused by the accusation. He

peered into the shadows, trying to make out his accuser's face. "I know you," he said finally. "You're that God-rotted Paddy that made trouble for me this trip. Come for your licking, have you?" Suddenly he rushed forward and grappled with his assailant, who had time only for a half-hearted blow with the stick. The glancing blow to his shoulder seemed both to sober the bo'sun and enrage him.

"You would, would you, you pig-fucker! God damn your eyes, I'll slice you to ribbons for that! I'll cut off your balls and feed them to the dogs!" He loosened his hold to reach back along his waist, and felt his wrist caught in an iron grip.

The two men veered across the wharf in a macabre dance, each clasping the other's right wrist, then one of them tripped and they fell together to the muddy ground, twisting and rolling in the foul-smelling muck. By sheer accident, the head of the blackthorn stick rammed the bo'sun under the chin. He grunted and loosened his hold for a moment. Instantly his attacker sprang to his feet and raised the stick to strike him. Stockman rolled away, onto his hands and knees, and lunged forward to butt the other man in the belly just as the stick grazed his hip. He staggered upright, grabbed the other man, who was bent over and retching, and shoved him backward in the direction of the watchman.

"Grab him and hold him, Coleman," he shouted, "or I'll have a strip off your back!" Coleman caught the dazed assailant by the elbows while the bo'sun drew a long knife from the sheath strapped to his belt. The moonlight glinted off the blade as he advanced.

"Now, by God," he said in a tight voice, "I'll mark your face so your own mother wouldn't know you, and then I'll see the color of your innards!"

As he raised the knife to head height, his opponent recoiled and shoved his elbow into the watchman's gut. The watchman, who was more interested in following the fight than in joining it, let him go and retreated hastily. Stockman swore loudly and charged, but the other man ducked and thrust the blackthorn stick between the bo'sun's legs. The knife sailed twirling through the air while the bo'sun's forward momentum propelled him, completely off balance, across the wharf until a two-foot-high cast-iron bollard got in the way of his head. His body, suddenly limp, draped itself across a thick hawser and swayed this way and that as the ship tugged at its mooring lines. Then, quite undramatically, it slipped from the ropes and disappeared into the narrow gap between the ship and the granite wharf. The ship bobbed in the tide and creaked as its planks chafed against the stone.

"Jesus God," said Coleman in a tone of amazement and satisfaction, "you've gone and done it now, haven't you! The bastard is dead for certain. Hey, wait, come back here! Watch! Watch! Help, murder!" He gazed after the retreating victor, who had stopped just long enough to retrieve his stick before running off into the darkness. Then he crossed to the edge of the wharf and looked down toward the water, invisible in the night. "By God," he muttered, "I wouldn't have credited it if I hadn't been here to see it. Well, Iron Man," he added in a louder tone, "what did it get you, being such an out and out son of a bitch, flogging men till their ribs showed through?" A dark stream of tobacco juice arced toward the river.

Sean was asleep on the floor of the grog-shop, dreaming that some terrible force had captured their ship and kept it from rocking, when Liam tapped on the shutters. At first the discreet noise fitted itself into Sean's dream, but gradually he returned to awareness. Slipping from his blanket, he worked out the door fastenings by feel and unlocked them.

"It's I, Liam." On the tail of the whisper a vague form slipped through the opening and leaned against the door, shutting it again. "Can anyone hear us?"

"They're all asleep," Sean whispered in reply. "Liam, where have you been? It's almost dawn. We feared you had met with some mishap."

Liam laughed bitterly. The sound was shockingly loud in the empty room.

"Stand you easy, lads," Malone's voice said in a conversational tone. "I've a barker in me hand, primed and cocked, and I'd not want any accidents when I light me candle!" A light flared yellow in the doorway, then steadied to a glow. Malone stepped forward and looked at the two young men curiously. "Now then, what's to do? Is it sneak thieves ye are? Or maybe our fiddler has been for a visit to the stews? Speak up; I'm an understanding man, unless I'm riled."

"I . . . ," Liam swallowed convulsively and tried again. "I went out to find the man . . . the man who knocked my Mary down and killed her."

"Ah. And did ye find him then?"

Liam nodded once, sharply. "There was a fight."

"Only proper, considering the case," said Malone genially. "Well, man? Spit it out!"

"Stockman's dead. He went into the river." Suddenly his voice broke. "As Christ is my witness, I meant only to break his head," he cried. "I'd no mind to drown the man at all! I'd not wish such a death on Cromwell himself!"

"What's done is done," said Malone in a voice that was serious now, but not overly concerned. "Were ye seen, do you think?"

"Yes, the gangway watch saw the whole thing. He'll tell the peelers everything."

The saloonkeeper chuckled. "The police in this city are not overeager to do much except collect their presents. Still, they are not to be despised altogether."

Liam looked uneasily to ether side. "I must go away," he said in a shaky voice. "The music made me known on the ship, and someone may have noticed us leaving with you. I'll not bring a curse down on this house in reward for your hospitality. I'll go west. I meant to anyway, but I'll go now, this morning! How do I go?" he added pathetically.

"The Albany steamships leave from the North River piers. From Albany you ride the canalboats and the steamcars to wherever you are going. The North River is ten minutes away in that direction. Have ye the tin?"

Liam rattled the coins in his pocket. "Enough to travel on. It will have to serve till I find work."

Sean had stood by silently until now. "Liam man," he said quietly, "what of Tom?"

Liam turned pale. "Sweet Christ," he said in a voice full of anguish, "not one day yet in Amerikay and I'm forgetting my sacred vows! I can't desert the boy, and him after losing his only blood relation in the wide world! But what will become of him if I'm taken up and hanged!"

"Will you leave him with me?" Sean said impulsively. "I'll swear to guard him like my own brother until you can make a home for him. Do it, Liam! You can't stay here, as you said yourself, and he'll only hold you up if you're on the run."

Liam looked at him doubtfully. "Would you do this, Sean *a grá*? It's no light thing, caring for a child."

"A child is a blessing from God," Sean quoted stoutly. "He's a fine, well-behaved lad and no trouble at all, and I'll do it gladly."

Liam put his arms around his friend and hugged him. "Then I'll say yes, and bless your kindness always. I'll write as soon as I'm placed, and send money for his keep. You'll tell him I had to leave and that I'll come back for him? I'd not have him think that I've run away from him."

"I'll tell him," Sean promised.

"You'd best be off," Malone interjected. "The sun is up already." Liam collected his fiddle from the back room; he had nothing else to take. At the door, Malone offered his hand; when he took it away, he had left a gleaming coin in Liam's palm. "For luck," he said briefly. "I like your way with a tune."

The streets were still empty, but to Liam's mind every window concealed a watcher, every alley a constable waiting to rush out and slap manacles on his wrists. He slinked along close to the buildings, presenting so villainous a picture with his mud-stained clothes, unshaven cheeks, and hunted eyes that any sensible policeman would have arrested him on suspicion of having done *something*. Fortunately for him, no sensible policeman of the time would have ventured from his bed at such an early hour.

He easily found the North River piers, but then halted, perplexed. Looking in either direction, he could see half a dozen or more steamboats, long low boats with tall black smokestacks towering over them. But which were going to Albany, and which was going first? A feathery plume of smoke from the stacks of a boat to the right decided him, and he began to walk in that direction.

"Bedad if it's not a fellow son of Erin!"

Liam hunched his shoulders as if for a blow, then looked around. A red-cheeked man in a battered hat and a green cravat was looking at him with an engaging smile. "You'll be wanting to go West, isn't it?" he continued. "Och, it's a grand country out there, a grand country."

"I was wondering which boat goes first to Albany," said Liam cautiously.

"Albany, bedad! Sure and you'll be wanting the *New World*, the pride of the People's Line, and a fine name that is to be sure! But they'll not sell the ticket on board, you know. No, no, you must seek out an authorized agent and buy from him, or you'll not be allowed to go."

Liam's face did not reveal his snap decision to let the comedy continue. "But where would I find such an agent?"

The runner pulled an impressive-looking document from his pocket and flourished its gold seals. "You've the luck of the Irish today, my lad, for I'm the very man, James Patrick Hennessy, duly appointed agent for passages west, and it's the merest chance that you find me here and not in my place of business on Broadway! Where was it you were going?"

"West. What's the next big place west of Albany?"

Hennessy's expression hinted that he knew even less geography than Liam, but he confidently replied, "Buffalo's the very place, a city of manufactures and shipping, with healthful ocean breezes and pleasant winters! I can give ye a combined ticket for only five dollars, only because I have one on hand that a wealthy horse dealer decided not to use."

"Five dollars? What is that in sterling?"

"You don't have dollars? Oh dear, and the rate after falling only yesterday and all! But I'll absorb the loss meself and give you the ticket for three pounds."

Liam's face hardened. He had taken the trouble, before leaving Liverpool, to learn that the pound sterling was worth roughly five American dollars. The runner had just tried to triple his price. "One gold sovereign is all I can spare," he said, holding the glittering coin between thumb and forefinger. "Yes or no?"

"For the sake of the ould sod, yes!" He snatched the coin, thrust a piece of pasteboard into Liam's hand, and scuttled off. Liam examined the ticket; the haste with which the runner had taken his offer suggested that it was much more than the ticket was worth. As promised, it was for passage to Albany on the *New World* and canalboat passage Albany to Buffalo. There were even, as an aid to the illiterate, woodcuts at the top of a steamboat with smoke pouring from its stacks and of a canal barge with three horses straining at the towropes. Liam shrugged and hurried up the broad street toward the pier where the *New World* was getting up steam.

Promptly on time, the huge paddlewheels on either side of the hull began to turn. The boat backed into the river, gave a shrill blast from its whistle, and began its journey upstream. The North, or Hudson's River, was immensely wide, as wide as a large lake, and bordered on one side by the thickly forested hills of Manhattan and on the other by the looming gray cliffs of Jersey. The steamer moved quickly, casting a white bow-wave to either side and exciting admiring comments from the passengers who thronged the rail to watch the hamlets on the New York shore glide past.

Liam was not among them. The moment he boarded the boat he had sought out a secluded area and stretched out full length on the deck. For almost three weeks, since the terrible moment he had seen his wife lying dead in her own gore, he had felt himself to be nothing but a vessel for bitter anger and a thirst for just vengeance. He had wrapped the sinews of his mind tightly around himself, to keep the vessel from bursting under the fierce internal pressure. He had moved through each day as if he and the rest of the world were substances of different orders, able to occupy the same space but unable to act on each other.

Now, with Stockman's death, he was an empty vessel. He imagined that if he stood with the breeze passing over him, he would give forth a low drowsy hum, like a distant swarm of bees. Or was he the head of the lion, that Samson slew and the bees took for a hive? He was not Samson, that was certain, for it was only by good fortune that he met the dawn as a murderer and not a victim. His thoughts balked at the awful word, *murderer,* but he forced them on like a skittish team of horses. He had blood on his hands, there was no shirking that, though it was true as true that he'd not meant to put it there. Still, in some fashion the blood on his hands, the bo'sun's blood, was washed away by the blood on his head, the blood of his sweet lost Maire and their poor unborn child. Though he was empty, hollow, *nothing,* he was not guilty. And he slept.

The sun woke him an hour or two later. He shook the confusion from his brain and followed his nose to a simmering cauldron where, for a penny, he bought a bowl of rich soup. He carried it to the railing and ate it slowly. His stomach had long since forgotten how to deal with meat and such, and he must re-accustom it to the task carefully.

Another customer, a man not much older than himself in a suit that was well cared for but threadbare, joined him at the railing. "A fine day to be on the river," he said.

"It is that."

The stranger gestured toward the bank with his spoon. "Prosperous country around here. I like to see that, for the poor can't buy my goods. I travel in fine silks," he added. He caught Liam's skeptical glance at his frayed cuffs. "I've not been at it so very long, I admit, but it's a fine upstanding trade and takes me into the best circles. Ye're a fiddler, I see." He seemed happy to change the subject.

"My uncle was a fine hand with the fiddle," he continued, "and brought dozens of the old tunes in his head when he came to America. He played the pipes, too, though he hadn't a set of his own. You're Irish, by the sound of ye?"

Liam agreed, and gave his name and county.

"And I'm Caleb Chisholm, late of the town of Sydney, Cape Breton Island. Another son of the Gael, if ye like. Do you have the Gaelic?" he asked in the Scottish form of that language.

Liam answered in the dialect of Connacht. Chisholm listened intently, then shook his head.

"Aye, I ken what ye're saying well enough, but it's not easy for me. I'd not want to get traveling directions or dispute a nice point in theology in the tongue, for I'd be sure to miss something and end up in . . . the other place."

Liam smiled at the witty use of the common euphemism for Hell. "Speaking of traveling, how far do you go on this boat—to Albany?"

"No, only to Hudson. You're traveling far?"

"I bought passage to Buffalo, but one place is like another to me. I seek work at decent pay, that's all." He paused. "Perhaps you can ease my mind. I saw when I came onto the boat that the man eyed my ticket strangely. Do you see anything amiss with it?" He handed Chisholm the pasteboard. The young Scot glanced at it, then looked more closely. His face grew solemn.

"Ye paid good money for this, did ye?"

"I did." His expression was grim. "Five dollars."

Chisholm whistled. "Mon, mon, the fare tae Buffalo is nae mair nor half that!" Excitement, or indignation, broadened his accent to the point that Liam had trouble following his words. "Och but they're a gey lot of villains, waur nor ony that hae scaped the gallus! And for a' that the wee ticket is nae guid! It's a forgery!"

Liam understood that. "A forgery! But they let me on the boat!"

"Oh, aye. Yer ticket is guid enough to Albany, but it'll no carry you to Buffalo, or anywhere else beyond. The canal company winna honor it."

"How do you know?" He clung to the faint hope that Chisholm was mistaken, though a part of him had recognized the truth at once. A forged ticket was exactly what he should have expected from a knave of a runner. Instead he had assumed that, in catching Hennessy's attempted swindle with the exchange rate, he had pulled his teeth. His smugness had put him off-guard; now, it seemed, he would pay for it.

Chisholm pointed to the woodcut at the head of the ticket. "Look at the wee boat with the three horses pulling it. Ye'd hae no way tae ken, bein' a stranger tae these parts, but the passenger boats on the Erie Canal are always pulled by *two* horses, and they're shown that way on the tickets. So this you hold is forged."

Liam took back the useless ticket and turned to lean over the railing. The steamboat was approaching the most magnificent stretch of the Hudson Highlands. The bay, bordered on the left by the heights of the Dunderberg, seemed to end just ahead at the town of Peekskill. Suddenly the sidewheeler turned its bow confidently to the left, and a narrow gorge opened up. The right bank rose sheer for hundreds of feet to the height called Anthony's Nose; at its base, crews of navvies were hard at work, creating the roadbed on which the tracks of the Hudson River Rail Road soon would run. On the left, the Dunderberg was succeeded by the even loftier Bear Mountain, and the river narrowed even further.

"There's talk," Chisholm said as he named the landmarks to Liam, "of constructing a great bridge from Bear Mountain to Anthony's Nose, to allow the railroad to reach New York City with coal from the Pennsylvania mines. The cars cannot cross the river south of Albany now, except by lighter. It'll no come to pass, though, in my opinion. Goods reach New York by barge now, except in winter, and three months' business winna pay for such a construction. That's the fort of West Point ahead, where they school the officers for the Army."

Liam obediently glanced at the stone buildings on the height above them, but his mind was not on the scenery or his companion's commentary. Most of his money had gone for the forged ticket and he had still to live until he found work. Traveling farther than Albany seemed out of the question, for he did not have the fare. Once he had thought that he decided his actions for himself, but now he felt no more independent than that piece of battered plank bobbing in the stream.

"What of Albany?" he said suddenly, interrupting a description of the wonders of Storm King Mountain. "Is it a town a man can thrive in?"

For a moment Chisholm looked affronted by Liam's lack of interest in his poetic narrative, but then his face took on a cautious, canny expression. "I'll no say aye or nay tae that," he began, "for some men thrive and some wither in any place. It's a busy town, wi' mills and railroads and the traffic of river and canal, and an important town, the capitol o' New York state."

"But . . . ?"

"I've no direct knowledge, mind, only what my common sense tells me, but it's no a place I'd look tae find work quickly. Look around ye, mon! I've nae doubt there's two hundred or mair o' your Irish lads on this boat alone, and the most o' them will stop at Albany, for the steamboat is cheap and the canal boat is dearer. What then? They'll all want work, and before ye know it they'll be cracking each other's heads over the few jobs there are, just as they did over in Pennsylvania and down in Maryland. No, in your place I'd no stay on the boat tae Albany, for a' that ye've paid your way there ten times over."

The *New World* was slowing down, edging toward the west bank, where the buildings of a substantial town rose, terrace after terrace, from the river to a height of three hundred feet or more. People and wagons waited on the wharf. Liam eyed them curiously. The moment the boat tied up, a man in canvas trousers and heavy leather boots stepped forward and cupped his hands to his mouth.

"I need fifty men," he shouted, "who can handle a spade and aren't afraid of hard work! A dollar a day and find your own keep!"

Liam looked quickly at Chisholm, who maintained an impassive expression and refused to meet his eye.

"I'm your man, Captain," he cried, and saw that his companion nodded soberly. He clasped the young Scot's hand and bade him farewell, then, as an afterthought, asked, "What town is this?"

"This? It is called Newburgh."

dear Brother,

Nvbr 19, 1848

I recved Uncle Sean's letter telling of yr progress in learning and was very proud to hear of it. You must make sure to get all the learning you can, for an ignorant man is his own enemy and an educated man can go as far as he wants in this land of liberty.

I have gone West from Newburgh city, to a place called Middletown that is in the middle of rich farms and near hills and forests, tho the nights are cold and too dark for the walks I liked before. Still I am building roads as before, but I have moved up, bringing a dozen fellows with me from Newb'g and being in charge of them at a higher wage. I put aside all I can, also the little bits that come when I play of an evening at the shebeen at the bottom of the hill, and soon hope

*to have enough to make a home where you can
live with me. In Newb'g or here or elsewhere if
the work is there.*

*Tell yr Uncle Sean and Aunt Sheila that I
wanted to play at the wedding but will keep my
fiddle warm for a christening. I've some new tunes
for them, as there's a lad from Mayo here that is
a dab hand at the whistle. I must close now as
the dark comes on early but will write again next
Sunday and hope to hear news of you soon, send
as per direction. My very kind love to all, from*

*yr brother
Liam.*

He put down the pen and stretched his cramped
muscles. He always forgot, from week to week, how
much work it was to write—to think of what to say,
and put it in words a child of nine would understand,
and to leave out what was not fit for the boy to hear,
took thought and care. He wondered once more what
explanation they had given Tom for his disappearance
and whether he could ever bring himself to tell him the
truth about it. Sheila's uncle had asked a few discreet
questions and found out that the old watchman had
sworn that Stockman fell over the edge of the wharf
while drunk. In the eyes of the world, the incident was
closed; but Liam still had dreams about it.

The picture he gave the boy of his life left much
out too. He spoke of the work in a sentence or two, but
it stretched from first light to last light, hard, dull,
mind-destroying labor with mattock and spade and
axe, clearing the right of way, digging and filling for
the roadbed, spiking the heavy planks to the sleeper

logs. The men returned to town after dusk, filled themselves with heavy, starchy food, and went straight to sleep. They knew that the next day would begin all too soon.

On Saturday nights they stayed up, but there was nothing for them to do but drink and fight. The night before had been typical. Liam had gone down to the grog-shop a little after nine, greeted the men he knew, accepted a dram from the proprietor, and started playing. Bobby Dolan, the whistle player he had mentioned in his letter to Tom, joined him around ten. At ten forty-five, or thereabouts, a Derry lad on his way outside to take a piss brushed by a fellow from Cork and knocked his beer into his lap. The Corkonian immediately knocked him to the floor. Moments later he was grappling with two other northerners, or Fardowners as they were known. More Corkonians joined the fray. Inevitably, one of the combatants hit a bystander from Connacht by mistake, and the battle became general.

Liam and Bobby stood at the back of the room, ready to dodge or duck but uninvolved otherwise. Perhaps as musicians they had inherited some of the personal immunity enjoyed by the harpers and poets of ancient Erin, or perhaps it was simply that no one wanted to damage one of the few sources of entertainment they had. Whatever the reason, when one bloody-nosed spalpeen caromed off the wall into them, he wiped his face and apologized nicely before flinging himself at a passing stranger.

It was just as well. Ever since that terrible night at Coenties' Slip, Liam took no joy at all in a good fight. As he watched the brawl, he thought sourly that he would never be able to explain it to an outsider. How could an American be expected to understand that two men from the same country were bitter enemies for no other reason than that one came from the North and the other from the South? To any civilized person, the idea was barbarous.

Yet, though Liam agreed with that judgment, he still retained a secret belief that, of all the Irish, the people of Connacht remained the closest to the true old Milesian race. To his mind, there was far too much of the Saxon in Ulster and of the Spaniard in Cork.

The brawl ended, as abruptly as it had begun, when the tavernkeeper shouted that he would close the place for the night if it continued. While the battered customers tried to fix their ripped clothing and eyed each other sheepishly, he hurried over to Liam and Bobby. "Play," he said under his breath. "Something to calm them down, for Christ's sake!"

Liam took his fiddle from its case and struck up "Who Dares to Speak of Ninety-Eight." Bobby tootled valiantly along right behind him. As he had hoped, the patriotic air helped the lads to put aside their sectional rivalries and recall their common heritage of oppression and rebellion.

When he finished, a barrel-chested carter from County Meath with a balding head and a fine tenor voice sang a sentimental ballad about a white-haired mother by a turf-built fire who dreamt of her son across the sea. From pugnacious, the mood of the room turned to maudlin. Bobby kept it going with a melancholy air that he filled with gracefully-executed runs and turns. Liam shared an ale with the relieved landlord and watched men who minutes before had been throttling each other stand side by side and listen to the music with tears in their eyes. There was no more trouble that night, and when Liam went home he was able to add nearly a dollar to his little store of savings.

By spring Liam was foreman of a crew of over fifty men. The contractor had seen that he was responsible and intelligent, and that he was accepted fairly well by Fardowners and Corkonians alike, and promoted him over several other possible candidates. One of these, Big Tom Byrne, resented this slight and challenged Liam the first time he gave an order. Liam's attempt to persuade him met only truculence, but a fast knee to the brisket and an elbow to the back of the neck convinced Big Tom that Liam was in charge and meant to stay that way. No one else seemed to need convincing after that.

He enjoyed the chance to use his mind a bit, though his shoulders and thighs were still much more important, and he quickly gained the name of a fair man. As the weeks went on, though, he became more and more uneasy. Something was going on that he didn't understand. Supplies were not being restocked as fast as they were being used up. When he spoke to Mr. Bentley about it, the contractor replied that some shipments had been held up by the late thaw. His manner suggested that Liam was meddling in matters that were not his business.

Then there were the rumors. Almost every week a new one was passed among the men: how the Connachtmen on a railroad crew in Pennsylvania had thrown a man from Fairhill into the river, where he drowned; how the Corkonians on a canal project in

Ohio had formed a secret society bound by oath to exclude all but their members from work on the project; how the Belfast men building the Hudson River Rail Road were secretly buying guns and diverting explosives from the worksites in readiness for an attack on the camps that housed Corkonians and Connachtmen. All the rumors had one thing in common, that they inflamed sectional irritations and generated a mood of fear, anger, and distrust among the men.

There were rumors among the townspeople, too, but instead of focusing on violence among the different factions of Irishmen, they whispered of Irish riots, of plots directed from Rome to overturn the Protestant faith and install the Pope as king of America, of sinister rites and midnight orgies in Catholic convents and churches. Mrs. Layton, the widow who owned the boardinghouse where Liam was staying, asked him one evening, in a quavering voice, if he expected trouble.

He was puzzled by the question. "Trouble, missus? What sort of trouble might you mean?"

"At the store I heard talk of an uprising," she said hesitantly. "I couldn't make it out, but it was something to do with that Kossuth feller and . . . well, and the Irishmen. I thought you'd know about it. There's talk of calling up the militia."

As he went out for his nightly stroll, Liam was more than usually thoughtful. He knew that there was agitation among the Irish communities of New York and Boston, aimed at winning reprieves for the imprisoned Young Ireland leaders, but a rising? In America? The idea was laughable! But how would somebody like Mrs. Layton know that? She knew very well that the

Irish started brawls weekly; was it unlikely that such quarrelsome men might stage a rebellion one day?

A few days later, Liam left the worksite with Ezra Minton, the young engineer from the Rensselaer Institute, to inspect a piece of marshy ground that lay across the path of the road and discuss how they would deal with it. Returning, he knew there was trouble long before he could see the worksite. Instead of the ring of axes and sledgehammers, he heard only a buzz of voices.

The men were gathered in a tight circle, and their voices were getting louder and angrier. Bobby Dolan saw Liam and hurried over to him. "They're saying we'll not be paid tomorrow for the month's work," he said. "Some of the lads mean to tear up the roadway as a protest. It's the Corkonians who are hottest for it, and some are saying as well that you mean to see that we Connachtmen get our wages at their expense. They're all daft, Liam, and some are drunk besides."

"Drunk! On the job? How?"

Bobby's brow furrowed. "It's surely a curious thing, but one of the kegs held whiskey instead of iron spikes. We all had a swallow or two, and some had a deal more than that. You'd best do something, before someone swings his spade and opens a fellow's skull."

Grabbing a spade himself, Liam strode across the clearing and leapt onto the back of a wagon. "Here!" he shouted. "Attend to me, you men! Tell me the matter!"

"Where's our wages?" someone yelled back.

"Tomorrow's payday, not today. You know that!"

"Today or tomorrow, there's no money!" A sullen

growl greeted the statement, and the crowd pushed a few inches closer to the wagon.

"Who says that!" Liam demanded. "Who told you this?"

"Is it true?" "Tell us!" "The truth now!!"

He held up his hand. "The truth, then: I don't know." Another growl, more savage, and cries of "Smash the road!" He overrode them. "We've been paid on time for five months, lads, but who can say what might happen tomorrow? I don't know,"—he paused impressively —"and neither do those who said there'll be no pay! But I do know this: destroy a single foot of the roadway and they'll stop all our pay and turn us away from the job, at gunpoint if they have to. And there won't be one bleeding thing to do about it!"

Big Tom stepped out of the crowd and turned to face the men. "He'd say that, wouldn't he! Bentley bought him when he made him overseer! I say show them we can wreck as soon as build, and put some fear into them! They'll pay us soon enough then, see if they don't!"

Liam's heart sank. Big Tom's fellow Corkonians were sifting through to the side of the crowd nearest the roadway. The tinder was dry and well placed, and needed only a spark to set off a real riot. "You lads all know me," he shouted. "Am I a man to back the master at all costs, or have I tried to see you fair? I've said I don't know if there's money for our pay, and I don't, but I do know there's something right quare going on! Is there a man among you who could mistake a keg of poteen for a keg of nails?" That got a laugh, and he continued over it. "Who carries all these tales, of riots and plots and dark deeds? *Who gains if we riot?*"

The question stymied them. After a silence, a voice said, "We do," but it lacked all conviction.

"In a pig's arse we do! Out a month's wages, haring through the woods with the militia on our tails, blacklisted from here to Chicago? That's no gain to my mind! No, I'll tell you who stands to gain: Mr. Bentley! Touch that roadway and you are handing him two thousand dollars, the pay he'll keep from us with every law on his side! Is that what you want?"

His eye, watching their reactions, caught the movement of a figure furtively kneeling and rising again. "Rory Malone," he said loudly, "if you throw that clod at me, I will break each of your arms in four places!" Everyone turned to look, and Malone let the clod fall from his hand and tried to look innocently indignant. He was not much of a actor.

Liam sensed that the mood was swinging toward him. "Now listen, and I'll tell you what we should do. We should go back to town, not as a mob, but with discipline and dignity, and tell the mayor what we fear. Bentley works for the town, after all, so it is the town's responsibility in the end."

The Corkonians, urged on by Big Tom, held out until they saw that all the others were won over, but finally they too agreed to follow Liam's plan "until," as one of them ominously put it, "we see it for the sell I t'ink it is. We'll know what to do then."

They marched into town in column formation, spades and picks at shoulder port. Householders stared, then hastily slammed their doors against the wild

Hibernians. The news of their coming ran ahead of them. When they turned onto the block-long main street of the town, the mayor, who also owned the livery stable and the wheelwright's shop, was waiting for them in the middle of the block. Behind him, in a line that stretched across the street, were a dozen or so scared-looking farmers' sons with squirrel rifles and duck guns in their hands. Liam held up his hand, and the column stopped, then flowed to either side of him to make a line two men deep.

"Stay here, lads," Liam said quietly. "And whatever you do, *don't provoke them.*" He took a step forward and three of the militiamen aimed their weapons at him. Stopping, he held his hands out, palms forward, and called, "I'd like to talk to Your Honor. We come peacefully."

The mayor looked dubious. He had never thought, when he agreed to serve, that he might find himself in the middle between armed but untrained militia and a mob of savage Micks. Still, if he could settle this dispute peacefully, he might find himself elected to the State Assembly, where a canny man could make a fortune in a single term. He took a few steps forward and motioned for the Irish boy to come over. From a distance he didn't look old enough to vote, but as he came closer the mayor saw lines in his face and a certain look to the eye that made it clear he was a full-grown man.

"What's going on here?" he blustered. "Why aren't you men at work? You'll be docked for this, you know."

"Begging Your Honor's pardon," the Irishman said, "but the men are upset by a rumor that there's no money to pay them tomorrow. There were some angry words passed, but they were persuaded to bring their worry to you."

"Why me? Jack Bentley's the man to talk to. He's the contractor you're working for."

"Yes, sir. But if the men could be sure that the money is there, it would ease their minds and stop the trouble before it starts."

"Trouble?" He looked across at the mob and imagined what those picks and shovels could do to his town. "Um. Yes, well, I can send for Bentley, I guess."

"I'm not so sure the men would believe him."

"This is a joke! If you people won't believe your own employer, who will you believe? The president of the bank?"

Liam was implacable. "Yes, sir, I believe so."

"Oh, for God's sake!" He turned and motioned to the end man of the militia. "Here, Will! Go tell Mr. Lucas at the bank and Mr. Bentley to come over here. Make it quick!"

While they waited, Liam noticed that more and more spectators were gathering at each end of the block and along the sides of the street. God help them as if one of the militiamen was startled into firing; there'd be a massacre.

Bentley came bustling along, with the banker just behind him. He saw Liam and shook his head sadly. "I'm sorry to see you throwing your lot in with rioters, O'Donnell. I expected better from you. Well, Mayor, didn't I warn you that there'd be trouble? Why haven't you ordered them to disperse?"

"Plenty of time for that," the mayor replied. "You don't mind telling those men over there if you have the money to pay their wages tomorrow, do you? There's a tale going around that you don't. You tell them it's all right, with Lucas backing you up, and maybe they'll go home peacefully."

Bentley turned scarlet. "Are you questioning my honor?" he gobbled. "I've called men out for less!"

"Nope. Your honor's no concern of mine. Just tell them, and we'll *all* go home peacefully. Unless you've got some reason not to, of course."

Bentley glared at him, then turned his glare on Liam. Finally he took a deep breath, stepped forward, and shouted, "You fellows! Your wages will be paid tomorrow, same as always! There's no trouble about the money, whatever you've heard! It's all ready for you, waiting at the bank!"

Liam noticed that Lucas jumped a little at that last statement.

"Now just to ease any last doubts you have," Bentley continued, "Mr. Lucas, the president of the bank, will confirm what I just told you. Jim?"

Lucas gave him a sidelong glance as he stepped forward. "Mr. Bentley is correct in saying that there was enough money, more than enough, in his account to cover your month's wages."

"What do you mean, *was*?" someone shouted.

"Just what I said. Mr. Bentley withdrew essentially all his funds earlier today. My teller informed me of this as I was leaving to come here."

The mutter from the crowd was inarticulate, but its meaning was clear.

Bentley stepped forward hastily. "Of course I withdrew the money," he cried. "I needed to get it ready for tomorrow. It's in the safe in my office right now!"

"Liar!" "Thief!" The angry crowd edged forward. The militiamen, who had relaxed, straightened up and brought their guns to bear on them.

"Jack," the mayor said quickly, "maybe that money would be safer back at the bank. It's a pretty big sum to trust to an office safe, isn't it? Tell you what: you just go over and move it now, and I'll send a couple of the boys along to make sure nobody holds you up." He called two of the militiamen over and gave them whispered instructions, after which they self-consciously followed Bentley through the crowd and out of sight.

There was a long, awkward pause during which no one knew what to do or where to look. When Liam accidentally met the mayor's eye, they both colored and glanced away, though neither could have explained the reason for his embarrassment. Then, down the street, the two militiamen reappeared, looking nervously from side to side and seeming to pretend that their rifles belonged to someone else entirely.

The mayor waited. "Well?" he said in a low voice, as soon as they were close enough. "Where's Bentley?"

They shuffled their feet. Finally one of them said, "Tell you the truth, Uncle Bill, we don't exactly know."

"You look at me, Jed Webster! And don't call me Uncle Bill in public! Now, what do you mean, you don't know?"

"Well, Un— Your Honor, we went to his office with him, like you said, and he showed us the satchel from the bank, with the money in it. But then he said there was some papers he needed from the back room. After a while, when he didn't come back, we took a gander, but he wasn't there."

"You just let him get away like that! You nincom-poops!"

Jed Webster looked hurt; his companion tried to look unconcerned.

"And what about the money? The city's money? Where is *that*? Did one of you run after Bentley to give it to him!"

"No sir, we didn't think of it. We took it to the bank, the way you said. You didn't tell us we were sup-posed to watch Mr. Bentley; I thought we were pro-tecting him against the Paddies!"

"Never mind, I'll deal with you later." He turned to face the restless road gang. "Men," he shouted, "your wages are safe. You'll be paid tomorrow, in full, in the regular way. And because of the peculiar circum-stances, you won't be docked for this afternoon, pro-vided you go back to work right away. You have my word on that. O'Donnell," he added in an undertone, "get them moving, won't you? We're not out of the woods yet."

Assured of their pay, the lads were willing enough to get back to the worksite. It was not comfortable to stand so long face to face with rifles and shotguns, and in any case they felt that they had won. None of them had yet thought to wonder what would come of their jobs now that their employer had run away. Liam could think of little else. The flood of emigrants was still continuing, making jobs scarce and driving wages down. Bentley's flight might put matters in such a tan-gle of confusion that they would all be laid off indefi-nitely. If that happened, he didn't know where he would go next to find work, but wherever it was, he couldn't hope to get a foreman's post again. It was back to the pick and spade for him. The prospect was so dispiriting that he hardly noticed Ezra Minton deep in earnest conversation with Lucas, the banker.

When he called the roll, back at the roadhead, Big Tom and two other leading Corkonians did not answer. Whether they were actively involved in Bentley's plan or only feared that the men would believe it of them, they had not wanted to face either Liam's tongue or his fists. He was content to see the last of them. If the job continued, he was going to have to fight the spreading factionalism head-on, and the three missing men had been among the most active promoters of it.

Half an hour later Ezra entered the clearing and looked around for Liam. His face radiated triumph as he walked over and took Liam aside. "It's settled!" he cried.

"It's glad I am to hear it. And what might *it* be?"

"The road project, of course. We have the bank behind us, and the mayor gave his agreement, though it'll be a day or two before the new papers are ready. Still, we won't lose a single day's work. Isn't it wonderful!"

Liam sighed with relief. Apparently his job was safe for at least two more months, and by the time it ended he might have heard of something else. "It is that," he replied soberly. "And the lads will be glad of it as well. Work is not so plentiful just now. They've found someone to take over from Bentley, then, have they? I hope it's not another twister."

The boyish engineer stared at him. "Liam," he said, "you don't understand. *We're* taking over. You and I. Partners. I know I should have spoken to you first, but it wasn't an opportunity to miss. Mr. Lucas was afraid that the project would fall through, and he and the mayor were both impressed by the way you handled everything, so when I suggested it they agreed right on the spot. As of this afternoon, *we* are the contractors for this road!"

It was Liam's turn to stare. His thoughts tumbled over each other, and he started to speak three times before he finally said, "But Ezra, you are the engineer. Construction is your profession. I am a musician, earning his bread as best I may. I know nothing of contracts and papers and plans."

"You know how to handle men," said Ezra stoutly, "and that's half of any construction project. I couldn't handle this alone, and they wouldn't let me anyway. I'm too young, to their way of thinking. So are you, for that matter. But between us we add up to one forty-year-old contractor! And a damned good one, too!"

8

One warm day in July the firm of Minton & O'Donnell, Contractors, moved its headquarters from Middletown to Newburgh. In practice, this meant that Ezra thrust three bundles of papers into the trunk with his clothes and the two partners took the next eastbound stage. The road project was done, and work seemed more likely to come their way in a larger town.

Liam was subdued on the journey. He had spent most of the night before with the lads at a cross between a celebration and a wake. The whiskey, supplied by him, flowed freely and the music, also supplied mostly by him, added its own cheer. Still he had come away saddened from the experience. Beyond the fact that, the job over, the men were scattering in all directions, he felt a deeper, more fundamental separation from them. Though he still spoke their language, dressed like them, and worked by their side, they were beginning to treat him like gentry. Their jokes and comments were more restrained when he was around. The most of them listened to his tunes with careful appreciation in place of the easy enthusiasm he was used to. Why, they did not even fight when he was in the room! And these were men who had known him a few months before when he was just another common laborer. How would it be from now on, with those who knew him only as the gaffer, the boss? Would they invite him to their parties, then wait for him to leave so the fun could begin? He would hate that!

A hundred years before, Newburgh had been an important place. General Washington made his headquarters there at one point during the American Revolution. But the opening of the Erie Canal had hit it hard, diverting or destroying the trade that had been its reason for being. Like the other Hudson River ports—Tarrytown, Peekskill, Poughkeepsie, Hudson—it still had not recovered from the blow. Unlike the others, it was on the west shore of the river, which meant that the new railroad from New York to Albany, which ran along the east shore, would only do more damage instead of helping.

The bill in the Legislature to encourage the building of plank roads seemed like a last hope for the town. The easier it was for farmers to bring their produce to Newburgh, the likelier they were to do it, and to buy their supplies in town as well. With proper planning, there was no reason the town couldn't dominate the whole area north of the Hudson Highlands and east of the Shawangunk Mountains.

Liam and Ezra arrived at just the right moment.

Even their lack of political connections didn't keep them from getting work. There were so many jobs, so much money, that the important firms, the "big bugs," decided not to bother with those that were too small or too tricky. Several of these were given to Minton & O'Donnell. As one of the town aldermen observed over a sherry flip one afternoon, "These damn Micks are thicker than fleas on a dog, and every damn one of them is taking out citizenship papers. It won't hurt us to show we got nothing against the bastards. And Minton's uncle is a judge up in Troy, too. You never know when you'll need a judge."

Word of Liam's musical talents reached the town almost as soon as he did. Not long afterwards, he was asked to play at the wedding celebration of Terence Waterford's youngest daughter. Waterford was the best known and most successful lawyer of Irish origin in the entire Hudson Valley. As a young man he had studied law with Thomas Emmet, the exiled leader of the United Irishmen, friend of Wolfe Tone, and older brother of the martyred Robert Emmet. Through Emmet he had also known MacNeven and Sampson, the other notable exiles from the crushed Rising of 1798, and still retold the stories he had heard from them about that glorious and tragic time. His revolutionary sentiments about Ireland did not prevent him from being an important figure in the more conservative wing of the New York Democratic Party.

Liam learned all this from Ezra, who had received an invitation of his own to the celebration. His college degree and his relationship to a judge automatically made him one of the more eligible bachelors of the area, and almost every day brought another invitation, to a ball, or a picnic, or a small dinner, from people he had never heard of. Waterford's invitation was doubly an exception, both because he knew of the man, though they had never met, and because he accepted it.

"It's his last daughter," he explained self-consciously to Liam, "so I won't have to be on my guard so much. And the men who'll be there are just the sort who ought to have a chance to get to know us."

"Lawyers, bankers, and politicians."

"That's the way of the world. We have to live with it."

"Don't I know that as well as me own name?" Liam dropped his joking tone. "But is it wise for me to accept as well? You go as a guest, but I do not. Back in Ireland I would know my place, which was respected by high and low alike, but here many treat a musician as something between a servant and a performing dog. That is not how we want to present ourselves, I'm thinking."

Ezra frowned. "I see what you mean. Let me look into it a little before you decide."

Liam never found out what "looking into it" included, but two days later he received a note on fine heavy stationery.

> *My dear Mr. O'Donnell* [*it read*]:
> *It occurs to me that the invitation I gave you for my daughter's wedding is open to an unfortunate misconstruction. As I told you, we hope very much that you will favor us with some of the fine old music of Ireland for which you have won such a name.*

*However, even if you are not able to do so, I
hope that you will consent to join us on this happy
occasion. I look forward to making your acquaintance, as I am sure many of my friends do.*

*Hoping for the favor of an early and favorable
reply, I am, Sir,*

*Your ob't servant,
Terence Waterford*

Waterford lived in a substantial brick house at the
northern edge of town. From the grounds there was
a thrilling view of the river and of the village of Beacon on the opposite shore. As Ezra and Liam turned in
at the gate, they could see a Day Line steamboat,
toylike from that height, whipping the water to froth
as it pulled away from the town wharf on its way
downriver to New York City. Soon, Liam thought,
soon he would be on such a boat, going south to see
his friends again and to bring back Tom. At last he
would carry out his pledge to be a father to the boy.

They were directed around to the back of the house,
where a gaily colored canvas marquee had been erect-
ed on the lawn. Waterford, a squarely built man with
steel gray hair and muttonchop whiskers of the pur-
est white, stepped over to welcome them. Directing
a servant girl to take Liam's fiddle case to the marquee, he escorted the young partners over to a group
that included the town's leading feed merchant, an
officer of the local bank, and Father Dillon, the Catholic priest.

The men acknowledged the introduction, then continued their conversation about the adventures of a
mutual acquaintance in the war with Mexico that had

ended a year earlier. "He was very struck," the grain merchant said, "by the bravery of the Irish boys. There was quite a number of companies of them, it seems, including one from Albany named for your old friend Emmet."

"For his brother, I believe," their host replied. "But why was he so astonished? Irishmen have been the backbone of more than one nation's army for hundreds of years. The marshals of France depended on their Irish brigades in the old days, just as the English generals in India do today."

"Yes, of course, but—" He broke off in embarrassment.

"But what, for goodness sake? Come, come, Moody, out with it, man!"

"Well . . . Mexico is after all a Catholic country, isn't it?" He glanced quickly at Father Dillon, then away again. "A lot of people wondered. . . . And then there was that scoundrel Riley and his Foreign Legion."

"Deserters and drunkards," Waterford said quickly, "of every nationality, who were captured and hanged by the forces under General James Shields, late of County Tyrone in Ireland, and Colonel Bennet Riley of St. Mary's County, Maryland, good Catholics both."

"Deplore it though I may," Father Dillon added softly, "the fact is that armies of Catholics have been fighting each other for many centuries. The men who volunteered to go to Mexico went out of gratitude to the country that took them in when their need was dire, and many of them proved their sincerity with the supreme sacrifice. Those who foolishly or wickedly hold that Catholics and Irishmen cannot be loyal

Americans should read the names on the graves in the shadow of Chapultepec."

"Of course," said Moody, alarmed by the depths his casual words had led him into, "I meant no disrespect to their memory or their religion. Every man is responsible to his own conscience."

"Every man is responsible to God," Father Dillon corrected him.

Liam turned away. The feed merchant's thoughtless prejudice offended him, though it seemed all too common in America, but he was also bothered by the priest's air of certainty. For himself, Liam knew that he had far more questions about life and the world than answers, and he was inclined to believe that getting wisdom consisted in discovering more profound questions. Father Dillon, he knew, would call that bad doctrine, but he believed it all the same.

His host had crossed the lawn behind him and came up to him near the marquee. "Will you take some refreshment, Mr. O'Donnell?"

"Thank you, sir." He followed him to a table near the house, where a servant in livery stood behind a huge silver punch bowl. Lumps of ice, cut from the river the previous winter and preserved in sawdust through the hot summer days, floated in the claret-colored beverage. Liam accepted a glass and took a cautious sip. He detected the rasp of whiskey hidden under the tastes of wine and lemons. "My compliments, Mr. Waterford; a very cooling drink."

To his surprise, Waterford winked in reply and took a glass for himself. "This is the fourth daughter I've married," he confided. "Four girls, each more darling than the last, and now they'll all be gone from me. Are you a married man, Mr. O'Donnell?"

"No, sir, a widower." It occurred to him that the lawyer had been at the punch more than was good for him.

"I'm sorry for it." Liam's bald statement must have changed the course of his thoughts, for he continued, "I am looking forward to your music, sir. It's little enough of it we hear these days. There is to be a light collation in a short while; perhaps afterwards you will grace us with a few tunes?"

The "light collation," when it appeared, included a whole suckling pig with the traditional apple in its mouth, a cold round of beef, and roast capons as well as several varieties of cold meat pies. Liam ate and enjoyed it, but he was unable to banish completely the recollection that millions of his countrymen, even before the Famine, had tasted meat perhaps twice a year, at Christmas and Easter.

He remembered, a few months earlier, helping one of the road gang compose a letter home. The man insisted on telling his relatives back in Tipperary that he had meat with his meal twice a week. "But Mike," Liam had protested, "why are you saying that? You know you have meat once or twice a day." "I know," Mike replied in a subdued voice, "but sure, if I tell them that they'll be thinking me a great liar!"

By now there were quite a number of guests scattered about the lawn or sitting at the small tables under the tent. The men looked drab, almost funereal, in their dark trousers, long dark coats, and tall dark hats, but the ladies in their billowy summer dresses and matching parasols made an unforgettable picture against the soft green grass and the distant sheen of the river. When Waterford came for him, Liam was relieved to learn that he was to play from the back steps of the house under open sky, and not in the dreary shade of the marquee.

To Liam, who knew that his host had not yet heard him play, Waterford's introduction was too flattering to please, but it served to gather an audience of three dozen or so guests. He strongly suspected that most of them were neither Irish nor particularly musical, so he began with a charming melody called "Sí Bheag, Sí Mhór," reputed to be the first piece ever composed by the blind harper O'Carolan, to put them into a proper frame of mind. He followed it with a pair of jigs, then, at the listeners' insistence, another pair of jigs.

As he played, he watched his audience curiously. Some of them had the air of listening because they knew it was what they were expected to do. They neither took pleasure in it nor missed taking pleasure. Others held themselves very still, as if they were afraid that otherwise they would lose caste by tapping their feet or even breaking into dance.

Only one of the listeners enjoyed the music frankly and openly, a young lady with light brown hair and very white teeth that flashed when she smiled. Gradually Liam found that he was playing *to her*, making subtle changes in the tunes in response to the subtle movements of her body. And though she could not have been aware of what he was doing, she responded to it nonetheless. Her red lips parted slightly, and her breath quickened, and her hips swayed almost imperceptibly. He moved into a hornpipe, "The Flowers of Spring,' 'in an irresistably bouncy one-two rhythm ornamented with fast rippling triplets, and knew as if they had grown up together that she was aching to fling herself into violent motion.

He ended with a flourish and acknowledged the patter of polite applause. As he was putting his fiddle away, she came up to him and said, "You've a rare gift for the music." He heard the lilt and knew that his instinct had been correct. "Will you think me overbold, Mr. O'Donnell," she continued, "if I introduce myself? I can fetch Mr. Waterford to do the deed if you prefer." Her eyes laughed at him.

"No need for my part," he laughed back. "We can pretend to be meeting in a country lane, in one of the old songs, and I'll ask your name, me pretty fair maid."

"Margaret O'Malley, kind sir," she replied. She dropped him a slight curtsey and giggled under her breath.

"Liam O'Donnell, at your service, Miss O'Malley."

"Fie, sir, not Miss if you please! I'm a married woman, I'll have you know!"

He looked at her in unfeigned surprise. He would not have put her age at past twenty, and she hadn't the air of a girl recently wed. There was a wildness in her, not far from the surface, that he would have expected more in a young girl just becoming aware of men. He glanced around and wondered which of the gentlemen around the lawn was her mate.

She easily discerned his thought. "If it's O'Malley you're seeking, divvil a bit you'll see of him, nor meself these twelvemonth or more since he went off to the boozer one Saturday night and didn't come home. As

well for him he didn't, after stealing the silver ring
I had from me mither and selling it for drink, for I
was waiting with the flatiron under the pillow for him,
to smooth out his face a bit! In my opinion," she added, dropping the exaggerated brogue but retaining
her native lilt, "he tripped over his own feet, the great
lug, and went into the river, for I'm sure he would
have come back if he still lived."

Liam gave her a look full of admiration. "He'd have
been a fool not to."

"I meant there were still bits of things for him to
steal." Though her expression was mocking, her neck
turned pink with pleasure at Liam's compliment. "So
here am I, nor maid nor wife nor widow, and a weary
state it is, too. Is Father Dillon looking at us?"

He glanced cautiously across the lawn. "No, he is
talking to some people with his back to us."

"Good. My unusual situation worries the mannie,
and I would lose my living if he took away my good
name."

Once again Liam was surprised. Those of Waterford's guests whom he had met were well-to-do, even
rich, not the sort whose female connections had to
speak of getting a living or preserving their good
name. "Would I be rude to ask?"

"What I do?" She laughed easily. "When O'Malley
disappeared, I thought I would have to go out as a
servant or worse till it came to me that I had something to sell." She broke off to laugh again at his puzzlement. "You'll not guess, Mr. O'Donnell, so leave
off! As a wee girl I had six years with the nuns, learning the secrets of lace-making and cutwork, and here
in America I find that's thought a genteel sort of way

for young ladies to pass their time. For a fee I instruct them, and as a bonus their parents often buy my better work to have about as inspiration. If it's passed off betimes as their daughter's own, it's no concern of mine. Oh Jaysus," she said in a changed voice, "here comes the priest!"

"May I see you home after this?"

"Thank you, sir." Her tone was flat, and all the life was schooled out of her face. She scarcely seemed the same animated girl he had been flirting with a moment before. "An escort will be very welcome."

"I'll search you out, then." Conscious that Father Dillon was close behind him, he bowed slightly. "Good day, madam."

She nodded distantly. "Sir."

Later, as they walked into town together, she bubbled over with mischievous laughter remembering the exchange. "I thought of a girl I knew, one Katie O'Neill, who had a poker for a spine and a firm belief that she of all around her was the descendent of princes. For all I know she was, but the descent from Tara to her daddy's byre was a long one indeed! Still and all, she had an air about her that would freeze the warmest blood. I borrowed a bit of it to impress Father, and I think I must have done so, for after you took your leave he commended me for having a proper regard for my position!"

"And so you do, though not in just the way he meant it!"

Margaret shared a small cottage off Liberty Street with an elderly deaf widow, but by unspoken agreement they continued past the turning and strolled down to the riverfront. The warehouses and coalyards were not very picturesque, but the area was empty and quiet at that time of day, and Liam dusted off a crude bench that faced the water. For a while they sat in silence, watching the unhurried flow of the river. Liam's mind, by contrast, was roiled by unruly thoughts. Margaret, by her looks more than her words, had as good as invited him to her bed. He found himself deeply stirred by the closeness of her, in a way he had not experienced since— He hastily blocked off that path into his memories.

But what should he do? She was no flighty, inexperienced girl, for all her youth. She knew her own mind, and she was ready to follow it within the limits set by prudence. He would not be taking advantage of her at all, deluding her with implied promises of marriage, for she sought none. He certainly thought the act no sin, for all the priests might say of it. If they wished to choose celibacy, it was their affair, but *he* had never taken such an oath.

The nub of the matter was simple. Was he thinking of a disloyalty to his dead wife's memory? A year had passed since that terrible time, but the pain of it still festered. When, at rare moments, he thought about the subject, he acknowledged that he was likely to wed again some day, but it seemed a very distant problem to be taken up when once he had made his way in the world. The other part had not come up until now. Women of the streets did not attract him, and the isolated world of the road gang did not bring him into contact with any other sort.

Mary and Margaret would have gotten along well with each other. He was sure of that, and he was also sure that it somehow mattered very much. If his Mary was somewhere watching him, he did not want to do anything that would bring her shame or lead her to think that she could be easily replaced. And if she was not . . . well, there was such a thing as loyalty to one's own better self.

"I should be getting home. The night will be upon us soon."

He looked up, suddenly aware that his long silence had been discourteous. Had she thought him unwilling to be in her company? "Forgive me. In watching the river I forgot myself entirely."

She smiled enigmatically. "It can do that. I count myself lucky that my room has the only window to look toward the river. I sit by it when I am at my lacemaking, and look up from the work to watch the boats go by. Sometimes I dream of taking one back to Kerry, though it's well I know they go only to Albany and New York City. Do you think of going home?"

"Where is home? Knocknarea and Ben Bulben still guard Sligo Bay, but the folks I once knew are all gone, I'm sure—starved or drowned or slaving for pennies on an American railroad, and their farms thrown together to make a sheep run. And yet . . . someday, maybe, I'll go back, to walk the hills I walked as a child and watch the rains come in off the sea, and I'll play some of the old songs in the land where they were born. But Sligo is not home to me any longer, for all the memories it holds."

"And America?" she asked softly.

Liam shook his head. "I'm a stranger here. I've met

some grand people, but they are not my people. They know it as well as I, though some may pretend otherwise out of kindness. No, I expect to live and die a sojourning stranger, an exile 'far from the land'. I'll relish me dinner all the same," he concluded with a smile, hoping to lighten the pall his words had cast over the both of them.

Margaret smiled back, but the sadness stayed in her eyes. Liam got to his feet and offered her his arm.

The sky was still light when they reached Liberty Street, but the hills to the west cast their long shadows over the land. Before they entered the gate, she led him a little way down the side street and pointed to a window at the rear of the house. "You see how fortunate I am, to be able to see the water. Mrs. Spiker's room is quite at the other end of the house, and looks onto nothing but the street. Not that it matters much to her, for she goes there only to sleep and she is the soundest sleeper ever I knew. I envy her, for isn't it meself that wakes at the slightest noise at all."

Liam gave her a sardonic look. She lowered her eyes and suddenly went crimson. Mumbling a farewell, she fled into the house. Liam walked off, whistling "The Bonnie Wee Lassie That Couldn't Say No."

By eleven the cottage was dark. He waited a few more minutes in the shadow of a tree, then moved softly around to the rear and tapped lightly on the window. There was no response. He was beginning to wonder if he had imagined the invitation in her words when the window opened and she whispered, "I'll unbar the back door." A hand, ghostly in the moonlight, motioned him to the left.

As he waited by the door, he realized that his pulse was pounding at the tempo of a fast reel and his mouth was dry as the morning after. Then Margaret was leading him through the darkened house and he had no attention to spare for his own nervousness.

In her room, she closed the door, then turned to him. Her face was only a pale, featureless oval in the spill of moonlight from the window. He held out his arms and she flowed into them, meeting him with an urgency that matched his own. *What a fool that O'Malley was,* he thought; then he lost himself in the moment. He pressed his lips to hers with bruising power, then nibbled along the line of her jaw to the soft hollows of her neck. She gasped out his name, and her hands tightened convulsively on his shoulders.

He stroked her long flank, rejoicing in the unconfined richness concealed beneath the rough linen nightdress. She molded herself to him, the full length of her body touching his, and he reached up to cup her generous breast, feeling the convoluted hardness of the nipple even through the thick cloth. Dizzy with longing, sure that he would burst if he did not have her at once, he stooped quickly and lifted her into his arms and carried her across the room to her narrow bed. As he lowered himself onto her, she arched her back to meet him and wrapped her legs around his hips, moaning softly. It seemed to him that she took over every nerve of his body and played it, just as he played hers.

Such urgency could not last. Too soon, he was lying limp against her, only half conscious of the confusion of images that raced through his mind. His hands explored more deliberately now, and he sensed her flesh awakening once more to his touch and his own responding to that awakening. Her fingers kneaded the long muscles of his back and moved down to his hips, teasing, retreating, digging sharp nails in.

He leaned away from her and tugged at the voluminous nightdress, pushing it above her waist and lifting her shoulders to pull it off entirely. For a moment, her convent training asserted itself and she struggled against him. Then, with a low, throaty laugh she raised her arms and allowed him to take it off. The moon shone through the window and fell directly on the bed, both revealing and concealing the riches of her body. Gently he cupped her cheek, then traced a line down the side of her long neck, between the breasts so proudly offered, to the patch of darkness where her thighs met. She gasped loudly and closed her teeth over her lower lip. Her legs locked powerfully, painfully, around his questing hand, then opened in welcome. Once more he fell upon her, with a hunger less pressing but no less strong, and they wove a net that tightened around them until the separation between them thinned and seemed about to vanish entirely. When the explosion came, it carried both of them away with it.

Margaret cautiously shifted her weight and Liam opened his eyes. For a few seconds he seemed confused, then he smiled, pressed his lips to hers, and rolled over to the side of the bed. She fondly brushed the hair from his forehead. "You must leave soon," she whispered. "I'd dearly love you to stay, *a grá mo chroí*, but I daren't take such a risk."

"I know, *mo cuisle*. Don't worry, I'll do naught to

take away your character." He chuckled softly. "Though if you agree, I'll soon be wearing a path through the grass to your door, for all to see and wonder at!"

9

Liam stopped pacing to watch a raft of canal boats, five abreast and nearly half a mile long, being towed downriver on the ebbing tide. A man sat on the roof of the nearest boat, smoking his pipe and entirely at his ease; on the next, a woman was pinning red flannel shirts to a clothesline. Barks and treble shouts revealed that one of the boats nearer the center of the raft harbored children and dogs. It was, Liam realized, a small town of its own, afloat from Albany to New York, where each component would go its own way, then regroup for the trip upriver to the Erie Canal. What a strange life it must be, to live always in the same dwelling but to find it always in different places! The bright flowers in window boxes and the gaily striped awnings on cabin roofs made it clear that these were homes, not merely devices for moving wheat and cheese from Buffalo to New York City. The notes

of a flute reached him across the water; did the ca-
nalers, like the tinkers and traveling people of Ireland,
have a music of their own? He resolved to ask the
next time he saw one in a local groggery.

Once more his eyes turned downriver, and this
time there was a smudge of smoke on the southern
horizon. It might be some other boat than the *Hendrik
Hudson*, of course, but he did not really think that
the pride of the Day Line, fresh from its great race
with the *Alida*, would be behind its schedule. He resumed pacing along the wharf.

Would he know Tom when he saw him? And would
the boy know him? A year was a long time in the life
of a child. Time enough, he hoped, for the recollection of his leaving to have faded; he still thought
sometimes of what it must have been, waking on your
first morning in a strange house, in a strange country,
to find that the only remaining fixed point in your
world had vanished during the night. Did Tom hate
him for that desertion? Sean and Sheila had explained
it to him, of course. And there was no resentment in
his letters to Liam. But did anyone really know what
passed in the mind of a child?

The steamboat was in sight now, its wheelhouse
towering over the three open decks. There were few
boats that large on the river; it must be the *Hendrik
Hudson*. As the bow swung out of midstream toward
the wharf, a string of possibilities circled through
Liam's mind. Tom had been waylaid and robbed of
his passage money. He had slipped overboard when
no one was watching and drowned. He was dead of
cholera long since, and Sean had kept the knowledge

from Liam out of misplaced kindness. He lived still, but Liam's disappearance had softened his brain and left him a gibbering idiot.

He flinched as a heavy hawser flew through the air and was caught and looped over a bollard by a long-shoreman. Already the gangway was in place and passengers were filing ashore; crack steamboats did not dawdle along the route. A new possibility assailed Liam: Tom would not reach the gangway in time and would be carried upriver and disappear. He hurried toward the line of passengers, scanning it as he went.

Suddenly he drew a sharp breath and held it. Tom's features, his small nose and thick black hair and piercing blue eyes, were Mary's all over. Not recognize him? Liam would have known him anywhere. The worst was that his face was white and pinched, just as hers had been as she lay dying in Liam's arms. Could he stand to have that face before him all the time, in the world as well as in his dreams? Or would he be forced to pawn the boy off onto Sean and Sheila once again?

Tom's eyes met Liam's. He blinked rapidly, and his body seemed to gather itself for a wild dash, but with a visible effort he stood very still, waiting.

Why, the poor tyke is terrified, Liam thought. *He's unsure of his welcome, as well he might be with me so caught up with myself that I've no time to think of a poor orphan.* He smiled broadly and waved, and started toward the boy. As if on signal, Tom came racing across the wharf and flung himself into Liam's arms. Liam caught him under the arms and lifted him high into the air, as he had so often in the past. *The lad has grown,* he thought ruefully; *I'll not be able to do this very much longer*. He picked up the satchel where Tom had let it fall, put his other arm around the boy's shoulders, and led him up the road to town. The road to his new home.

Liam was lodging with Mrs. Noonan, who had come to America from Belfast twenty years before, raised four children on her earnings as a laundress, and seen them all make starts for themselves in the world. Liam was just the age of her second son, who had followed the lure of gold to California, half a world away. As a result, Liam got the choicer bits at supper and found something waiting in the oven if his work kept him late. He accepted the special treatment cheerfully, reasoning that the fates had allotted enough of the other sort to him to make it fair. Once he flustered Mrs. Noonan completely by saying "G'night, ma" and giving her a peck on the cheek before going to his room.

She was hovering near the door when he arrived with Tom. "And is this him, then, Mr. O'Donnell," she exclaimed. "Bless us, how big he is! You told me he was a child, but isn't he the next thing to a man! You must be hungry after such a long trip—would you like some bread and honey?"

Tom looked at her with big eyes. "Yes, please."

"Listen to the darlin' boy!" She swept Tom into her arms and pressed him to her, then let him go and tousled his hair. He accepted the treatment passively, but his expression was perplexed, as if the experience was entirely new to him.

That night he woke sobbing from a nightmare. Liam had to hold him and stroke his thin body until he was calm enough to go back to sleep. As the days passed, though, he grew more and more at home, treating Mrs. Noonan with a breezy affection that made her beam and beginning, slowly, to take Liam for granted. His eyes no longer got tense and frantic each time Liam had to leave the house, though once Liam returned from an early morning visit to the outhouse to find Tom sitting up in bed with tears streaming down his blanched cheeks.

With the end of summer, Liam enrolled Tom in school, though he protested that lots of boys his age were working and earning money. "Aye, so they are," Liam replied only half in jest, "so since you earn no money from your schooling, you must work all the harder at it." Because he could not quite understand this, Tom was greatly impressed by it.

Gradually, as the boy relaxed, he revealed more and more of his life in New York City. The divisions and feuds that Liam had found on the road gang were mirrored on the mean streets of the city, drawing even the youngest children into the battles among Connachtmen, Corkonians, and Fardowners. Gangs of boys still chubby with baby fat fought with clubs and broken bricks, and woe to the child who was caught alone away from his own street.

Sean had tried to exercise some control over Tom, but what was he to do? Their quarters were overcrowded even when all of them were asleep; there was certainly no room for an active boy to play, and he could not pass all his waking hours in the grog shop. His friends and playmates were in the street, chasing each other, stealing fruit from the pushcarts, jumping onto the back of a horsecar and dodging the driver's whip, making fun of the swells in their fancy carriages. Hunger, disease, and death were as familiar to them as a glass of milk to a child in Newburgh, and they were as knowing about corruption and vice as they were ignorant about grace and beauty. The more Liam learned, the greater his relief that Tom had escaped, and the greater his sorrow that thousands of others had not. The Famine had destroyed a generation, and now the slums of the New World were destroying the next. Ireland's English rulers had much to answer for.

On Sundays Liam took Tom for long rambles in the countryside. One week they followed the bank of the river, looking for interesting flotsam cast up on the shore. Tom went home with an oddly-shaped piece of greenish glass, worn utterly smooth by the river, and a tree limb, bleached white and incredibly light, that he shaped and polished for a walking stick. Another Sunday Margaret O'Malley joined them, giving Liam a great basket of willow withies to carry. She showed them a path to a place where they could see the town, and the river, and the forests on the other shore. When Tom turned around from taking in the view, he found that she had laid a cloth on the grass and spread it with cold meat pies, and fruit, and thin slices of pink ham. He liked Margaret all right, she was nice, but he wished Liam wouldn't spend so much time *looking* at her when there were so many other things to look at.

On one of these Sunday walks, Tom's habit of looking at things had an unexpected result. A sharp early frost had hastened the turning of the leaves, and a rain storm with high winds had scattered them from the trees. The rolling woods they were walking through looked very different without their thick curtain of green. Tom practiced chucking stones at the trunks of trees, once shifting his aim to an unwary squirrel. The squirrel flashed up to a high branch and turned to chitter angrily. Tom started to shy another stone at him, but then he stopped and glanced around in puzzlement.

"Liam?"

"Yes, *drihaurín?*" Liam replied, using an affectionate Gaelic term for little brother.

"Why do the trees stop?"

"Stop? How, stop?"

"Look." The boy pointed. "All around are trees, but on that hill they stop. Why?"

He was right. The entire slope was covered only with low bushes and grasses, though every other hill was thickly wooded. Liam scratched his head, as puzzled as Tom. "Perhaps the soil," he said. He realized how lame this answer sounded, and added, "Let us go and look. Watch where you go; the ground is boggy and you'll not want to ruin your shoes."

A few minutes later they stood three-quarters of the way up the slope, no wiser than before. The view was tantalizingly familiar to Liam, but it was some time before he realized that the irregular line through the forest, just visible in the gap between two nearby hills, marked the course of the plank road that he and Ezra were building. Approaching from the south, he had not realized where he was. The walk home would be easier for that discovery.

Tom had a handful of small round stones and was tossing them idly at a bush. Liam reached over for one, to try his own skill, and noticed that it looked very much like the gravel he and Ezra were bringing in by the barge-load for their roadbeds. The other stones Tom held were the same, small, hard, and smoothly rounded, what he had known in Ireland as shingle.

"Where did you find these stones, *mo grá?*"

"On the ground. Why? Are they diamonds?"

"No, no, only stones! Where, on the ground?"

"Why, here." He scuffed his foot over a tuft of grass, which pulled away roots and all, then reached down and held out another handful of stones. Liam stared down at them, so long that Tom started to wonder if he had done something wrong, then straightened up and looked around as if he had just awoken.

"I know a game we can play," he said. "Let us see how many places on this hill we can find stones like these. Do you go that way and I'll this, and we'll meet at the top."

Tom opened his mouth to say something, perhaps that it did not sound like much of a game to him, but something in Liam's face silenced him. He trotted across the slope to the left and stopped about twenty yards along to dig up more stones. Liam watched for a moment, then turned to the right.

In half an hour, his unspoken question was answered, and so was the question of Tom's that led to it. The hill was bare of trees because its soil was only the thinnest of layers over a mountain of gravel. A mountain, moreover, that was less than a quarter of a mile from a fine new road and not far distant by that road from a river port. In the proper hands—and he meant to see that it came into the proper hands!— it would be worth, if not a fortune, a great deal of money.

Before they left, he took careful note of the location, leaving an unobtrusive cairn by the side of the plank road, and on the walk home he cautioned Tom not to talk of the day's adventures to anyone. The next morning he left the straw boss in charge of the work gang and set off through the woods with a map and compass in his jacket pocket, striking out for the gravel hill only when he was sure that he was out of sight. And on Tuesday he went by Terence Waterford's office.

"I want to buy some land that lies next to the road we're building," he explained, "but if I appear in it I fear the price will climb beyond my means. Can you discover who owns it and inquire if he will sell?"

"It's not a task that's entirely new to me," the lawyer replied dryly. "Is there a particular tract you want?"

"There is." He opened his map and pointed to the penciled circle. For safety's sake, he had drawn it larger than the hill and off-center, and included more of the road frontage than he needed; anyone looking at it would think that was his reason for wanting it.

Waterford raised the pince-nez that dangled on a cord around his neck and studied the map. "Um," he said. "Pray excuse me a moment." He stood up and crossed to the shelves that covered the wall to the ceiling, and selected one of a row of japanned deed boxes. Drawing a map from it, he compared it with Liam's for a moment, then returned to his desk. "Yes, I thought so. A client of mine once owned all that area, and I think I know the present owner, though I'll want to check the plats at the courthouse to be sure. Will you come to see me on Friday, O'Donnell? I'll know something by then."

The week passed very slowly. It seemed to Liam that he counted over his little store of savings a dozen times, and each time it seemed smaller and his hopes more preposterous. At last Friday came, and he presented himself at Waterford's office. After the usual preliminaries, the attorney cleared his throat several times.

"Well, sir, I've news for you, though whether you'll find it good or bad I cannot say. The land you want is owned by a man in Cornwall who has no great use for it that I can tell. I doubt if he has seen it more than once, if that. He is willing to sell, and at a price that seems in accord with the market for the timber it holds."

Liam opened his mouth to speak, and Waterford held up an admonishing finger. "So far," he continued, "so good. *But* . . . he will only consider an offer for the entire tract, some two hundred fifty acres, more or less. I suspect that he regrets buying it and wants it off his mind altogether."

Liam gulped. He had been figuring on buying twenty acres, thirty at most, not two hundred fifty. "And what sort of money, now, would we be talking about?" he asked faintly.

"He mentioned twenty-five hundred dollars, but I believe you could get it for fifteen or eighteen."

"I see. Yes. Yes. I must consider this carefully. Thank you, Mr. Waterford, you have been very obliging. I shall speak of this again on Monday next. Thank you."

He was never quite sure how he found his way out of the office and onto the street. Fifteen hundred dollars! It was more than a laborer might earn in five

years or more of working on the rail road! Where was
he to get such a great sum, he who had stinted himself
to save a quarter of that in the course of a year? He
must give up the idea, or put it aside for an indefinitely
long time. And anyone might come along and make
the same discovery at any moment. He had the terrible feeling that fate had given him a great chance
to better himself and that he was letting it slip from
his grasp.

No! He must find the money, that was all. But
where, and how? Until the land was his own, he dared
not reveal the reason he wanted it. Who in his right
mind would lend a large sum to a poor Irishman and
not insist on knowing what it was for? And if he admitted that he wanted to buy a large stretch of scrub
forest, apparently no different than any other? They
would think him mad! But if he told Waterford, for
example, that he thought the land held valuable
mineral deposits, what was to stop Waterford from
declining to lend him money, then buying the land on
his own account? Only the fear that Liam might do
him an injury or set a torch to his barn, Whiteboy-
style. A realistic fear, Liam decided.

No, the lawyer did not seem like a good prospect.
But there was another possibility. He found Ezra in
their tiny office above the hardware store. His partner
looked surprised to see him in town in the middle
of the afternoon.

"Does the firm have any money," he asked without
preliminaries, "that I might borrow in a case of need?"

"Is Tom sick? What is the matter?"

Liam shook his head impatiently. "Nothing of the

sort. I'm asking for me own information, in case a need should arise."

"Oh. I see." He obviously didn't. "Well, I suppose there is some money you could draw against if you had to. Two, perhaps three hundred dollars, I imagine. And the bank might give you as much as that against your share of the firm. You haven't been playing cards, have you? You shouldn't. I had a cousin who blew his brains out after losing the family farm in a game of cards."

"I don't care for cards," said Liam. He did not for a moment believe in Ezra's gambling cousin and refused to waste any breath on condolences. "Another question: how are we obliged to the gravel company?"

"Another bargeload has been contracted for and is to arrive in two weeks' time. Liam, what is this? Why are you asking such peculiar questions?"

"If we could buy our gravel for, say, fifteen per cent less, what then?"

Ezra snorted. "Then we'd make more money on the road project, of course."

"Will you write an affidavit that we would buy so much gravel at so much a ton, delivered, and sign it?"

Ezra stared, as much at the desperate earnestness of Liam's tone as at the oddity of his request. Finally he said, "Of course I would. Do you want me to?" He drew a sheet of paper from the drawer and opened his inkwell.

The next morning Liam was on board the *Thomas Powell*, that ran between Newburgh and New York, and by mid-afternoon he was finding his way through the streets of Five Points to Pat Malone's saloon. Malone himself was behind the bar when Liam walked in. He stared, trying to place the face, then smiled broadly. "Sure, if it isn't—" he paused imperceptibly, obviously recalling the circumstances of Liam's flight the year before—"Mr. Murphy from Mullingar! And how is the cobbling trade in Philadelphia, Mr. Murphy?" He winked broadly, proud of his conspiratorial skills, and poured Liam a dram of fiery poteen.

"*Slainte*. It's that I wished to have speech with you about, Mr. Malone, when you've a moment to spare from your fine, flourishing business."

"No time like the present. *Jimmy!*" He untied his heavy duck apron and tossed it to the boy who appeared in the doorway. "Take the bar; I'll be away for a bit."

He led Liam to the back room. The moment they were out of sight of the grog shop, he turned and took Liam's hand in a powerful grip. "Man, but it's good to see you once more. How's the lad? As much an imp of Satan as ever?"

Liam laughed. "He grows an inch every time I turn me back! And your nieces? And grand-niece too, I hear?"

"You'll see for yourself soon enough. When they learn of your presence, they'll be all over you. Little Maura still pines for her playmate, though; faith, she's not so little any more. But are you here on a visit, or have you business in truth?"

"Business." He proceeded to tell Malone about Tom's discovery and his own estimate of the amount of gravel in the hillside, though he was rather vague about the location of the find. Ezra's affidavit was produced and studied, and a table of estimated costs and profits that Liam had worked on half the night. Finally Malone leaned back in his chair and stared at the wall. After a long silence, he said, "You'll be needing some two thousand dollars then."

"A thousand will do me."

"Oh aye, to buy the land perhaps, but then how will you hire men and wagons and all?" Liam was silenced. "If you are asking me to lend it to you, the short answer is I won't."

"I'll pay any interest you name!"

Malone scowled. "Do you take me for a gombeen man who'll suck you dry slowly and call it a favor? No. I'll not lend it at any interest, but I'll give it to you if you'll take Sheila and Maura in as silent partners. Say a third-interest between them? If the endeavor does not flourish, they need never know, and if it succeeds it will make a nice surprise for them. What say you, O'Donnell *a grá*?"

The proposition came too suddenly for Liam to take it in all at once. "Let me be sure I understand," he said slowly, stalling while he turned the idea over in his mind. "You want to pay two thousand dollars for a one-third share of the new gravel company. I will own two thirds and your nieces will own the rest, but will not be active in it. And you?"

"Will have no connection with it at all," said Malone gravely. "I don't wish my name to appear anywhere in this."

At the time, Malone's passion for anonymity seemed peculiar to Liam. Later, when O'Donnell Sand & Gravel began to get large orders at premium prices from various government bodies in New York and Albany, he remembered Malone's political connections and understood. Of course the saloonkeeper's name could not appear in connection with the company, but he was keeping the profits in the family all the same.

Even without the state contracts, though, the gravel business was an immediate success. The roads that Liam and Ezra were building helped it survive the first months, but then the contractors for the Hudson River Rail Road learned that Liam's company was nearby, dependable, and cheaper. Soon trains of heavily laden wagons were rumbling down the plank road to Newburgh, where the stone was transferred to barges for the trip across the river. The best of it was that the gravel company took up very little of Liam's time, leaving him free to give most of his attention to the construction firm.

One spring day this fact took on new importance. He and Ezra were walking back to town from a work site. He was listening to the birds and trying to recall an air that imitated a thrush when he heard Ezra sasy, "Liam, I've taken a job with a railroad. I'll be leaving for Chicago next week."

"What!" Ezra repeated what he had said. "But why? Is it money, man? We already have all the work we can do."

Ezra shook his head. "No, Liam. It's not money at all. Look, I'm an engineer. I want to do things—to build a bridge across the Mississippi, to blast a tunnel through the heart of the Rocky Mountains. I'm wasting my life designing culverts and drainage ditches, so I'm moving on."

"Bridge the Hudson! Tunnel through the Berkshires

to Boston! Man, there are challenges enough to spend a life on them right here! You don't have to leave."

Ezra clapped him on the shoulder. "Don't think I'll be glad to go, partner. But out west the railroad promoters are daring men. They have to be, the country demands it. They will bridge the Mississippi long before any span crosses the Hudson south of Albany, mark what I say. And they are willing to listen to young, untried engineers like me. Here, if it weren't for you, I would be assistant designer of a road from nowhere to nowhere until my hair was gray enough to command respect. There, I will be construction engineer in charge of a hundred-mile stretch of mainline railroad. There's no choice."

"I see that," Liam cried, "but what of the firm! I've no training, no skills! Without you I'm nothing!"

"You are no engineer, it's true, but you're a builder and a damn fine one too. When did I last have to use my training? You've done it all with little need of my help. In fact, I think my greatest assets for the success of the firm have been my college degree and my uncle. I can't do anything about Uncle, but if you insist I can find you a Rensselaer graduate to hire. You needn't listen to him, just pay his salary and hang his diploma in a prominent place."

Liam argued for the rest of the afternoon and into the evening, but it was no use. The next Monday he stood on the wharf and watched the steamboat *Oregon* carry his former partner on the first leg of his journey to the Wild West. Then he and Tom trudged hand in hand up the hill. Halfway up, Tom said, "Liam, when summer comes, can I work for the company?"

"Maybe, *mo grá*, but would you not rather spend the time playing?"

"I don't think so. Now that Ezra's gone, I don't want you to be lonely. If I'm there, you won't be, will you?"

II

I wish I was a butterfly, I'd fly to my love's breast
I wish I was a linnet and I'd sing my love to rest
I wish I was a blue cuckoo, I'd sing till morning clear
I'd sing for you, my Irish girl, that now I love so dear.

10

Shortly after daybreak, the volunteer companies began to assemble on the sidestreets south of Canal Street. The men wore their new green uniforms with a mixture of selfconsciousness and pride and greeted each latecomer with a derisory cheer and an offer of a sip from the stone jug. The air still held its night chill, and the March wind off the river was cold enough to redden their noses and bring tears to their eyes. They hugged themselves, stamped their feet, and gathered six-deep around fires lit in the middle of the street and fed with rubbish and scraps of lumber.

At last a whistle blew. With much jostling, they formed their ranks of four and made ready to march. From Broadway they heard the shouts as the first units, the Napper Tandy Light Artillery and the Fitzgerald Dragoons, rode into view. Then it was their turn. A flourish from the band, and they stepped out, marching with a military swagger, heads high and eyes ahead. Above each company floated the emerald green flag with its golden harp, side by side with the stars and stripes of their adopted land. Ornately embroidered banners waved gaily, displaying symbolic figures—a robed woman with harp in one hand and sword in the other—or portraits of heroes such as Wolfe Tone, Robert Emmet, and Lord Edward Fitzgerald.

The sidewalks were a sea of green, pretty girls in green dresses and bonnets, men with broad green scarves about their shoulders and green cravats about their necks, children waving green flags. They cheered each volunteer company as it passed, the Smith O'Brien Guard, the Irish Rifles, the Emerald Rangers, but their loudest shouts were saved for the pride of the Irish, the 9th Regiment, the 69th Regiment, and the 75th Regiment of the New York Militia. The bands played "Garryowen" and "The Wearin' o' the Green," the banners snapped in the breeze, and the sound of thousands of boots hitting cobblestone at the same instant reverberated off the houses.

Not all the spectators were enthusiastic. The doorways of the great dry-goods emporiums around Astor Place were crowded with well-dressed women who looked on the parade with nervous disdain and regretted the leniency that had led them to give Bridget the day off. Farther north, businessmen found their customary paths blocked by paraders, onlookers, and the traffic jams they were causing.

"Look at them," one man said to his companion. They stood, slightly apart from the crowd, at the corner of Broadway and 19th Street. "All brag and bounce and bluster, and by sunset half of them will be sprawled in a gutter, besotted by drink. And this is the future of the Republic! I despair for my country, Wainwright, in the hands of an ignorant, venal, drunken mob."

"Come, come, Morton," his companion replied uncomfortably. "I think they make a fine, soldier-like show. You with your knowledge of history should appreciate that, as you have taught the rest of us to appreciate it."

John Tyler Morton was one of the best-known authors in the United States. His books on Napoleon's marshals, on Benedict Arnold, on General Ireton and the English Civil War, sold thousands of copies. If professional historians muttered that the works contained more color than research, at least no one accused them of being dull or of lacking martial spirit. This was the point of his friend's retort, and it seemed to score, for Morton's neck reddened.

"I do not object to them fighting for the United States, if they are willing to do so, though they would find a vast difference between Broadway and the battlefield. What I deplore is that they enable corrupt men to gain power, through their own ignorance and corruption. That is what endangers the nation."

"A bit strong, surely?"

"Strong!" A few heads turned toward them, and Morton lowered his voice. "See here, Wainwright, there are a hundred low saloons and grog shops in New York where any Paddy fresh from the bogs can get a paper instructing a magistrate to nationalize him at once. He can stagger straight from the boat to the polling place, and his vote will carry as much weight as that of a man who has thoughtfully weighed the issues. Is that sensible? Is that what the Founding Fathers fought for?"

"Put like that, perhaps not, but what of democracy? Is that not an essential part of what they fought for?"

"Of course, but consider: Americans are not allowed to swear allegiance to a foreign prince. What do you call the Pope of Rome, if not a foreign prince? Our democratic system rests on an independent, educated, informed electorate, who have learned in their town meetings and congregations to exercise their rights carefully and responsibly. But now the country is being flooded by a lazy, superstitious, priest-ridden rabble that sell their votes with the same cheerful ease that they would sell their sisters!"

Wainwright was shocked. "Steady on, Morton! Surely there are a few bad apples in every barrel, but would you condemn a whole nation? Why, I've some Irish in my own family tree, I believe."

"Scotch-Irish, I'm sure; not the same thing at all. A canny, hard-working Protestant folk, not a boozing, brawling mob. Wait until tonight and see the condition of these martial spirits who have so impressed you."

"Come, come," his friend laughed, "your Vermont plowboy or Kentucky backwoodsman is not above taking a drop or two in season, and I've seen you enjoy a sherry cobbler or a cocktail often enough! For that matter, there was that temperance priest who came over from Ireland a few years ago and gave the pledge to many thousands."

"Rubbish. It's as natural for a Paddy to drink as for his pig to grunt. And once he's drunk, to start a brawl. If we want to save this country from mob rule and dictatorship by corrupt Democratic politicians, we're going to have to show these fellows a firm hand. It's the only language they know."

Wainwright sighed. "I suppose you mean all that Know-Nothing business you got involved with a couple of years ago. I thought you'd have grown tired of it by now."

"I have the honor to be the American Party candidate for the Congress in my district," Morton said stiffly, "and I have every confidence that I will be elected."

"Really? This new Republican party hasn't made much progress in Newburgh, then."

"People recognize that they are the party of slaves, just as the Democrats are the party of slaveowners. My party is the only one that stands solidly for freeborn Americans."

"Of course. How do you like living in the country?"

For a moment, Morton's public face was laid aside. "It's wonderful! I write so much more easily away from the bustle and clamor of the city, where I have fresh air and green prospects to rest my eyes, and fruits from my own garden to brighten my table. I've started a vineyard, too, and hope to make my own wine in a few years. And yet, when my affairs call me to the city, as they did today, I am only hours away by fast boat."

"You make it sound idyllic!"

"And so it could be. But . . ." His face hardened again. "No place is really safe from these elements." He nodded toward the passing parade. "More and more of them are finding their way to Newburgh, crowding into shanties hardly fit for pigs, taking work away from our native sons, and bringing with them the same political corruption that has made this city such a blot on the landscape. I left the city because I could not stand what these canaille had turned it into. Now I see it happening in my new home, but I have done with running. I and my fellow members of the American Party are determined to keep our country safe for its citizens by whatever means are necessary. And God help any filthy bogtrotter that gets in our way!"

Behind the Irish regiments in the great parade came the dozens upon dozens of civic organizations, great and small. There were benevolent societies and burial societies, fraternal lodges and religious sodalities, sporting clubs and political clubs. Each proclaimed its identity proudly on a colorful banner borne by the front rank of its members, and each in turn was cheered impartially by the crowds that lined the street. The loudest cheers were saved for the County Associations that did so much to make the immigrant's lot easier. And if the factions among the bystanders tried to cheer the loudest when the banner of their own county passed, for today at least the rivalry was good-spirited.

John Tyler Morton, member of the Know-Nothing Party and candidate for the United States Congress, was not the only resident of Newburgh who had come to New York City that Saint Patrick's Day. Liam O'Donnell was in town as well, visiting his old friends and reporting on the state of the firm to his silent partners Sheila and Maura. He brought Tom Flynn with him, of course; he couldn't deny his young brother-in-law a chance to see his old playmate Maura again.

Sean MacMahon was marching with his volunteer company, the Wolfe Tone Fusiliers. Liam readily agreed to escort Sheila and her sister, who were planning to walk with the County Clare Association. Sectional loyalties meant less to him than to many, he knew no one in the County Sligo Association, and in any case, he reasoned, Clare *was* west of the Shannon, even if historical accident had attached it to the principality of Munster rather than Connacht. And fine folk they turned out to be, these from Clare. One neighbor on the march was with the city Water Department and had some amusing stories to tell about the new aqueduct from Croton. Another admitted that he played the uilleann pipes and promised to come by Pat Malone's saloon with them the following night.

Tom had a less pleasant time of it on the parade. It was an agony to be so close to Maura and still have her take him so much for granted. She had grown into a real beauty. Her dark hair flowed down over her shoulders, and her serious gray eyes flashed roguishly when he least expected it. He wasn't the only one to notice the change in her. It seemed that every lad in their section of the parade had some urgent business that brought him alongside her. Tom stubbornly refused to let anyone edge between him and Maura, but he could not stop her from talking to whoever walked next to her on the other side. It seemed to him that she spent almost all her time doing just that, too. He grew more and more silent, brooding morosely on the unfairness of it all.

Maura noticed his silence, of course. She knew him too well not to. She tossed her head and talked with even more animation to John Kavanagh, who was nearly twenty-one and expected an appointment to the police force through the father of his older brother's wife. What right did Tom have to ruin her day with his black looks and blacker moods? She enjoyed the attention she was getting, and she meant to go on enjoying it, and Master Thomas Flynn had best get used to it if he wanted any kindness from her!

At 23rd Street the parade turned west, as far as the Eighth Avenue, then south through Chelsea and Greenwich Village. At Canal Street Sheila decided to wait for one of the carriages that brought up the rear, but Maura insisted that she was not a bit tired. After a short, silent debate, Sheila entrusted her to Liam and stepped out of the line of march. To Maura's chagrin, Liam saw it as his duty to walk next to her, on the other side from Tom, and to keep her would-be beaux at a distance. Her isolation left her no choice but to talk to Tom.

"Have you left school then?"

He looked sidelong at her, half-expecting a barb in her question. She smiled, and his heart turned over. What had she asked him? "Not yet. Liam says I must finish the high school, to hold my own against the others. After school I work at the gravel pit though, and this summer I will join a road gang." From his tone it seemed that a road gang ranked just a little lower in his mind than the Red Branch Knights of antique fame.

Maura sighed. "I wanted to go into service this year, but Uncle Pat would not allow it. He still treats me as a child, though there are girls enough my age with husbands and babies."

"You could get both easy enough if you wanted," Tom said daringly.

Maura said nothing, but pink blossomed in her cheek as she remembered some of the games she and Tom had played together before they were old enough to know better. Suddenly she was sure that he was remembering too, and her embarrassed confusion turned to anger. "That's no way to be talking to a decent girl," she said with a frown. "I'll thank you to keep your foul thoughts to yourself from now on!"

Tom's face reflected his surprise. "Och, *a stoir,* I meant no harm," he protested. "Must we quarrel, when we see each other so seldom?"

"Quarrel? Quarrel? Is it quarrelsome you'll be calling me now, you unmannerly spalpeen?"

"Devil a bit of it, for all that it's yourself that is calling names! I thought we met as friends, but I fear your beauty has made you proud."

Under the combined pressure of the compliment and the well-merited accusation, Maura's little chin started to tremble and her gray eyes became pools. Tom was her oldest and closest friend and her hateful vanity was driving him away! Why was she so cross-grained? A fat tear traced its way down her cheek.

Tom saw it and was horrified. *"Ta brón orm, a mhúir-nín,"* he murmured. "I'm sorry, my darling. Don't cry, Maura."

She sniffed once and brushed her hand across her cheek, then turned and gave him a brilliant smile. Once again his heart turned over, but he was more confused than ever. What was the proverb Liam had quoted? "Three kinds of men who do not understand

women: the young man, the old man, and the middle-aged man." He was just sixteen, but under Maura's influence he felt that he was aging rapidly.

That evening the six County Associations of Munster sponsored a ball together, in the grand ballroom of one of the big hotels on Broadway. Pat Malone's entrance, with Liam and the others in his train, was like a royal procession. He seemed to know everyone and to greet most of them by name, and not a one but was glad to be noticed by him. Sean and Sheila had seen this a hundred times, but Liam was amazed by it, and amazed too at the length of time it took them to cross the room, what with bits of news and questions about family members and the occasional whispered request or loudly spoken thanks for a favor. He noticed, too, that Malone greeted some of the other guests with more respect than joviality, particularly one John Kelly, Captain of the Emmet Guards and, he gathered, a growing power in Tammany Hall.

During the sober, inaudible conversation between Kelly and Malone, Liam's mind wandered. He scanned the crowd, noting appreciatively the great number of well-turned-out young women. He was finding life increasingly lonely. Now that Tom was no longer a child, he was thinking of a family of his own. He could afford it; between the sand and gravel company and the contracting firm, he was a man of some substance, one of the rising young capitalists of the Hudson Valley. Mothers of marriageable girls were taking notice of him in growing numbers. Not only Irish mothers, either; just before leaving for New York he had received an invitation to dine with Doctor Pendleton, whose many children included a pretty, shy

daughter of nineteen or so. Liam had been sorry to have to decline. He liked the doctor's dry humor, and Louisa was appealing, if hardly more than a child.

Once again he found himself wishing that Maggie O'Malley had not gone away like that. She had been very dear to him. But in the eyes of the Church she was a married woman. Every time they were together, they risked her reputation and his as well. In the end, the strain was too great. She told him that she was going off to look for O'Malley but had no answer when Liam asked what she would do if she found him. His own belief was that she moved to another part of the country where no one would know about her putative marriage. A little matter of bigamy, if it came to that, would rest easy on her conscience, he was sure. He would have offered himself were it not that everyone in Newburgh knew about O'Malley. As it was, he missed her, and wished her well wherever she was.

Sean touched his arm and roused him from his reverie. "Liam, here's someone I would have you meet. This is Thomas Aherne, of Tralee, a fine hand on the flute. Liam is the fiddler I've told you of so often, Tom."

Aherne was a stocky man a few years older than Liam, with a studious air to him. As they shook hands, he said, "O'Donnell is it? From County Clare perhaps?"

"No, though I marched with Clare today, in company with Sean's wife and her sister."

"Oh? That's fitting, then, for know that the O'Domhnaills were lords of Corcabaskin in Clare until they were dispossessed by the MacMahons."

"Was this recently at all?"

"A matter of four hundred years or so," Aherne admitted. Sean and Liam laughed. Aherne looked slightly miffed. "That's not so very long ago," he protested. "Our race has a long history, but I'll not speak for its future. Too many want only to forget and grow rich, for all they'll wear the green on St. Patrick's Day."

He looked around the crowded ballroom with a sort of gloomy disdain.

"Thomas has a great interest in the old ways," Sean explained to Liam in an undertone.

"Look at them," he continued. "They'll go to the theatre to cheer Barney Williams in his latest play, and they will weep buckets to hear "The Last Rose of Summer," but what do they really care for their suffering motherland? In twenty years their children will know no more of the Gaelic than *Slainte* and *Erin go bráth*! Ah well, as the proverb has it, *Ní dhéanfadh a' saoghal capall rása d'asal.*" He looked sharply at Liam to see if he understood his words, which meant only that "the whole world can't make a racehorse out of a donkey."

Liam smiled. *"Is minic a bhí braimichín giobalach 'na chapaillín cumasach.* A ragged colt often grows into a fine horse." As he said it he too looked around the room, as if to point to all the "ragged colts" he meant. The truth was that he might enjoy a conversation or a battle of wits with Sean's learned friend on some other occasion. Tonight he was more interested in dancing.

Aherne must have sensed his withdrawal, for rather than replying to Liam's sally, he asked, "Will you be in town for long, Mr. O'Donnell?"

"A few days."

"I'll look you up if I may. We have much to talk about, but this is not the place." He nodded abruptly and vanished into the crowd.

Liam was taken aback. "I hope I've not offended your friend," he said to Sean.

"I doubt it. Likely he saw someone he had to speak to. Thomas is thick with Meagher and Mitchel and the other Young Irelanders and is much concerned in their affairs. But I'll say no more of that. Are you not going to dance then?"

"That I will, if Sheila will stand up with me and you give your permission."

He had one dance with Sheila, who treated him like a brother, then a pair of dances with Maura, who treated him like an uncle. He loved the both of them dearly, but he was glad enough to accept an introduction to the sister of a friend of Sean's and lead her onto the floor. Although she did not greatly interest him, it was a delight to have someone in his arms who recognized that he was a man and not simply a benign and sexless relation.

After that dance, they made their way to the refreshment room, at one side of the ballroom, and he edged through the crowd to fetch two glasses of punch. As he was returning with them, he glanced across the room. It was the sash he saw first, of a brilliant green satin, that crossed the bodice of the white dress and was pinned at the left shoulder like the plaid of a Highland Scot. A green stone set in curiously wrought silver held it there. Her hair was pure gold, falling forward to conceal her face as she leaned over to study her dance card. Was it that shining hair, or something about the set of her shoulders that made him stop where he was and watch her? All he knew was that he dared not lose sight of her for a moment.

Some special sense must have alerted her. She raised her head, and their eyes met. Liam's jaw dropped in surprise. He knew that face, and yet he didn't! His scalp tingled with superstitious dread. Had he dreamt her? It must have been a powerful dream, to have left such a jangle of feelings behind.

Her eyebrows drew together, perhaps from vexation at being stared at, but perhaps not. She too seemed puzzled and confused, as if trying to revitalize some long-buried memory. She modestly lowered her eyes, but a moment later she was looking at him once more. Two red spots flamed in her cheeks, but she continued to stare.

Liam was not aware of moving, but he found himself standing in front of her, offering her one of the glasses of punch. She accepted with a hint of a curtsy, still gazing earnestly into his eyes. Her head was tilted just a bit to one side, and her full red lips were slightly parted. Liam inhaled deeply, to keep himself from reaching for her right there in the crowded ballroom. A faint aroma lingered in his nostrils. He swallowed convulsively, gnawed at his lower lip, at last managed to say, "Would it be forward of me to ask you to dance?"

"Yes," she said huskily. She set her untasted glass on the tray of a passing waiter and raised her arms to him.

"I must go," she said, some time later, still looking deep into his eyes. He had lost track of the number of dances, forgotten even where he was, and the idea of parting came as a great shock. "I have tarried overlong already."

"But—" She lifted her index finger gently to his lips and silenced his protest, then turned and walked quickly away, her head lowered.

Liam was too stunned even to move. In his mind it was still a moment earlier, and her warmth still filled his arms. How could she walk away like that? Had she been merely toying with him? He could swear not; she had been as overthrown by the meeting as he. But then why? He called up the energy to follow her, but it was too late. She had already disappeared. He stood near the entrance, gazing out into the night, until someone tapped his arm and asked him to step aside. He was blocking the doorway.

He muttered an apology and went back inside, where Pat Malone gave him a quirky smile. "So, lad, you're back with us, are you? It's certain I was that Queen Cliodhna of the *daoine sídhe* had enticed your spirit away to her city under the hill!" His two companions, strangers to Liam, chuckled at this reference to the tale of how the queen of the fairies of West Cork had bewitched Sean 'ach Séamais, one of the Fitzgeralds of Desmond, and held him captive in Carraig Chliodhna until his father the Earl enlisted the help of Máirín Dubh to set him free.

Liam knew the story as well as anyone, but he did not understand the reference. Malone took pity on his bafflement. "Three times," he explained, "you passed me dancing, and three times I greeted the both of yez, and sorra a word in return did I get from you or the *cailín óg*! Not that I blame you, mind, for I'll not deny she's as handsome as any in the room, barring me own nieces of course."

"You know her?" asked Liam eagerly.

"Know her? Not to say *know* her," Malone replied deliberately. Liam's nails were digging into his palms from impatience. "Now you seemed to know her very well, meaning no offence."

"But I don't!" Liam cried. "I don't even know her name! And now she's left without a word!"

Malone gave a quick snort of amusement, then turned serious as he observed Liam's agony. "Her name I can tell you, though not the reason for her actions. It's Edith Holmes. Her mother, God rest her soul, was an O'Casey from Cork city, and her father's a Sasanach. She takes after her mother, I hear, and the father ill-treats her in consequence, not that he's noted for his kindness to anyone."

A small lump of ice formed in Liam's middle and rapidly grew. "Holmes . . ." he said slowly. "It's a common name, surely."

"I wouldn't know. He is George Holmes, and he owns a shipping agency."

"Pedlock & Holmes," said Liam in a faraway voice.

"Aye, though Pedlock went to his reward some years since. You know him, then?"

As if it had been only the day before, Liam recalled the feel of the deck b eath his feet, the intense blue of the afternoon sky, the small blonde girl who listened so intently as he played "The Trip to Sligo." And below, in the foul darkness of the hold, his Máire bled her life away, a victim of the greedy shipowner as surely as if he had dashed her brains out with a stone! That such men lived on, unpunished for their crimes!

And he, what was he that he had forgotten so easily!

"Liam, man, what is it? Are you ill?"

He brushed Malone's hand from his shoulder and walked unsteadily from the room and out into the street, seeking to pull the blanket of night around himself. More than one passerby stopped to stare at the intense young Irishman, then turned away under the impact of his fierce glare. Soon, though, he found his way to a warren of unlighted streets where his lack of caution made everyone else fear and avoid him. He wanted no eye to mark his face, for his rage was shaping itself into an aim so vile that even in the midst of his anger he felt the creeping tendrils of shame.

11

m y dear Miss Holmes,

March 18, 1856

Although we have not been formally introduced, I had the honor of dancing with you at the
Ball last evening. I unaccountably neglected to
ask leave to call while I remain in the City, so
take the opportunity of these lines to do so. I
must return to my home and business in Newburgh on Friday next, but until then a word in
care of the Astor House, Broadway, will reach me.
I have the honor to remain, etc.,

Yr obt servant,
Liam O'Donnell.

He read over the note with grim satisfaction before
folding and sealing it. The next morning he had his
answer: her engraved calling card, with the penned
words "At Home. Wednesday." in the lower left cor-

ner. He sat on the windowsill, looking out over Broadway and tapping the card against his front teeth. Now that his plan was beginning to move forward, he was not so sure of himself. Would it not be more honorable to tear up the card, go home to Newburgh, and forget that such a person as Edith Holmes existed? Perhaps so, but honor had two opponents to contend with: an attraction so deep that he ached with it, and an oath sworn in blood. Either might have been overcome singly, but their unnatural alliance outweighed his scruples. He sprang up from the windowsill and opened the doors of the clothespress. He intended to look his very best that afternoon.

When he emerged from the Astor House, he was a striking figure. His boots gleamed, his linen was dazzlingly white under his superfine broadcloth suit, and his beaver hat was freshly brushed. Across the w /, the fountain in City Hall Park sent its jet sixty eet into the air, a spectacle the equal of any in F rope, but Broadway as usual was ankle-deep in m d and dung. Liam raised his gold-headed walking tick and a horsecab swerved over to the sidewalk.

The Holmes residence was one of a row of new brownstone houses on West 19th Street. Liam paid off his cab, climbed the flight of steps to the carved oak front door, and tugged at the brass bellpull. The door swung wide and a scared-looking little Irish girl in black dress and frilly white apron and cap bobbed to him, then held out a small silver tray. He dropped his card onto it and followed her into the hallway. The tall pierglass mirror on the wall showed as immaculate a reflection as the one over the chest of drawers at the Astor House, but he was abruptly aware that his shirt was soaked under the armpits and his heart was pounding.

The maid returned, accepted his hat, gloves, and stick, and silently led him to a set of double doors. Beyond was the parlor. Edith Holmes was seated behind a silver tea set, looking toward the entrance with something like dread. Her eyes were wide and her cheeks were drained of color. She parted her lips to speak, then closed them and motioned him to a chair next to her.

"Thank you," he said. "Good afternoon." His words rang like a shout in the empty room. "It's a fine day, isn't it?"

"Yes," she replied faintly. "Tea, Mr. O'Donnell?"

"Thank you." He accepted the cup and watched her prepare one for herself. The little maid scurried in with a plate of hot muffins, caught his eye, blushed, and scurried out again. He turned back to his hostess, started to speak, and saw that she was about to speak. Each waited for the other.

"I beg your pardon. You were about to say . . . ?"

"No, please continue."

"I insist. The fault was mine."

"Not at all." A long pause. "More tea?"

He looked down at his untouched cup, then back at her. She turned her face away, red with vexation. He thought seriously of rising and taking his leave. Her pride would be wounded, no doubt, but it might be kinder in the long run. But now that he was near her again, the thought of leaving was intolerable.

"It was very bold of me to intrude on you like this."

She turned back, slightly alarmed. "You don't intrude, sir. If anyone has been unconventional, it was

I, for going unescorted to a public ball. I think your behavior has been perfectly correct."

He bowed from his chair. "On a great holiday, the unconventional is the rule. And what holiday should be great if not St. Patrick's? You wore the green very handsomely, Miss Holmes."

"Thank you." The color in her face was from shy pleasure now. Liam's heart turned over. She looked like a little girl who had just received a present. Was he really going to succeed so easily? If so, his guilt would be all the greater.

"It's very strange," she continued, "but I felt at once that we were not strangers. We haven't met before, though, have we? I don't think I would have forgotten."

"No, we haven't." He quieted his conscience with the thought that this was strictly true; the daughter of Holmes & Pedlock would never have been allowed to meet a poor passenger from steerage.

"I can't account for it at all, then, but the feeling is as strong as ever. I believe you mentioned in your note that you live in Newburgh. That is up the Hudson, is it not? I've never been there."

"It's a pleasant town, close enough to the country for a sight of green now and then, but with the conveniences of a small city."

"How nice. Have you always lived there?"

"I was born in Sligo, but I've been in Newburgh since coming to America."

"Sligo? Weren't you attending the wrong ball, Mr. O'Donnell?"

"If so, it's a mistake I'll never regret, Miss Holmes."

She looked down in confusion. "My mother was from

Cork," she said rapidly, "and I was born there, but I've lived most of my life in New York. I wish I knew Ireland better—there is something about it that attracts me greatly."

"The only thing greater than its beauty is its distress, and I fear that will not change in our lifetimes. I hope to return on a visit some day, but America has been kinder to me than my native land ever was or could have been."

"You mentioned your business . . . ?"

"I own a construction firm in Newburgh, building roads, canals, railways, and so forth."

"That must be very interesting for you. Were you brought up to the trade?"

He laughed. "Far from it. I was trained as a musician. But America has more need of a well-made road than a well-played reel!"

As she laughed at his remark, something passed behind her eyes, perhaps an association to the idea of a well-played reel, but she gave her head a shake and it was lost. The conversation moved onto safer topics and wound finally to a close. Neither she nor Liam mentioned her father once.

That evening Liam escorted her to the theatre, and the next day he hired a gig and they drove up along the river, past the villages of Bloomingdale and Harlem, all the way to the century-old Dyckman house, then back to the Claremont Inn for a light meal. Afterwards they strolled through the gardens down to the riverbank. The weather as well as the calendar proclaimed that it was the first day of Spring. The trees were covered with a haze of green, and birds were everywhere. Though the air still retained winter's chill, the ground was warm in the afternoon sun. Out on the river, white-sailed schooners passed like great sea-birds and a deep-noted horn announced the approach of one of the steamboats from upriver.

Liam found a secluded nook and spread his topcoat on the grass. Edith hesitated and looked at him doubtfully. When she sat, she held herself very straight and faced the river in such a way that her shoulder was between them. Liam smiled to himself and made easy conversation, though it was a trouble to him to keep his breathing even. Gradually she relaxed, leaning back on her arms to gaze up at the flawless sky. He placed his hand gently on her shoulder, and she turned her head to look at him. Her eyes were bluer than the March sky, and though they held a question, he saw no trace of fear in them. A single blonde curl had escaped to drape itself across her cheek. He leaned closer to brush it back and caught the faint scent of her flower-water.

Taking a deep breath, he shifted his hand from her cheek to the back of her neck and pulled her toward him. She stiffened, but he insisted, crushing his lips down on hers. His arm was around her now, pressing her pliant body against his hard chest. It seemed to him that she welcomed and met his approach, turning subtly at the waist to bring herself into fuller rapport with him. His hand slipped down, instinctively avoiding the rigidity of her whalebone stays for the soft fullness of her hip, and felt her writhe under his touch.

Without warning she twisted free of his embrace and sat up, back to him, gulping for breath. He reached for her once more, but she brushed his hand aside and stumbled to her feet. "Please take me home,

Mr. O'Donnell." When he didn't answer, she added in a stronger voice, "Unless you agree, I shall leave you here and hire a cab. Don't try to hinder me or I shall cry out for assistance."

Liam stood up and retrieved his grass-stained top-coat. "There's no need for that at all, Miss Holmes. I meant no harm. We are both adults, after all."

"Yes, and as such, able to rein in our unruly impulses if need be." She led the way up the hill to the inn, ignoring the knowing looks of other strollers, and was silent during the long ride south to 19th Street. He asked if he might call again before leaving the city the next day, but she said that she was fatigued and somewhat indisposed, and planned to pass the next day in her room. At the last moment, as he was turning to descend the steps of her father's house, she relented to the extent of inviting him to call on his next visit to the city. He bowed coldly and did not answer.

That evening, for the first time in his life, he visited one of the joy-houses on the lower west side. The house was well-conducted, and the exercise relieved the ache in his groin, but it did nothing to soothe his inflamed emotions. Even the next day, on the boat back to Newburgh, his mind was a cauldron of conflicting desires. The strongest still was a lust to avenge himself on Holmes, by way of his daughter's body. Added to that was the anger he felt at being rejected. He had imagined that the force of his impulse would carry all before it, that in one day he would manage either to seduce or violate her. The ease with which she brushed him aside was only an added humiliation that made him grind his teeth in rage.

And yet . . . he had not needed to war against himself to try to win her. The attraction he had felt, before he had discovered who she was, persisted, strengthened by the hours he had since passed with her. Sitting next to her in the gig had been intensely disturbing. Each time their bodies touched, he burned with it. And even in the midst of that fierceness, he had felt a strange ease with her, as if they had known each other for many years. He had had to remind himself constantly of who she was: a stranger and the child of an enemy, his lawful prey if he chose.

He needed the reminder for other reasons as well. He knew the Biblical and Classical precedents for the revenge he planned on Holmes, but it still shamed him to look at it squarely. To rape a foe's daughter might have been appropriate for the Jews, Greeks, and Romans of antique days, but it seemed unworthy of an Irish gentleman. Shooting Holmes from behind a hedge would be more honorable. Most disturbing was the thought that Mary would have been appalled and disgusted by his scheme. How then was it a decent way to respect her memory?

This constant wrestling with himself made the voyage pass quickly. As the boat nosed in toward the wharf, he strolled back to the gate where the gangway would be placed. Several other Newburgh-bound passengers were waiting there. He recognized one of them, a man named Morton who wrote books about war. Morton had bought a place just outside of town a few months before and seemed eager to be treated as gentry, if the word had any meaning in America. Terence Waterford had introduced them not long after

Morton arrived in town and had later explained to Liam that the writer had vague political ambitions that bore watching.

Liam caught Morton's eye and nodded casually. Morton stared straight ahead, feigning not to see him. For a moment Liam believed that he truly had not noticed, then something in the stiffness of his back made it obvious that the slight had been deliberate. The muscles in Liam's neck and shoulders tightened and his eyes narrowed. He gripped his walking stick so tightly that his knuckles turned white. Morton saw the motion and flinched, then gave Liam a look of concentrated hatred for having witnessed his timidity.

Tom returned on Sunday afternoon with his eyes full of stars and spent the next week trying to find words that rhymed with Maura. The best he was able to do was *flora* and *aurora*. Liam offered *begorra*, but Tom was not amused by the suggestion. When he received a letter a few days later, he pointedly stuffed it in his pocket and stalked out of the house, as if he feared that Liam was about to creep up behind him and read over his shoulder. Liam went in search of him just before supper and found him lying on his stomach in the grass at the top of the hill, staring southward as though his vision could reach all the way to New York City. When he got to his feet, he was shivering violently from the chill. Liam started to put an arm around him, then reminded himself that at sixteen Tom would not relish being treated as a child.

April and May were busy months. After several fruitless attempts, and some careful string-pulling, the firm was awarded a contract to build several short spurs for the Erie Railroad. The work promised to be both rather difficult and very profitable, and Liam had to give it a great deal of attention. The other jobs, if less important, also made their demands, as did the gravel business. He found himself spending the daylight hours in the saddle, riding from one worksite to another, and the evening in the office planning the work ahead and bringing the records up to date. From the office he went directly to his bed and fell asleep almost before he had stretched full-length. If the thought of Edith Holmes crossed his mind at all, he set it aside as a project to be considered again when he was less occupied building rail lines.

He thought of her one evening in June, as he walked home from the office. It was a warm, still night, and the air was redolent with the fragrance of flowers. A half-moon floated above a line of clouds to the east and besilvered each ripple on the face of the river. His steps slowed and he breathed deeply, aware of strange longings. This was not the life he had wanted, working sixteen hours a day at an occupation that did not much interest him, then returning to his room in a boarding house. Tom would be striking out on his own soon, and he would be left alone, he who had always imagined himself surrounded by a large, laughing family. But now, when he thought of a family, he saw Edith's face and form and golden curls beside him, and the idea of such a betrayal of Mary's memory chilled him.

Mrs. Noonan was waiting for him near the door, looking apprehensive. "Mr. O'Donnell," she whispered, "you have a visitor these many hours. I didn't know what to do, if I should send word to you."

"Is it Tom? Has something happened to him?"

"No, no, the lad's upstairs asleep, don't fret yourself. No, it's just . . . well, see for yourself." She motioned toward the door to the parlor. Liam crossed the hall and peered in.

Edith Holmes was huddled up in a big chair, asleep. A half-full cup of tea rested on the little table beside her. Her gown was creased, and her face was tired and drawn.

Even through his astonishment, Liam felt once more that bone-deep attraction that had brought him across a crowded room. His projects for revenge now seemed, in her presence, childish and nasty. But what was she doing here?

The pressure of his gaze woke her. She looked around, dazed, and seemed to be asking herself the same question. Then her eyes fell on him. She sat up and struggled to compose herself. "I—" She licked her lips and tried again. "I imagine you are surprised to see me here." He bowed silently and waited. "I have no right to intrude like this, Mr. O'Donnell. I do know that. But I had nowhere else to turn."

Mrs. Noonan appeared with a tray of tea things and a plate of bread-and-butter sandwiches, then discreetly withdrew and closed the door behind her. Edith looked at the tray helplessly, but she accepted a sandwich and a cup of tea when Liam handed them to her.

"I expect you will think me very foolish and forward. I suppose I am. But . . . I left my father's house this morning, never to return. On that I am adamant. But I know the likely fate of an unprotected female in the city. I thought of you, and thought to seek your advice. I want to be able to support myself in some respectable manner, however humble or toilsome."

Liam gained time by sipping his tea. The irony of her throwing herself on his mercy appalled him. "Was there no one closer to home you could have asked for help?"

"No one. We never spoke of my father, you and I. You must take my word that his occupation, manners, and choice of diversions have driven away all with a shred of decency left to them."

"Yet you stayed."

"I did, God help me. Though I watched his cruelty kill my mother, I vainly imagined that I could soften and reform him. I suppose that is the pride we are told goes before a fall, though in all truth, what choice had I but to stay? I have no other family to shelter me."

She lowered her head, screening her face with her hair, and spoke in so low a voice that Liam strained to hear her. "But last night he came home deep in liquor. I am used to that, but last night he . . . he behaved unspeakably. I passed the night in my room, wide awake, fully clothed, with the door locked and a chair wedged under the knob, and I fled at first light."

Liam thoughtlessly reached out to touch her hand. She gasped and recoiled, then visibly fought to regain her control. "I don't know what freak led me here," she said at last. "I know we did not part on the best of terms, you and I. But something told me that I could rely on your kindness. I do not think you are a man who would take advantage of the helpless."

He sprang up and strode to the window, to stand with his back to her staring into the night. The great chasm between her idea of him and what he knew himself to be shamed him deeply. He could not face her. He snorted as a further irony occurred to him. He had schemed to take revenge on her father through her, but from what she said—and what she left unsaid —George Holmes was a man who could not be injured that way. If Liam's plan had succeeded, as thank God it had not, who would have been harmed but an innocent girl and Liam himself?

He turned back. "You must be very tired," he said gravely. "Mrs. Noonan has a bed to spare, I know, and we can talk better in the morning, when you are rested. Will you let me call her now?"

She raised her hand, palm upward, in an odd, defeated gesture, and let it fall to her lap.

Though her room was on the other side of the house from his own, Liam seemed to sense her presence as he lay on his bed unable to sleep. It was wonderful to him, and somehow inevitable, that she, like him, was her father's victim. They shared that, as they shared so much else. And as he was finally drifting into sleep, a strange idea seized him. On that terrible day when Mary died, had something of her departing spirit become lodged in the young girl who listened so intently to her husband's music? Was that the reason they had recognized each other immediately, the night of the ball?

In the morning the idea evaporated like the fragment of a dream, but after breakfast he took out his fiddle and began to play. Without thinking, he moved into "The Trip to Sligo." He had never played it since Mary's death, but his fingers still knew it perfectly. As he finished the repetition of the second section, a noise distracted him. He opened his eyes to see Edith clutching the doorpost, her face a ghastly white. He stopped playing and jumped up in alarm.

"No," she gasped, "I'm all right. It's just— That music. It was very beautiful, but for some reason it made me unbearably sad. You once told me that you were trained as a musician, but I had no idea you were such an artist. Will you play something more? Please?"

Liam retrieved his fiddle and began an air called "The Autumn Stubble." As he played, the Gaelic words ran through his mind, a story of two young lovers who escape from their families and go off together. When the last note died away, he looked up to find that Edith's cheeks were damp. Her eyes regarded him with that same grave intensity he remembered so well, and in that instant his resolve was formed.

"Will you walk with me? There is a grand view from the hill."

As they started up the grassy slope, she took his arm. Her touch was light, but it stirred him far more than the kiss he had taken from her that March afternoon in New York. At the top, she turned and cried, "Oh, it's beautiful!"

The valley of the Hudson spread itself at their feet, green and blooming in the mild summer air. Beyond the river, the hills of Dutchess County rolled eastward toward Connecticut, and to the south Storm King and Breakneck Ridge loured at each other across the narrows. From a nearby field came the drowsy hum of bees and the scent of clover.

Liam cleared his throat. "I've thought much of what you told me," he said carefully. She looked over her shoulder with a doubtful expression. "Your difficulties will be much lessened if you'll agree to my proposal, I believe."

"Oh, I knew I could rely on you!" She turned to face him fully. "I'll do anything—anything that's not dishonorable."

Liam removed his hat. "You refer to honor. Will you do me the honor of becoming my wife?"

She stared at him, as though wondering if she had heard him correctly, or if she was the object of some incomprehensible joke. Her eyes searched his face and found only earnestness there. Frowning with bewilderment, she said, "This is very sudden, Mr. O'Donnell. We hardly know each other."

"There you are wrong, *mo cuisle*, for our souls have known each other forever. The rest doesn't matter. Will you deny that you knew something had happened in that moment we first saw each other? Sure, I tried to deny it myself, but it was stronger than the both of us. Didn't it bring you here to me, as unlikely an event as any in the old songs?"

Her bewilderment deepened. "I don't even know your given name!" she wailed. "How can I be your wife?"

He bowed solemnly. "I am Liam Dermot O'Donnell, and I have loved you since first I saw you. Though I own I did not know it meself until last night." He extended his hand toward her, palm upward, and waited.

She flinched. Her gaze moved back and forth between his face and the proffered hand.

"*Tabhair dom do lámh, a stóir.* Give me thy hand, my treasure."

Slowly, almost without volition, her hand rose, hesitated, retreated, and settled trembling on his. For a long moment they stood like that, palms barely touching, eyes locked in a gaze both serious and charged with passion, almost forgetting to breathe in the intensity of the instant. Then, with no transition, her arms were around his neck and his around her waist, and she was sobbing against his chest while he kissed the top of her head and pressed her closer to ease her sorrow. It was too soon to expect joy, but that too would come.

Liam's friends were happy to hear the news. If they were also surprised, they hid it well. His Newburgh acquaintances assumed that he had courted Edith in New York, and his friends in New York knew little enough of his day to day life to let them assume what they liked. Nor was the possibility of his remarriage so remote to them. Sean let slip that he and Sheila had talked of eligible girls they might introduce him to on his next trip to the city, then added diplomatically that Liam had done much better for himself than they could have done for him.

The person who was most affected by the news, of course, was Tom. For what seemed to him all his life, he had been Liam's closest relation. The prospect of losing that distinction confused and frightened him. He was nearly of an age to go off on his own, it was true, but that was far different from being banished. Edith, however, made a special effort to become friends with the lad and to draw him into the preparations for the wedding. At first he was inclined to be withdrawn and resentful, but she persisted. In the end, he loved Liam too much not to open his heart to her as well. When the wedding day came, he was cheerful as a lark.

The celebration after the wedding was notable for several reasons. Liam handed his fiddle to Sean and refused to take it back. He had played at enough weddings already, he said, and meant this once to listen and dance while others did the work. Pat Malone and Terence Waterford, after circling each other like a pair of strange dogs, started talking and discovered that Tammany politics and the upstate variety were more alike than different. Sean's brother Kevin and sister Grainne, the last of his family to be brought to America, hung about shyly on the outskirts until the music started, then joined in with a verve that had the others clapping and cheering. Tom followed Maura behind the shrubbery and kissed her. She pushed him off and ran away, but by some strange mistake ran deeper into the shrubbery. Caitlín, Sean's and Sheila's seven-year-old daughter, burst into tears because *she* wanted to marry Liam, and had to be consoled with a kiss and a special piece of cake.

At the end of it all, the guests followed the carriage down to the river, where Edith and Liam took the ferry across to Beacon and the steam train north and west, all the way across the state to Niagara Falls. As the scenery drifted past, Liam reflected that, but for a forged ticket, he might have made this journey eight years before, to end, like so many of his countrymen, in an unmarked grave on the western plains. Then he put such thoughts behind him and turned to Edith— his present and his future.

12

Most of the wedding guests reassembled in Newburgh a year later, for the christening of Robert Emmet O'Donnell. The baby had a grave face and a cap of dark hair that formed a widow's peak. All agreed that he looked more like Liam than like Edith. To Liam's eye, fond though it was, he simply looked like a baby, chubby and pink and generally asleep. In later years, as his experience with babies grew, he realized that he had not properly appreciated Robert's placidity.

After cooing over the new baby, the visitors were expected to take a tour of the new house. Liam had built it on the same hill where he had proposed to Edith, with the same sweeping view of the valley. A roofed porch surrounded the first floor, and there were two more floors of bedrooms and a capacious attic as well. Liam was especially proud of his study, a dark-paneled room on the second floor of the circular tower that dominated the southeast corner of the house. It was there that he took Sean when his friend asked to speak privately with him.

Sean accepted a cigar and took his time lighting it. "I like your son's name," he said at last.

Liam grinned. "As do I, or we'd not have given it to him. Come on, Sean *a grá*, what's to do? Is it in need of a loan you are, or a job for one of your brothers?"

"No, but . . . I mention the boy's name because for several years I have been a member of the Emmet Monument Association. I don't know if you've heard of it?"

Liam hadn't, but he realized the significance of the organization's name at once. In his last speech after the English had condemned him to death, Robert Emmet had commanded that no man write his epitaph until his country had taken her place among the nations of the earth. If Sean's group meant to raise a monument to Emmet, they must mean first to free Ireland of English rule.

"We have many members among the volunteer militia," Sean continued, "who are pledged to use the martial skills they gain for the sake of their country."

Liam raised a hand. "Don't tell me more than you mean to. I am not of your association."

"But you support its goals."

"And doubt its means. I honor Emmet's memory; my own child proves that. But a more laughable excuse for a rebellion than his is hard to imagine, or was until Smith O'Brien led his army of a dozen old men to Ballingarry nine years ago. We already have martyrs enough for any five nations. Would you have me help to create more? That's not an enterprise that is to my taste at all."

Sean heard him out. "This time is different. The boldest and most resolute of our people are here, in America, free to speak, to organize, to arm and train themselves without looking constantly to be informed against and sent to the gallows or to Australia. And here we have more than liberty, we begin to have wealth as well. Wealth to support organizers, to print newspapers, to buy muskets and pikes."

"And warships?" Liam asked dryly. "A musket in a warehouse in Brooklyn is not much use to a cotter in Mullingar."

"If need be, yes! But muskets can be found closer to home than Brooklyn, as close as Sheffield and Manchester. All that is needed is gold and a firm resolve to strike when the moment is right."

"I won't ask what would make the moment right, for I've no wish to know your secrets."

"Nor would I divulge them to any not bound by our oath, no matter how close a friend he was. But consider this: the Sasanachs are at war in China, and their Indian colonies are in revolt. How if another war comes to Europe? Already the loss of our Irish lads has damaged recruitment to their army—look at the way they broke American law to gain soldiers for the war with Russia. Each new adventure spreads their forces thinner and makes our opportunity greater. Anyone can see that."

Liam sighed. "You may be right. I hope you are. But governments can always find men to fight for them for pay, more of them than you might expect. And fewer than you might expect will come out when a rising is called. It is one thing to take an oath of a Saturday night in the public house, and another to face a squad of dragoons with naught but a home-made pike to your hands."

"And so the training and drilling is important. A regiment of a thousand well-trained men is worth more than a mob of ten times their number. But those back at home, who cannot drill and train, must still be reached and prepared for the time to come. They need our support, now more than ever."

Liam unlocked his desk, fetched the strongbox from a lower drawer, and opened it with a small key on his watchchain. "In honor of my son, and of his namesake, then." He counted out twenty dollars and handed them to Sean. "I wish it could be more, for with all my doubts and questions, the cause is dear to me. But business is very shaky just now."

Sean was startled. He was now running Pat Malone's string of saloons while Pat devoted himself to politics, but the grog business was not very sensitive to currents in the larger economy. "Shaky?" he repeated. "Do you expect a smash?"

"God knows. The craze for railroad shares must end in a disaster of some sort. The profits can't support such prices for the stocks for very long. And once the shares collapse, new construction stops and my business becomes a thing of the air. Did you see the fine garden I've planted at the back of the house? What-ever comes, I don't mean for us to starve this time."

He stood up. "Now, man, will you come downstairs and join me in wetting the baby's head?"

"I will then. It's dry work speaking of politics."

* * *

196

On August 24, the Ohio Life Insurance and Trust Company of Cincinnati was unable to meet its debts, and closed its doors. Like a line of chained prisoners along a cliff, one financial institution after another was pulled into the disaster. Banks failed, whole industries went bankrupt. By the middle of October the Panic reached Wall Street and the stock market collapsed. One of the casualties went almost unremarked. George Holmes, Edith's father, had ventured almost everything on a railroad speculation. When it failed, he went back to the house on 19th Street and put a pistol ball through his temple. It was several days before he was found.

Liam's companies did not go under, though they had a tight squeeze of it. Not long after his conversation with Sean, Liam had begun to pull in his horns. He factored as many of his accounts receivable as he could, even when he had to accept deep discounts on them. He had a long-term contract with the firm that hauled his sand and gravel, but now he bought out of it and put their dealings on a week to week basis. Gradually, carefully, he drew all his funds out of the local bank and put the rolls of ten and twenty-dollar gold pieces into the patent safe in the wall of his study.

The failure of the bank ruined most of the businesses in town. Liam was one of the few men in a position to help, and to advance his own interests at the same time. He saved the haulier from bankruptcy by buying, for cash, a substantial interest in the company. It cost him less than he would have had to pay in a month under the old contract. When his old patron Terence Waterford found himself in difficulties, Liam took several downtown buildings off his hands for what was, considering the state of the economy, a very fair price. By the time the Panic began to ease, early in 1858, he had become a substantial power in the economy of the town.

Popular rumor made him out to be even more powerful than he was. He had Morton, the author, to thank for that. Morton had won election to the legislature two years before on the Know-Nothing ticket. Since then the joke in town was that it should have been the Do-Nothing ticket. Now he was up for reelection, and his political party had disappeared completely. His hatred for the Democrats was matched by theirs for him, and the newly formed Republican party was trying to attract immigrant support by keeping its distance from nativists like Morton. He could have retired to his estate and written another book, but everyone would have seen that as the retreat it was. Like one of the generals he was so fond of writing about, he decided instead to attack. To attack the Irish, and in particular to attack "the *fons et origo* of corrupt profiteering, the enemies of every true American working man, the hidden masters of the Democrat despoilers," Terence Waterford and Liam O'Donnell. Morton's listeners were not sure what a *fons et origo* might be, but they were certain that it was nasty and foreign.

Liam tried to ignore Morton's slanders, assuming that any reply would only help spread them and give Morton the public notice he was seeking. Even when someone fired a shot through a window of his house one night, he did nothing more than buy a mastiff to prowl the grounds and frighten intruders with its fierce bark. By day, Prince was a playmate for the baby, who loved to climb on its back and hold on to its ears while the big dog paced slowly around the porch.

Then one day Tom limped up the hill to the house. Edith's scream brought Liam running from his study. The boy's face was badly bruised, he had a deep cut under one eye, and the clothes were half torn from his body.

"It was the Leaguers," he said as he sat in the kitchen while Edith tended his injuries. "Four of them set upon me near South Street. They called me a dirty Mick and said they were going to tar and feather me, but I kicked one of them in the middle and got away. I think this tooth is loose."

"Let it be. It will tighten itself in time." He turned away.

"Liam!" Edith called out. "Where are you going?"

"To settle an overdue account." When he came back downstairs, he had a light rattan whip under his arm. Edith started to speak, but when she saw his expression she closed her mouth again. She could not follow him, though she dearly wanted to. Like a soldier's wife, she had to trust in his good sense and skill and in her own prayers for his safety. She saw Tom to his bed, then settled into the swing on the front porch to wait.

The headquarters of Morton's League of Native Americans was a run-down saloon near the riverfront. Liam's route there, quite by chance, took him through the largest of Newburgh's shantytowns. One well provided water for the hundreds of poor Irish families who lived in the hovels, and open ditches on either side of the unpaved street carried off their sewage. In summer the entire area stank. Even now the reek carried Liam back to those terrible weeks in steerage, but the memory only strengthened his resolution.

Something must have shown in the way he held his shoulders. At a noise, he looked back. Half a dozen little clumps of Irish laborers were drifting along in his wake, and more were appearing from the doors of their shanties. Oddly, a number of them were carrying hods and spades on their shoulders, even though it was Sunday, and most of the others were walking with the aid of stout sticks. After a moment's thought, Liam shrugged and went on his way. Whatever came to pass, Morton had only himself to blame for it.

The crowd behind him continued to grow, until it numbered fifty or more. Some were simply curious to see what was happening, but most looked grim and determined. Tom wasn't the only Irishman who had been harassed by Morton's bullyboys. At the bottom of the hill, Liam turned onto the street that led to the League headquarters. Doors opened, heads peered out, and the doors were slammed shut. Those who lived in that neighborhood knew the look of trouble.

As he drew closer to the Eagle's Nest, about twenty men tumbled out the door and formed a ragged line in front of the saloon. Each one carried a hickory axe handle. Some wore truculent scowls; others were pale with fright. Liam stopped in the middle of the street and surveyed them one by one, tapping the rattan against his calf all the while. He knew without looking that the mob that had followed him was arrayed on the sidewalk behind him.

"Morton!" he called out. On the second floor of the Eagle's Nest, a curtain twitched, but there was no answer. "Morton! Four of your bastards attacked my brother Tom Flynn today. He got away, though he's only a lad. I'm here to see what they do against a grown man. Do you hear me, Morton? Send them out for the thrashing they deserve!" A low growl arose from behind him.

A noise distracted him. Father Daly was trotting down the hill, holding his soutane up above his knees. "Stop!" he panted. "Let no man lift his hand against another!"

"Your warning is overdue, Father," Liam replied.

"Would you break the peace of the Sabbath with riot?" He stopped, red-faced, in front of Liam, but he spoke loud enough for the others to hear.

"That I wouldn't, but some of those dogs broke it already. I mean to mend it and give them instruction for their future conduct." He whished the light cane back and forth.

"Don't bandy words with me, Liam O'Donnell! I see blood in your eye, and I tell you again, as your spiritual guide, to uphold the peace of God."

"And I tell you, Father, that I will uphold it by correcting those who break it. Didn't He say that He brought not peace but a sword?"

"You are perilously close to blasphemy, my son! Now, once and for all, will you come away?"

Liam was on the point of refusing the priest outright, whatever the consequences, when the initiative was taken away from him. A half brick sailed across the street and shattered the window next to the door of the saloon. At the sound of breaking glass, a whole volley of bricks and rocks filled the air. The Leaguers ducked and covered their heads, then ran into the street swinging their axe handles. The Irishmen were ready for them, blocking the blows with their shille- laghs and following through with their own in reply. The line of battle swayed, then moved back toward the Eagle's Nest as the greater number of the Irish made itself felt. Behind it, half a dozen men sat in the dust clasping their bloody heads, and one lay face down, oblivious to the random kicks of the combatants.

The moment the first brick flew, Liam pushed Father Daly to the ground and hovered over him. One of Morton's toughs took a swipe at him as he ran past, but Liam fended off the blow and sent his attacker sprawling with a well-timed kick to the ankle. The moment the skirmish line was past them, he grabbed the shaken priest around the chest and dragged him to one side, then stood him up and brushed him off. Father Daly was not as appreciative as he might have hoped.

"Now see what you've set off, you with your wild Connacht ways!" Father Daly was a Dubliner and had never been farther to the west of Ireland than the seminary at Maynooth. "What will they think of us after this!"

"That our tolerance for injuries and slights has a limit to it. And who are *they*, that we should care so greatly what they think? The ones who preach pa- tience and understanding, and will not have an honest Irish girl in their houses as a maid? The ones who condemn equally those who guard their churches with rifles in hand and those who try to put those churches to the torch?" Liam's gaze shifted from the priest's mulish face to something behind him. "Please excuse me, Father. I see someone I must speak to."

He set off at a run. Morton saw him coming and tried to duck back in the side door of the tavern, but Liam slammed his hand against it and kept it from closing. "I'd like a word with you, sir," he said. "Would you come out here for a moment?" He grabbed Morton's collar and pulled him through the doorway.

"Don't think you can bully me! Every native son of America will rise up to avenge an attack on their leader! Take your hands off me!"

"Very well." Liam released his grip so suddenly that Morton staggered and nearly fell. "But hark you, and heed what I say. You may tell what lies you like about me, for anyone with sense will know them for what they are. But if you or those you incite lay another hand on any of my family, Morton, I'll find you and thrash you though all the legions of Hell stand in the way! Do you understand?"

The Know-Nothing leader glared at him silently.

"*Do you understand?* Answer, or by God I'll give you a foretaste right now!"

Morton shied away from his upraised hand. "I hear you," he said sullenly.

"Then see that you remember." As he turned away, Morton slipped quickly through the side door and slammed it behind him.

In the meantime, his followers had managed to retreat into the saloon by the front door. There were shouts to break down the door and to burn the place down, but while the mob was milling around in the street, Father Daly was grabbing its members one by one and ordering them home. Within minutes, all of them were trudging back to Irishtown, turning occasionally to jeer or shake a fist at the battered Eagle's

Nest. None too soon, as it turned out: as the last of them was turning the corner, someone let off two shotgun blasts from an upper window of the saloon.

The Paddy Riot, as Morton named it, was a turning point in his campaign. As soon as everyone realized how shallow his support was, they began to ignore him. His followers still managed to start fights, but with their mystique gone, they lost more of them than they won. The last blow came when several prominent employers, Republicans all, denounced the League of Native Americans as an organization of troublemakers and hinted that its members would not be welcome in their firms. Two weeks later, Morton announced the dissolution of the League and his own retirement from politics. Instead of running for re-election, he said, he was planning to start work on a new book, a Life of William of Orange, with particular attention to his military successes in Ireland against James II.

Every year, in late June, Pat Malone's Democratic Club in the Sixth Ward held a great all-day outing and picnic. Liam had a standing invitation to attend, of course, but had never found the time to accept. With the revival of construction after the Panic, however, there were several men he needed to meet with in New York. Even more influential, Tom had just completed his schooling and deserved a treat. So it was, one Thursday night, that Liam, Edith, Tom, and the baby all boarded the *Rip van Winkle* and were shown to their staterooms for a few hours of sleep before docking in New York.

On Friday Liam took care of business while Edith spent the day at A.T. Stewart's department store shopping and baby Robert was spoiled by both Maura and her niece Caitlín. Tom went off by himself and returned late, nor did he offer to say where he had been. For someone who was celebrating a great change in his life, thought Liam, the lad seemed remarkably subdued. But the picnic would change that.

The great day started early, with a brass band parading through the streets of the precinct. Each tenement disgorged its crowds of inmates, all smiling and chattering and dressed in their best. Malone knew them all by name, from the wizened granny to the wide-eyed toddler, and he made sure that they knew it too, greeting each new arrival loudly. By the time the procession reached the East River and the chartered steamer, it was nearly a thousand strong.

The voyage up the river and through Hell Gate to the Long Island Sound took over an hour. By the time the boat docked at College Point, everyone was more than ready for breakfast. And it was ready for them—smoking cauldrons of eggs, huge platters of ham, bacon, beefsteak, and fish, tea and coffee by the vatful, not to mention small beer for those who wanted it, all laid out on row after row of long tables. The picnickers quickly found places, while the sixty waiters ran back and forth bringing refills.

After breakfast the games began. There were sack races and three-legged races, hopping contests and crawling contests, a hammer-throw for the serious athletes among the men, and even a brief game of cricket. And of course there were prizes for every event, distributed to great applause by Pat himself. Those who did not want to compete were free to watch, or to stroll around the wooded grounds, or simply to sit in the shade and start on the day's supply of free beer.

Tom spent much of the morning wandering aimlessly. More than one young girl noticed his dark good looks and air of smouldering passion and tried to get acquainted with him, but to no avail. If he was aware of their interest, he certainly didn't seem to return it. There was only one girl at the picnic—or in the world—that interested him, and perversely he avoided her, though he was never far from her either.

Maura had a busy time of it. In addition to looking after her nieces and nephews, she had to share in the duties of a hostess, dispensing smiles and cheerful greetings and listening to long, sometimes pointless, stories. One gaffer mumbled toothlessly at her for a quarter of an hour, detailing his obscure grievances against former President Fillmore, who had turned down his petition for a job or a pension, Maura couldn't tell which. He seemed to think that her Uncle Pat was easily the equal of a President in such matters and should have done something about it. Sheila finally noticed her plight and called her away.

Through all this, Maura was very aware of Tom Flynn, but every time she looked over at him, he was staring off in some other direction. At first she was hurt by this, but gradually she began to fume. She couldn't imagine why he would deliberately ignore her, but she certainly was not going to take it meekly. She turned her shoulder to him and did not glance his way again, even when her steps took her within two feet of him. If the day seemed suddenly dreary to her, at least she was not humiliating herself by courting neglect.

As Liam would have said, though: *níl bealach 'un 'a coille nach bhfuil bealach 'un a fágardh*. For every path into the forest, a path out of the forest. After a lunch of staggering proportions, the main event of the afternoon was an oldfashioned ceilidh. Three lads with button accordion, fiddle, and flute supplied the music, and the caller coaxed everyone he could onto their feet for a long dance in jig-time from Kerry. The lead couples in each line balanced, circled right and left hands-across, danced up the center and back, and moved to the next place in line to start the first repetition. Old and young bobbed and skipped, and those who would not dance watched and clapped in time. The figures repeated until all the couples were dancing and the lines came back around to their original order.

By then, all but the most energetic were ready to rest a while, but the caller announced an eight-hand reel and the musicians struck up "The Wind That Shakes the Barley." Maura looked up to find Tom standing before her, bowing with hand over heart in the most approved dancing-master fashion.

"Will you stand up with me then, Maurín?" His face was impassive, but there was a quaver in his voice.

She held out her right hand and let him lead her to an unfilled set. As they danced, they gazed at each other constantly, and when they touched, to dance up the center or do a hands-round, she caught her breath in sudden wonder at the strange ache she felt.

The emotions surging through her combined with the vigor of the reel to leave her pale and weak by the end of the dance. She fell into a chair and fanned herself. Tom stood nearby, awkward and unsure of himself, and looked as if he was about to flee. Maura sat up straighter and took a deep breath.

"I think it must be cooler by the water," she said. "Will you walk me there?"

"Of course," Tom stammered. "I'd be pleased."

It *was* cooler by the water. They walked slowly, and gradually she recovered her composure. Tom, however, did not. When she tried to get him to talk about his plans, now that he was finished with school, he stuttered something about going West, then refused to explain. Nor did he seem at ease talking about anything else. Maura's patience started to curl up at the edges.

Their steps had led them past the wharf and into a grove of elms. Across the Sound, the farms of the South Bronx stretched down to the water, dozing peacefully in the summer sunlight. Maura abruptly broke stride and stood still. Tom turned in surprise. His surprise turned to shock when she reached up with both hands, grabbed his ears, and pulled his head down to kiss him soundly. After a moment, his arms went around her and he returned the kiss with a depth of passion that left them both shaken and gasping.

She rested her head on his breast and he clasped her more tightly, breathing in the scent of her sun-dappled hair. "Maura, *mo stoir,*" he murmured. "*Mo cuisle, mo chroi.* . . . I never want to let you go, never!" He bent over to find her lips again, and she met him gladly. It was long before they spoke again.

"Maurín," he said dreamily, "you're of an age to marry. Are you of a mind to as well?"

"I am not . . . unless it's you that is asking it."

"And if it is?" he teased, chucking her under the chin.

"Then ask it properly," she replied tartly, "and I will give what answer I please!"

He tried to kiss her again, but she pushed him away and stood with crossed arms, her head cocked at a challenging angle, with a look in her eyes that was almost anger. He nodded as if to himself and stood straighter.

"Maura, you own my heart. Will you give me your hand in return? I will cherish you forever."

"I will that, *mo grá*, for my hand must go where my own heart has gone already."

A look of utter astonishment came over Tom's face. "You *will*? You mean it?!" He jumped up into the air, clicking his heels together and crowing aloud in a triumph so comical that she burst out laughing. Even when she was in his arms again with her heart pounding as though it would explode, the memory of his face made her giggle helplessly.

All their relatives had linked Tom and Maura in their minds for so many years that, paradoxically, their first reaction to the news was to question the wisdom of the match. Maura had to make almost frantic avowals of her love for Tom to win her sister's blessing, and Tom had an equally difficult time persuading Liam that he was old enough to know his own mind and that he was not simply doing what was expected of him.

In the end, everyone recognized that there was no reason to oppose or to delay the marriage, and the ceremony took place at the end of July. Liam gave the couple a cottage just down the hill from his own house, and to Tom he gave a one-sixth interest in the gravel company. This was doubly fitting, since he intended to turn the management of the business over to Tom and since the most important part of Maura's dowry was her own one-sixth interest in the company. Though the match might have been made in heaven, Liam calculated that it was more likely to thrive if the husband was not merely an employee of a firm in which his wife was a partner.

13

Michael Joseph Flynn was born on April 6, 1861, in Newburgh. Six days later, in far-off South Carolina, the Secessionist forces under General Beauregard opened fire on Fort Sumter, and two days after that, the fort's commander hauled down the Stars and Stripes and surrendered to the rebels. A civil war had begun that would touch every life in America.

Edith was sitting on the porch nursing six-month-old Patrick and enjoying the first warm day of spring when she saw Liam striding up the hill. Her first thought was that something had happened to Tom, but Liam did not turn aside at the Flynn house. As he drew closer, she could see that his expression was grim, but not distraught. She stood up and waited at the top of the steps. Patrick complained loudly, but he soon found the nipple again and gurgled with contentment. She adjusted her shawl to the requirements of modesty.

"Fort Sumter has fallen," Liam called as he neared the foot of the steps. "The news came over the wire just this morning."

The baby wriggled as she unintentionally tightened her grip. "Oh Liam, what does this mean?"

"It means a war, I fear. There's no turning back now. The rebellion will have to be put down by force, and it will not be as easy as some think. Damn them! Damn them for a pack of fools and madmen! Any reasonable man can see that slavery's day is past, but those damned planters think they can keep it alive, and those double-damned abolitionists are not content to let it die naturally. Between them they will drench this land in blood!"

The most directly affected by the outbreak of war was Sean MacMahon. The militia regiment of which his company of volunteers was a part was one of the first to be called up. By the end of May they were encamped somewhere near Washington. He wrote Liam a long letter explaining his views on the war.

". . . they make no secret that they expect England to support them, for the sake of their cotton of course, but from a sympathy of spirit too. If I had no other reason to fight them, that alone would convince me. However, the projects we have talked of yield another motive. I am now a brevetted lieutenant and am gaining priceless martial skills with every day that passes. There are many thousands of us who are thus being turned into soldiers. The battlefield will doubtless claim some, but most will survive to fight another day *in an-*

other place. A war between brothers is horrible to contemplate, but I console myself with the thought that in this case there are Brothers who will go on from this testing to a great triumph . . . My fondest greetings to your wife and sons, and to all the Flynns."

No one needed to explain to Liam that the "other place" Sean referred to was Ireland and that his odd phrase about Brothers was a discreet allusion to the Fenian Brotherhood, the secret revolutionary group that had succeeded the Emmet Monument Society. Liam was deliberately incurious about such matters, but he could not help knowing that Sean was deep in their conspiracies. He occasionally asked Liam for a contribution, and Liam always gave it, but it was understood between them that he would go no farther. He loved his native land and longed to see her free, but he had chosen America, and there he would make his life.

In any case, the war against the secessionists and the struggle to free Ireland both seemed far away from the white house on the hill in Newburgh. His worries were much more immediate. It was almost two years now since Edith had given birth to the girl they named Dierdre, only to see her carried off by an attack of diarrhea when scarcely a month old. Edith had seemed to get over the loss as well as could be expected, and had become positively cheerful when Patrick was born. But just the day before, Liam had come upon her in one of the spare rooms upstairs. She held a lacy white christening gown in her arms, and her face was wet with tears. When she heard Liam's step, she tried to hide both Dierdre's gown and her tears, but he put his arms around her and held her while she sobbed.

"She was so tiny," she said after a little. "She never had a chance. I keep thinking there is something I could have done, but there isn't, is there? Is there, Liam?" She leaned back to look up into his face.

"No, *mo cuisle*, nothing. You were all to her any mother could have been. Come down now. Isn't it nearly time for Maggie to bring you the baby? He's a hungry one, that lad. Screaming his head off, more than likely. I wager you'll be glad enough when he decides he prefers applesauce to milk."

He took the christening gown from her unresisting hands and returned it to its box, then put an arm around her shoulders. "Come, now. The past is past, and we can thank God for two fine sturdy sons who are probably downstairs this minute, wondering where we've gotten to. There is nothing here but old memories that are better left alone." Edith allowed him to urge her out of the room, but on the threshold Liam looked back at the unremarkable little box and his throat moved convulsively.

As Liam had predicted, Maggie, the nursemaid, was waiting in the parlor with Patrick asleep in her arms. Robbie, who was nearly four, was sitting on the carpet playing quietly with his blocks. He was a serious little fellow, and so unlike Edith with his turned-up nose and jet black hair that she sometimes swore, laughing, that some of the *daoine sidhe*, the "good people," had emigrated from Ireland and played their old trick of changing babies in the cradle.

Liam too found something uncanny about Robbie, for a reason that he could never mention to Edith. The boy's deep blue eyes, under that shock of dark hair, looked exactly like Liam's memory of Mary's eyes. He could almost have been the very child whose miscarriage killed Mary, come back ten years later. Yet there was no possible blood tie between Robbie and Mary Flynn. There was not even anyone of her family alive still, save Tom. For a moment Liam's eyes narrowed reflectively, then his mouth quirked in distaste as he caught up with the direction of his thoughts. The very idea was absurd; five years before Tom had been only sixteen, and he was as devoted to Liam as Edith was. But didn't Edith seem fonder of Patrick than of Robbie? The poor tyke; life was hard enough without having to compete with a darling new baby. Liam squatted down and began to build a fort out of blocks. Robbie seemed to ignore him, but when he needed an oblong block for a lintel, the boy gave it to him unasked.

When Liam completed his fort, Robbie stood up to survey it. He circled it, looking from every angle, and even lay down to peer through the gate. Then, slowly, delicately, he slid his foot through the gate and inched it forward. The gate fell, and the guardhouse, and then the great tower keep itself, all collapsing under the steady encroachment of the boy's bare, wriggling toes. Liam winced as a shower of wooden blocks hit Robbie's foot, reddening it.

"Now then, Master Robert!" A form in gray and white swooped down and hoisted the lad into the air. "Just look what you've done to your father's erection, and him so obliging to be playing with you and all! Aren't you ashamed?"

From the prison of Maggie's arms, Robbie looked at

his father. There was no shame in his face, no, nor defiance either, but a sort of challenge: was Liam man enough to allow his son to pull down what he had built? Liam searched himself, found small embers of anger and hurt ready to be puffed into flame, and carefully smothered them with affection. He took his eldest son from Maggie and lifted him high in the air.

"Would you be wrecking my castle then, Robbie lad?" he cried. His index fingers tickled the boy's ribs and made him break his silence for the first time. "I'll not let you down 'til you promise to build one twice as grand! Do you promise?"

The child crowed with helpless laughter until there were tears on his face. "Promise!" he gasped out. "Promise! Want down!" Liam lowered him to the ground, turning his little body in a complete flip on the way down. Robbie collapsed on the floor, panting, but only moments later he held up his arms. "Flip me again," he demanded. "Turn me over!"

"After you build your castle. You promised, remember? A man's word is his bond. Do you want any help?"

"No! I'll do it, like I said. Then you flip me. Promise?" He gave his father a fierce look.

"Indeed I do. Build well, and I'll flip you as much as you like."

"Won't so much attention spoil the boy?" Edith asked later, when they were alone.

"It may, I suppose, but I don't like to see him so solitary and silent. It can't be right for a lad his age. I could wish there were other boys his age in the neighborhood. Perhaps it will be different in a few years, when Paddy and Maura's Michael are older."

"Perhaps. Do you have to call the baby Paddy?"

"Why not? Isn't it his name? And his grandfather's before him, for the matter of that?"

"I know, but somehow it has such a low, coarse sound to it. Patrick is bad enough, but at least it's more genteel, not quite so—" She broke off in confusion.

"Not quite so Irish, you mean?" His voice had a touch of steel in it. "But he *is* Irish, and I don't mean for him to forget it either. And if a day comes when he seems ashamed of the fact, I'll lather his bottom with a cane, though he be a grown man! Still," he added more gently, "if it'll please you more, I'll try to call him Pat. It's no great odds either way—he wears the map of Erin on his face, and always will."

Those who predicted that the rebellion would collapse quickly were wrong. The war dragged on, far longer and far bloodier than anyone had expected. From the first, disastrous battle of Bull Run, the green flags of the Irish Brigade were in the thick of the fighting. Irish-Americans thrilled to read of its exploits and wept over the long lists of killed and wounded. Thomas Meagher, the Young Ireland leader from 1848, who had escaped from exile in Tasmania to come to the United States, now wore the star of a brigadier general in the Union Army and led five regiments of well-trained, battle-tested Irishmen. Like Meagher himself, most of his officers and many of the men were sworn members of the Fenian Brotherhood.

One of them was Sean MacMahon, whose regiment, the 69th New York Volunteers, had formed the nucleus of the Irish Brigade. December of 1862 found him and his men camped on a hillside in northern Virginia. The

Federal capitol of Washington lay fifty miles due north, and the Rebel capitol of Richmond was the same distance to their south. At the foot of the hill, just across the Rappahannock River, the little town of Fredericksburg slept. An uneasy sleep, for Sean's regiment was a tiny part of a great army, 120,000 strong, and in the hills beyond the town 80,000 Rebel troops were dug in, waiting confidently to slaughter any "Blue Bellies" who dared to attack them.

The first stage of the attack began that very night. Pioneer battalions started building pontoon bridges across the unfordable river, and Southern sharp-shooters, hidden in the brick houses of the town, drove them off by firing at the noise of their tools. With daylight, the snipers' job got even easier. The construction crews, what was left of them, pulled back while the Federal cannons flattened the little town. Even then, the Rebels had to be dug out of the rubble at bayonet point by troops who crossed the river lower down. It was a sign of what was to come, but the general commanding the Union forces didn't read it properly.

By noon of the next day, Sean and his men were making camp in the ruins of Fredericksburg and watching with astonishment as some of the other Union troops looted the town. An unshaven trooper from Ohio paraded by with a lace-trimmed silk cami-sole over his grubby blue uniform and an elegant be-feathered parasol on the shoulder where his musket should have been. In the distance, angry shouts marked the spot where two rival groups had uncov-ered some Southern gentleman's wine cellar. By con-trast, the soldiers of the Irish Brigade cleaned and polished their weapons and rechecked their supplies of cartridges, while General Meagher, limping from a badly-lanced boil on his knee, took his officers to a spot near the western edge of town to look over the terrain.

It was not encouraging. A low line of hills made a semicircle around the town, touching the river at both ends and creating an enclosed plain about a mile wide and seven miles long. The Rebs were dug in all along the top and the slope of that line of hills, and they had had time enough to sight in their artillery to sweep all the open ground between the town and the forward slope of the hills.

"I see now why they didn't try harder to keep us from crossing the river," Sean said in a low voice. His companion, Captain Francis Madigan of County Longford, raised a questioning eyebrow.

"They wanted us on this side," Sean continued. "We'll not find returning so easy, to my mind—if any of us are in a state to try."

"You expect Burnside to order us to charge their position straight on? The man's no fool, he might as well save powder and shot and feed us directly to a sausage-machine!"

"Ah, but what is the poor fellow to do after bringing all these grand divisions here? Would you have him turn around and leave without a fight and some blood spilt? Our blood, to be sure; but what's that to him?"

General Meagher, standing near enough to overhear, gave Sean a warning glance. Sean knew that Meagher was as disgusted as anyone with the "political" generals who came and went almost as rapidly as they lost battles and wasted soldiers' lives. But the Irish

Brigade had a sacred mission: to prove to every American who had ever listened sympathetically to the Know-Nothings or told an Irish joke or refused to hire a servant girl because she was Irish that Irishmen and Democrats would fight as fiercely for the Union as any Yankee Republican. However true Sean's comment might be, it sounded defeatist, and that could not be permitted. He took his commander's hint and said nothing more about the coming battle. But his friends noticed that he spent the evening huddled close to the lantern, writing letters home.

The next morning the sun rose shortly after seven, but it brought no warmth to the shivering troops in Fredericksburg. A dense, bone-chilling fog filled the valley of the Rappahannock from rim to rim, muffling the sounds as the Army of the Potomac made ready for battle. As the fog started to thin, General Meagher, "Meagher of the Sword," reviewed his troops and addressed them. For the first time they were going into battle without their famed green battle flags. The old flags were so tattered from a year and a half of war that they had been retired, and the new banners, contributed by admirers of the Brigade back in New York, were late in arriving. Even so, the soldier-orator told his men, their opponents would know them, to their cost. He ordered them to put sprigs of evergreen in the bands of their hats, as a token of their homeland, and set the example of being the first. As soon as the cheers died down, every boxwood hedge was stripped bare.

By ten-thirty, the fog had burned off and the valley was filled with brilliant sunlight. From the heights across the river, the long-range guns opened fire while the big yellow observation balloons bobbed and dipped high overhead. The Rebels were silent, waiting. They did not have to wait much longer. At eleven-thirty, the massed bluecoats left the shelter of the town and surged across the narrow plain toward the Confederate positions. Suddenly, in the middle of open ground, the charge stopped. From the hilltop in front of them, cannons hurled ball and exploding shell and deadly grapeshot down at them. Men tumbled in every direction like torn, bloody rag dolls.

Sean's company was toward the rear of the mass. To him, the sudden halt seemed unexplainable except as a mass impulse to commit suicide. A few minutes later he understood. A sort of millrace or canal crossed the center of the plain in front of them, and the Rebs had taken up the planks from the bridges across it but left the stringers in place. Thousands of Federal soldiers were crossing the thirty-foot-wide canal single-file, balancing like Blondin on his tightrope over Niagara Falls, while Lee's artillery poured death down on them.

That was bad, but worse was to come. As Sean's men crossed the millrace, the forward companies set off at a run toward the foot of the slope, firing at the Rebel positions as they went. Suddenly the ground in front of them vomited flame and smoke. The entire blue line crashed to earth, mowed down like a field of grass when the sickle passes. Their cries carried even over the ongoing roar of the guns, and their bodies carpeted the open field. Another charge was ordered. When it ended, moments later, the carpet of blue was thicker and wider, but no closer to the wooded hillside.

Sean and his men hugged the ground in a shallow

dip and tried to figure out what had happened. Now they could see a line of earth and stone along the foot of the slope that was a hidden enemy breastwork. Judging by the thickness of the rifle fire coming from behind it, it was heavily manned too. Even without the devastating cannonfire from above, the rifle volleys from the earthwork kept the Federals pinned down three hundred yards short of their objective.

Or would have if the commanding general had known or cared about the pointless slaughter. As it was, the order came for another assault. Sean's company, and a hundred others, stood up and ran shouting into a storm of bullets, trampling on the dead and wounded of the two earlier charges, then falling to join them or crawling back to the safety of the dip they had left moments before. Before sunset silenced the guns, the generals ordered three more charges, each of which broke before the wall of lead thrown by the hidden riffemen. By then, of the twelve hundred men who had put sprigs of boxwood in their caps that morning, almost a thousand were dead or wounded.

One of them was Captain Sean MacMahon. Twice he led his men in insane dashes across the open ground toward the hidden Southerners, only to be driven back. The third time, even the men of the Irish Brigade were slow to leave the safety of the shallow swale. Sean turned back, waving his sword over his head to urge them onward, and a Rebel bullet shattered his right wrist. His first thought, before he looked at it, was that he had slammed it against a tree. His last thought, as two of his men helped him off to the surgeon's tent, was that he would never play a jig or hornpipe again.

* * *

By the time Tom Flynn next visited New York, in early July, the slaughter at Fredericksburg had faded from everyone's mind. His fellow passengers on the boat could talk of nothing but the two great Union victories that were just appearing in the newspapers. Both, oddly enough, had occurred on the Fourth of July. In Pennsylvania, the Army of the Potomac had stopped Lee's daring invasion of the North at the little college town of Gettysburg and forced him to retreat back to Virginia. And at the other end of the country, Vicksburg, Mississippi, the "Gibraltar of the West," had surrendered to Grant after a six month campaign and a six week siege. The Union now controlled the Mississippi River along its entire length, cutting the Confederacy in two. Most of the men on Tom's boat agreed that the war would be over before Fall.

Tom dropped his grip off at a hotel in the West 20's, not far from the People's Line pier, then strolled across town to Sean's saloon on Second Avenue. As he walked east, he grew more and more uneasy, though he could not pin down the cause. Perhaps it was the expressions on the faces of the people who stood in little groups on streetcorners, or something carried in the tone of their voices, though the words were indistinct. Whatever the reason, he was relieved to see the hanging sign with its golden harp wreathed in shamrocks and to push through the swinging doors of the saloon. Here he was on familiar ground.

The place was jammed, as he had expected on a Saturday afternoon. Many of the patrons, he knew, were Fenians or veterans of the Irish Brigade who had made the saloon a gathering place out of respect and affection for their maimed comrade. Tom edged through to the back. As he expected, Sean was at his usual table. He sprang up when he caught sight of Tom and came forward to greet him. Once more Tom found himself not looking at the hook that ended Sean's right arm.

"Man, you're a sight for sore eyes," Sean exclaimed, pounding him on the back. "What brings you to town? How are Maura and my godson?"

"Both well, and Mick never stops running, now he knows how. It tires me just to watch him sometimes!" He went on to explain that he had business to discuss with the Erie Railroad people and to decline Sean's offer of hospitality on the grounds that he already had a hotel room. After a few moments, Sean stopped arguing the point and introduced him to the others at his table. They nodded neutrally and went on with their conversation.

"It's a great shame and a scandal," one was saying. "You'll have seen the lists and seen that three-quarters of the names are Irish. Will you be telling me that that's an accident? Faith, No. The draft boards are all Whigs and Republicans. If they cannot beat us at the polls, they will kill us off in their war!"

The others growled their agreement, and one added, "They were glad enough for our lads at Fredericksburg and Chancellorsville, but now they won't allow the Brigade leave to come home and recruit its numbers. There's more to this than meets the eye. The German brigades are treated well, though they've broken and run as often as they've stood and fought."

"It's the old story," said Sean. "If England intervenes

on the side of the Rebels or even recognizes them, the war may be lost. So the government in Washington will do anything to avoid offending the English. D'ye think Lord Palmerston didn't know what it meant to have Irishmen fighting under their own banners and officers? Stanton and Lincoln mean to break up the Irish Brigade and drive Meagher from the service, while conscripting our men and spreading them throughout the Federal armies as cannon fodder."

"But there are wealthy Republicans on the draft lists too," someone objected. A bark of sarcastic laughter greeted his comment.

"Aye, so there are," Sean said mildly. "And every one of them will find the three hundred dollars to hire a poor Irishman to go in his place while he stays home to make his fortune from shoddy uniforms, spoilt rations, and defective muskets. Make no mistake: the freedom that the Republicans are fighting for is the freedom to coin gold from our sweat and blood. They mean to free the slaves only to make slaves of us."

"Three boatloads of black men were brought over from Jersey yesterday to break the strike on the docks. Our lads tried to keep them from landing, but Kennedy's police drove them back."

"There you are then," said Sean, banging his hook on the table for emphasis. Tom winced. "They'll use the blacks to take away our work, until we'll hire ourselves for whatever pittance they choose to offer. It's worse than slavery, for a slaveowner is obliged to keep his property fed and housed, but these employers care not if we starve!"

Later Sean took Tom to the back room; he had something to show him. The "something" turned out to be a strange-looking musical instrument shaped a bit like a guitar, with three strings that ran over the edge of a narrow wheel and a row of wooden buttons along its length. A crank protruded from one end.

"It's a hurdy-gurdy," Sean said happily. "I'd not seen one since I was a boy. An old tinker named Barry played one at fairs and holidays, I remember. It all came back to me in hospital, wondering if there was any instrument I could play with one hand, but I couldn't find such a thing until two weeks ago when a friend found this in Providence. Listen."

He wedged his hook into the crank handle and started to turn it. The revolving wheel, like the bow of a fiddle, set the strings vibrating. Two of them made a steady drone while the third, fretted by the buttons Sean's left hand pressed, gave forth a melody. Tom recognized it as a song called "The Gaberlunzie Man." The effect was more like the pipes than a string instrument, as he told Sean when the tune ended.

"So it is. I've spent so much time with fiddlers, but now it seems I must turn my attention to pipers, though likely they'll turn their noses up at such a base contrivance as this." He patted the hurdy-gurdy affectionately. Tom thought that anyone, piper or not, who scorned Sean's determination to remain an active musician would be both insensitive and foolhardy.

After another tune, Tom said, "Will there be trouble? That was some fierce talk I heard before."

Sean stared silently at the wall. "You'll hear more than that before it's over. The draft law was bad enough, with its three-hundred-dollar exemptions and all, but it's as Donovan said out there: the lists have been stacked against us. I don't expect our people will take the news well."

Tom spent Sunday with Sheila and the kids in Central Park. It was a welcome escape from the close, hot, humid air of the streets, but as they rode the horse tram back downtown, his uneasiness returned redoubled. Even the horses seemed to sense the sullen anger and shy away from every passing crowd. The atmosphere in the saloon was a concentrated essence of that in the street. Yesterday men had voiced their resentment in low voices; today they were shouting.

"Why should we fight to free some nigger who'll only come north and take the bread from our families' mouths?"

"Yerra, what do we care for Lincoln and his fanatics? They care nothing for us. When they're not preaching about slavery, aren't they trying to destroy our religion?"

"It's as Mitchel says," another added. "The South is only wanting the same freedom we want for Ireland!" He was referring to John Mitchel, who had shared the leadership of Young Ireland with Meagher and Smith O'Brien back in '48, and who more recently had become an outspoken advocate of slavery and the Confederacy.

Sean pounded the bar with a bottle, demanding their attention. "I honor Mitchel for his devotion to our homeland," he said when the room quietened. "So should we all. But he can go astray as readily as anyone—more readily, it may be." Some who had personal knowledge of Mitchel's erratic ways laughed at that.

"Don't be misled about one thing: whatever you

think of Negro Emancipation or the Republican Party
or the Draft Act, the Secessionists are no friend to our
cause. If England succeeds in destroying the Union,
Ireland has lost its best hope of freedom. The Union
must be preserved!"

Sean's speech subdued them for some minutes, but
then the uproar mounted once again. From the soil of
anger and frustration, freely watered with poteen and
porter, grew the idea that, if the politicians were
shown that the Draft Act would not work, they would
have to withdraw it or at least change its most dis-
agreeable features. Conscription needed lists and files
and papers to function. If there should happen to be a
fire that destroyed those lists, though? Two local
boards had their offices not far away, one at Broadway
and 29th Street, the other at Third Avenue and 46th
Street, and both had announced that they would be
drawing the names from their wheels on Monday
morning.

Tom returned to his hotel room in an apprehensive
frame of mind. If the mood of the crowd in Sean's
place was anything to go by, the next morning would
bring serious trouble to New York City.

He spent most of the next day downtown, at the
offices of the Erie Railroad, arranging delivery dates
for the shipments of gravel they needed for a new
branch line. He had put aside his worries about disorders, but as he walked across to catch a Sixth Avenue
car, he heard the newsboys shouting of riot and rebellion, arson, pillage, and murder. He bought four different papers and read them on the way uptown. Apparently the two draft boards *had* been burnt to the
ground by what one of the papers called "mobs of

drunken Hibernians," who went on to beat a police official and tear up railroad and telegraph lines along Third Avenue before they were dispersed by police.

Looking ahead and to the right, Tom could see four thick columns of smoke against the pale evening sky. Frowning, he tried to estimate their exact distance and direction. Two he knew, and working back from them he decided that the farthest right must be on Second Avenue, very close to the house where Sean and Sheila now lived. As the horsecar crossed 14th Street, his alarm grew more acute. In his imagination, made more vivid by stress, he saw his little nephews and nieces trapped in an upstairs room while the flames licked closer and closer. He jumped down at the next stop and hurried eastward. Others were doing the same.

At Lexington Avenue the ground began to slope down to the East River. Tom stopped and stared at the spectacle. For blocks ahead the street was filled with people. Many held flaring torches over their heads. Others shook improvised weapons—cudgels, lengths of pipe, palings from a cast-iron fence. Farther along a huge placard bobbed up and down. NO DRAFT, it read. Two Union flags flanked it. A chant started, the same words as the placard, and rebounded off the building walls to form a rolling mass of undifferentiated sound. Suddenly it broke, to become cheers, as flames burst from a building a couple of blocks from where Tom stood. Remembering his fears, he began to make his way through the crowd, intending to reach Sean's home and give whatever help he could.

He was almost to Second Avenue when the note of the shouts changed. Someone pushed him sharply in the back. He whirled around, to see that the entire mass was recoiling, blindly fleeing some danger he could not see. Not ten feet from him a young girl screamed and lost her footing. Pressed from behind, the others could not stop to raise her up or avoid her underfoot. The pressure grew, as the voice of the crowd rose to a shrill scream, punctuated by a series of flat popping sounds. Tom realized with horror that he was hearing gunfire.

A low stone curb had saved him from the fleeing crowd, but it would be no protection against bullets. He pressed backward into a doorway, followed by a dozen or more others, women and children among them. One woman carried a small, weeping child wrapped in her shawl. "He's not mine," she explained, "but he'd lost his mum and was in a fair way to be trampled."

"They mean to kill us all," a short dark man said in a conversational tone. "It's true. I was near the edge over there. The last thing the sergeant said before they started hitting us was 'No arrests and no prisoners.' Here they are." He crossed himself and his lips began to move in an act of contrition.

Tom instinctively pulled back as the line of men in blue coats and gray pantaloons came running down the block, savagely swinging their locustwood clubs at the heads of stragglers. Behind him he felt the door give way. As he and the others huddled in the entranceway scuttled backwards to safety, he saw a shower of bricks fall toward the charging policemen from the line of rooftops. Instantly a dozen of them wheeled and thundered up the sidewalk. Their faces were red, and their eyes gleamed fury like something from a nightmare. The man who had overheard their orders was the only one not to run for the stairs. One of the police gave him a blow with his club that split his head like a pumpkin, spattering blood and brains on the wall.

No one thought of fighting back, only of escaping the blind rage suddenly loosed among them. Those women who knelt and cried for mercy were only shoved aside, not clubbed down. Those who ran were caught by the hair and flung down the stairs. All the men were treated equally; whether they surrendered or not, they were knocked to the ground and kicked repeatedly.

By chance Tom was one of the first to gain the stairs. A few seconds of watching from the first landing told him the danger he was in. He dashed up the remaining flights, followed closely by three or four others, and found the door to the roof. As he opened it, a brick flew past his head, thrown by one of the dozen fellows who were still pelting the police below. Moments later, boots thundered on the stairs. Tom backed away as the officers, maddened with blood-lust, charged onto the rooftop and flailed their clubs about. A pistol shot rang out. One of the policemen dropped his club and clutched his arm. With a low growl, his mates ran toward the group at the edge of the roof. Two screamed and went over the edge; the rest were knocked senseless or worse.

All the while Tom was crouched behind a chimney, hoping somehow to escape the storm. He might have, too; but as the policemen were starting downstairs to rejoin the rest of the force, one of them spotted him.

"There's another of the bastards," he shouted. He

ran over and grabbed Tom's arm; another wrenched the other arm behind Tom's back. He tried to speak, to protest, to plead, but a locust club knocked his teeth in. Terror finally overcame disbelief. He kicked out frantically as he felt them drag him toward the edge of the roof, but he was helpless.

"Come on, Paddy," one of them said, "show us how to fly!"

The riots continued for three more days. Fire and looting spread through Manhattan, and at least twelve helpless Negroes were lynched by angry mobs. Three policemen were killed, one of them shot by one of the soldiers called in to help suppress the riots. The exact death toll among the demonstrators was never known. The dead and wounded were carried off by their friends, to keep them from the hands of the police. City officials later estimated that twelve hundred citizens had been killed during the disorders.

Tom Flynn's body lay in the city morgue, unidentified, for three days. Just before it was slated to be buried in Potter's Field, Sean found and claimed it. On Friday, with a pall of smoke still hanging over the stricken city, he and Sheila escorted the lad who had been both son and brother to them up the river to his disbelieving widow and fatherless baby.

III

We've made the false Saxon yield
Many a red battlefield:
God on our side we will triumph again;
Pay them back woe for woe,
Give them back blow for blow—
Out and make way for the bold Fenian men!

—Michael Scanlan

14

Patrick O'Donnell cut a dashing figure as he strolled up through town from the steamboat landing. His flannels were spotless white, tied at the waist with a silk necktie, his blazer was brilliant scarlet with white piping, and he wore a straw boater at a jaunty angle over his pale yellow hair. He had left Newburgh a schoolboy, but he was returning a College Man.

No one had met him at the dock because he had not written to tell them when he was coming. He wanted to surprise them by sauntering up to the house like a casual visitor. If he had seen them waiting on the landing, he might have forgotten the sophistication he had worked so hard to acquire. He might even have shouted and waved and jumped up and down like a joyful child, and that simply wasn't done!

He tipped his hat to Mr. O'Rourke, the grocer, who hid his smile and bowed decorously to the boy he had been giving jawbreakers to not so very long ago. The

lad was filling out nicely, he thought; he'd be a credit
to his parents if he didn't start giving himself airs and
forgetting where he come from. Not like the older boy,
who burned with a dark flame like a lump of bewitched coal and whose pale eyes always seemed to
look past you or through you, never at you.

Patrick continued on his way, unaware of O'Rourke's
silent compliments to him or doubts about his brother
Robert. For even though he had been away at college
for a year, he was still of an age to take for granted
all those who had been fixtures of his childhood. Mr.
O'Rourke and his grocery were to his mind as fixed in
their courses as the North Star.

Panting a little—for the dashing red blazer was a
bit heavy for an uphill walk in June—he turned into
the lane that led past the Flynn cottage to the house.
It was odd that Father still called it the Flynn cottage;
it had been rented out for years, ever since Aunt
Maura died of influenza and Michael came to live with
them. Of course it did still belong to Michael. Father
had carefully banked the rent for him year after year.
It must be a tidy sum by now.

At the gate he hesitated. His breath quickened further, though not from the climb. He found himself
wishing that he had let them meet him at the dock.
Everyone knew what to do then. But when he walked
in on them like this? Would they be glad to see him?
Would they even recognize him? It had been a year,
after all, and people do change. He took a deep breath,
readjusted the tilt of his straw hat, and started up the
walk.

"Patrick!"

Bridget came running down the steps with her pigtails flying behind her and flung herself at his neck. He started to lift her into the air, the way he always did, then stopped himself. She was rapidly becoming a young lady. Even if it had been proper for him to do such a thing, he wasn't sure he still could.

"What are you doing here? Why didn't you tell us? Is your jacket new? Are all the fellows at college wearing them now? You look *very* grown-up!" She called over her shoulder, "Mommy, Ronnie! Here's Patrick!"

Twelve-year-old Veronica appeared in the doorway. Her strawberry blonde hair was tied back with a ribbon, and she wore a green dress that matched her eyes. Her expression, as always, was serious and considering, though she could enjoy fun as well as her bubbly older sister. She walked down the steps and tucked herself under Patrick's welcoming arm. "Hello," she said simply. "I'm glad you're home. I've missed you."

"We all have," Bridget said quickly. "Do you want to see my pet bunny? Mommy, I'm taking Patrick to see my bunny!"

He looked up. His mother stood at the top of the steps, looking at him with an expression in which pride, love, and a certain wry amusement were equally mixed. Seeing her after an absence, he suddenly realized that she was growing older—though he quickly told himself that she was no more than forty-five, the very prime of life. Still, he was shocked and upset by the new awareness. She and Father had been the unchanging center of his world. The knowledge that they too were subject to the passing years felt like a breath of mortality on the back of his neck.

He hurried up the stairs, setting aside both the sound of "Time's wingéd chariot" and a vague idea that College Men greeted their mothers by languidly shaking hands. There was no one to see him embracing her, except those who would have been confused to see him do anything else. Moments later he was doing the same to Maggie, who had nursed each of the six O'Donnell children in turn and who stayed on, she claimed, in the expectation that Master Robert and Master Patrick would soon settle down to the task of bringing along the next generation of O'Donnells for her to care for.

Maggie was blubbering with happiness, but when Patrick offered his handkerchief, she stopped herself and said, "And where are the others then?" Patrick, taken by surprise, turned nearly the shade of his glorious jacket. "Now then, Master Patrick," she continued sternly, "what is it I was always telling you? Gentry always carry three, one for show and one for use, and one for a maiden in distress. What else have you been forgetting, off at your grand university, I'd like to know?"

He leant over and planted a kiss on her cheek. It was her turn to blush. "It's not grand, and it's not a university, and I remember every word you ever said to me, Maggikins!"

She dimpled. "Go on wi' yer flatterin' ways, young Paddy, for I've seen through them this many a year. You'll be wanting a bite and a drop of something, I'm thinking. I'll go warn Cook."

Patrick gave his mother a short account of his trip home and fended off Bridget's efforts to drag him to the back yard to see her rabbit, all the while glancing around. Edith noticed, of course, and interpreted his glances correctly.

"Your father will be back by suppertime. He and Michael drove down to Vail's Gate this morning. There's talk of a new railway line and they wanted to look over the route."

Patrick felt a spasm of irritation that surprised and shamed him. He and Michael Flynn were as close as brothers—closer, in fact, than he had ever been to his real brother Robert. And he knew why his father was so attached to Michael. He had heard the awful tale of poor Uncle Thomas and his death at the hands of anti-Irish soldiers many times, and had seen his father's eyes fill with tears at each repetition. With him off at college and Michael at home, working full time in the family firm, it was natural that his father would come to rely on Michael, even though he was nearly a year younger than Patrick. It was natural, and only to be expected, but knowing that did not ease his feeling that he had been replaced.

Once more Edith interpreted the play of emotion on his features correctly, but she kept silent. Anything she might say could worsen the situation, while if she ignored it, the bonds of affection between Patrick and Michael, and between Patrick and Liam, would make themselves felt soon enough. She had been coping with similar situations for nearly fourteen years, after all. Ever since poor darling Maurín, God rest her soul, had been taken. By influenza, Doctor Childers said, but Edith knew that the dear child had never recovered from Tom's murder. She could still hear Maura's feverish voice murmuring over and over, "*Och mo bhrón.* Oh my sorrow." And even now the recollection brought tears of grief and anger and helplessness to Edith's eyes.

"Mother? What is it? Is something wrong?"

She blinked rapidly and forced herself back to the present. "Nothing," she said brightly, "nothing at all. Why are we all standing on the porch? Come inside, son, and sit down. Is your trunk down at the dock?"

"Kirby is bringing it up later. He said Robert left a few days ago?"

Edith led the way into the front parlor, turning back to say, "Bridget, tell Cook we'll have tea in here, and then you girls get back to your studies. You can talk to Patrick this evening." They protested, but they went.

"Now, what were we talking about? Seeing you has scattered my wits completely!"

Patrick grinned inwardly and refused to be diverted. "Robert. He was here, and left? A few days ago?"

"Yes, what a shame he missed you. But I expect he will be back in a month or so. He has a new position that involves a lot of traveling."

"A job? What sort of thing?" He hid his surprise. His older brother had always seemed a dashing, romantic sort of character to him, like someone from a book by Sir Walter Scott. He couldn't easily imagine him on a stool in a countinghouse with paper sleeve-guards on his wrists.

Edith looked away. "He explained it, but I was thinking of something else at the time. I believe he is a commercial traveler—the term he used was "drummer"—for a book publishing firm in Massachusetts. It must be very taxing work. When he left, he said that he was going to Chicago but making thirty stops along the way. I wanted addresses, you see, in case we needed to telegraph him. But he explained how difficult that would be."

Poor Robert, thought Patrick, hauling a heavy satchel of dull books from one tank town to another. What on earth had gotten into him, to take such a job?

At that moment, Robert Emmet O'Donnell was pushing through the doors of a run-down grog shop just off 55th Street in Cleveland, Ohio. A few heads turned, then turned back incuriously. He stepped up to the bar, ordered and paid for a beer, and sipped it quietly. After a few minutes, the landlord came over to stand beside him.

"I've not seen you here before, sir, have I now?"

"That you haven't," Robert agreed.

"We're glad of your custom. New to town, is it?"

"A traveler only. James Curran, representing the Messenger Publishing Company of Worcester, Massachusetts."

The landlord, suddenly alert, offered his hand. "Welcome to Cleveland, Mr. Curran. I'm Peter Sullivan. I don't recollect that I've heard of your company before."

"No? That's odd, then, for we're now virtually established in every state this side of the Mississippi."

Robert's curious choice of words echoed the oath of allegiance to "the Irish Republic now virtually established" sworn by every member of the Fenian Brotherhood and its successor, the Clan na Gael. That, together with the mention of the Fenian publishing house, identified him as the field organizer Sullivan had been warned to expect. He seemed terribly young for such a responsibility, the tavernkeeper thought, but the glint of dedication in his eye overbalanced his lack of years. It was mostly the young who were willing to throw away their private lives to serve the Cause anyway. Sullivan himself had been part of the botched Fenian invasion of Canada thirteen years before, but today, with a wife, five children, and a business to take care of, he was far from sure he would do it again.

"Now I come to think of it," he said carefully, "I think I once met an officer of your firm, name of Devoy."

"Very likely," said Robert. John Devoy, the exiled Fenian, was probably the single most influential figure in Irish-American revolutionary circles. The mention of his name meant that the tavernkeeper was confirming his recognition of Robert. "Has he many friends hereabouts? I could give them word of him, it may be, but I'm not in town for long."

"A good few who drop in of an evening, yes. Will you stay for supper?"

"I thank you, but I have calls to make on my firm's affairs. If I should return at eight, though?"

"You do that, lad. Mr. Curran, I mean. Will you be having another?"

When Robert returned, shortly after eight o'clock, he found a dozen men waiting for him in the back room of the tavern and two more casually guarding the door. He surveyed them quickly with an eye sharpened by practice. Half of them were most likely longshoremen and railway laborers, recent immigrants. A tubercular schoolteacher whose fervor seemed too great for his weakened frame. Sullivan, and two other small businessmen, grocers, tavernkeepers. Two young lads, students or clerks. A fellow of Robert's age completed the group. There was an air of quiet authority about him, though his hands were heavily calloused. A foreman, perhaps, or petty officer on a Lakes steamer. Whatever he was, Robert marked him as the most promising of this particular lot.

Sullivan introduced him briefly, and Robert came directly to business. "We have learned that up to seventy-five members of the Royal Irish Constabulary have been sent as supposed emigrants to this country, for the purpose of joining the ranks of our organization." That got some stares and a few nervous looks around the room. "We've always known that the rival firm will stoop to anything, however low, to frustrate our work. All this means is that we must be doubly, triply, careful. A new recruit must be known personally to at least one active and trusted member. If he's recently arrived, someone who knows his family over there must vouch for him."

"What if there isn't anyone?" one of the longshoremen objected. His accent placed him as from Belfast. "Sorra a single soul I knew when I came to this town, and there's many a one else in the same strait."

"Then they must be kept from our counsels. Better a score of stout loyal men be in the dark than a single R.I.C. be admitted to the light."

"That's good sense," someone muttered.

"Affairs are once more beginning to build toward a crisis, and we cannot afford to have informers in our ranks."

He stopped to pour a glass from the pitcher of ale on the table, and to judge how he was doing so far.

Well, he thought. His warning had impressed them, and the skepticism his youth always awoke seemed dispelled. Now to the more important part of his business here.

"You'll have read the papers," he said abruptly. "Half of Ireland is kept from starving by private charity, and in Cork, Kerry and Limerick it is more like nine out of ten. Evictions doubled last year, and bid fair to double again this year. The protections of Gladstone's Land Act of 1870 are of no use at all. Another wet summer and we'll see the Great Hunger all over again."

"Jesus, lad," one of the dockers said, "we know how dire it is, but what are we to do? No one I know but is sending back whatever he can spare to folks at home already."

"What Ireland needs is freedom, not charity!" he snapped, then softened his tone. "Of course we must help our kin however we can, but we here in this room have a larger goal as well. It is that I am here to speak of. I'm referring to the New Departure you'll have heard about. We, and our brothers across the water, have entered into an alliance with the most forward elements of the Home Rule agitation. With our support, they mean to bring the business of the Saxon Parliament to a standstill."

"What's Home Rule?" someone growled. "Up the Republic!"

"Aye, Up the Republic," Robert said swiftly, "but are we to sit in shebeens for the next forty years muttering that to each other? The organization has not reached the Irish people, and it will not if we do nothing but wait for the hour to strike for another Rising.

This is the news I have for you: this very week, our brother Michael Davitt will lead a national meeting on the land question at Westport, County Mayo."

"Davitt?" the schoolteacher said. "I knew him. I thought he was still in Dartmoor Prison."

Robert ignored the comment. "The meeting will create an organization to stop evictions and demand a general reduction in rents. And the chief speaker at the meeting will be Charles Stewart Parnell, M.P."

This was news indeed. Parnell, a handsome and wealthy young Protestant with a great estate in County Wicklow, was the undisputed leader of the Irish Party in Parliament, where he used every trick of procedure to hold up the passage of laws unfriendly to Ireland. English M.P.s called him unprintable names as a result, but the newspapers back home were starting to call him the Uncrowned King of Ireland. With his blessing, Davitt's Land League might succeed.

When the reaction to this information died down, Robert went on to say that two things were needed from America: money, and dedicated men willing to go back to Ireland to work with Davitt's group. "By preference," he added with a smile, "men who are not already well known to the R.I.C.!"

Afterwards, when the formal part of the meeting broke up, the fellow Robert had spotted at the beginning came over to him and introduced himself as Rory Clarke. "I'm ready to go," he said quietly.

"Why?"

He shrugged. "My people are from Clare, and I've cousins and all there still. I know how it is with them. I think I can be of more use there than staying here and sending dollars back."

"Do you have the Gaelic?" Robert asked in that language. It wasn't the first time he was thankful for his father's stubborn insistence that he learn to speak it.

"Some," Clarke replied, also in Gaelic. "I'm no scholar, though."

"Well enough. What might your trade be?"

"Locomotive engineer," he said, in English. "I don't know the Irish for that."

Robert grinned. "Neither do I. I doubt if there is any. Are you known to the police?"

He hesitated. "My da was a Fenian, but he brought us away to America when I was still a boy. To be safe, I might take my mother's name of Lynch, I suppose."

"Hm, yes." Robert was secretly amused by Clarke's assumption that he could only take a name he was entitled to in some fashion. "Well, I'll pass this along to the head office of the firm. I expect you will hear from them directly."

"Thank you, Mr. Curran."

"Call me Jim," said Robert genially.

At his own request, Patrick joined one of the work gangs as a laborer. He welcomed the exercise, but after three weeks of wielding an axe and a nine-pound sledgehammer in June heat, he gave in to Liam's insistence that he work in the company office. After some initial confusion, he began to find the demands both challenging and interesting. O'Donnell & Co. was carrying on several construction projects at once, and each had to have the supplies, tools, and men it required, at the right time. This meant shifting crews and equipment from one job to another, then back again, in a pattern as swift and complex as a jig or reel. When Patrick said as much to his father, Liam smiled.

"I've had the same thought myself now and again. Ah, Paddy," he went on, throwing an arm around his shoulders, "I think it a great shame none of you had a mind to learn an instrument. I would swear you have the feel for it in the blood. Still, new world, new ways, I suppose. Now, where do you mean to put the grader next week?"

If the work was a pleasure, though, at home he was starting to be concerned about his sister Bridget. She had been so excited the day he came home, but since then she had become more and more withdrawn and morose. He hated to see her moping so, but the only person she would talk to was Michael, and even he couldn't seem to bring her out of the dumps.

One evening after supper, he and Michael took a walk to town. After clearing his throat a few times, Patrick remarked that Bridget seemed a little downcast.

"I know," Michael replied. He seemed happy that Patrick had brought it up. "I think she still hasn't gotten over Thomas."

Of course. Patrick cursed himself for an insensitive hound. Thomas was his baby brother, the last of the O'Donnell children, and named for Michael's father. A year and a half before, when he was five and Bridget barely twelve, they had gone out sledding. Thomas ran out onto the frozen surface of the pond. Bridget frantically yelled at him to come back, but even as he turned around, the ice broke under him and he plunged into the freezing water. Michael saw it all from the top of the hill. He ran down, but by the time he got there the child was dead. It was all Michael could do to keep Bridget from going in after him.

"But we all know it wasn't her fault," Patrick said heatedly. "She can't still be blaming herself!"

"Can't she though? She was looking after him, and he died. That's no easy thing to have on your mind. She torments herself, asking if there was nothing she might have done to prevent it, or to save him once he had fallen in. There wasn't, I know, and it's often enough I've told her so. But haven't I asked myself the same questions too, and me so much farther away when it happened?"

Patrick was silent for a few moments, then he burst out, "Well, she must pull herself together, put all that behind her! That's all. I'd tell her so, too, but . . . well, girls change so quickly at her age, I hardly feel I know her. *You* must tell her, Mick; you're more like a brother to her than I am these days."

Michael started to speak, then stopped in confusion. Finally he said, "I don't think it's my place to say such a thing. We may have grown up together, but Biddy is no relation at all to me!"

"Well, of course not," Patrick replied, surprised by his friend's vehemence; "not if you mean by blood, but there's affection between you, isn't there?"

"And if there is? What of it?"

"Nothing, Mick! What's put a burr under your saddle? All I meant is that she'll listen to you like a big brother if you talk to her about Thomas. She's a nice kid, and I hate to see her so gloomy all the time when she should be out playing and having fun."

Michael gave him a strange look, but he did not make any further protest. The conversation seemed to have an effect, too, for over the next few days Patrick noticed that Bridget was starting to smile more often. Once he even heard her laugh aloud, though the moment he walked into the room she became very prim and missish. If he felt a bit hurt at being left out of the fun, he still was glad that she was having some once more.

Soon he had something else to think about than his little sister's moods. One day he returned from the office to find a letter waiting for him. He didn't know the hand, but his pulse jumped in recognition just the same. He carefully slid his penknife under the seal and unfolded the letter.

My dear Mr O'Donnell,

I know you'll think me terribly forward to write like this—at least the Mater would say so I'm sure—she's very big on the proprieties and is talking now of having me Presented at Court, not a judge sort of court but Queen Victoria Herself if you can imagine ME kneeling in front of The Queen—I confess I can't, but if it has to be done I suppose I'll go through with it.

It is a very wet afternoon as I write curled in the windowseat looking out at trees and the lawn and the rain coming down. I was reading Lord Tennyson's Idols of the King before but (promise not to tell a soul) I started to nod!! I *adore* Lord Tennyson too, so I think it must have been the sound of the rain that is to blame.

I have lately been learning two wonderful

games from England called badminton and sphairistike, which I can't pronounce at all and most people here are starting to call lawn tennis. Do you know either of them? They are similar in using racquets and nets, but I find lawn tennis much more difficult and strenuous. You must learn, so we can have a game the next time Will brings you on a visit.

Will is spending all summer working on a farm the Pater owns just outside town. It leaves him very tired and awfully dull—can you imagine that he refuses even to learn badminton, though that leaves me with no one to play with most of the time? It isn't my place to criticize my brother, but in someone else I would call that quite selfish! He tells me that you were planning to work for your father's railroad company. Is that interesting? More than farming, I imagine. Are you going to do that until you go back to College? Will said he might get you here on a visit in September, but he always forgets things like that until it is too late!

I must close now—it is nearly teatime, and I have horrid INK on my fingers which the Mater would not forgive at all! If you happen to write to Will, you might want to enclose a note for

Your friend,
Margaret FitzHugh

Patrick smiled as he read, and when he came to the passage about his father's railroad company he laughed aloud. But when he finished the letter he found that his pulse was unaccountably fast and his mouth was dry. It seemed an odd reaction to a casual letter from someone he hardly knew; maybe he was coming down with a summer cold.

As her letter indicated, Margaret FitzHugh was the younger sister of a classmate of Patrick's. Will and Patrick had first gotten acquainted because they were among the handful of Roman Catholic students at the college, and Patrick was happy to say yes when Will invited him to his home in western Pennsylvania for a long holiday weekend. It turned out to be the first of several visits.

Will's father was a doctor who had done well for himself in real estate. His strong, autocratic character was tempered by his absent-mindedness, and after the first day he treated Patrick as if he were simply another of the many FitzHugh offspring. For all Patrick could tell, he might actually have thought he was.

As for his wife, her chief occupation seemed to be upholding and glorifying the family honor of the Fitz-Hughs. She was the one who insisted that the Fitz-Hughs were Anglo-Norman, whatever that might be, and not, God forbid, *Irish*. When Doctor FitzHugh mentioned over dinner that his father had arrived in America from County Wicklow with scarcely a penny to his name, she was aghast. She preferred to believe that the family had left the ancestral castle and estates at the particular invitation of some official body—Congress, perhaps. The sound of Patrick's last name seemed to grate on her ears, and when she heard her son call him Pat, she actually winced.

Margaret was two years younger than Will and Patrick. She was a pretty girl with light brown hair and pale blue eyes and a fashionably light complexion.

She was sure that her life would be ruined because her nose reddened after a few minutes in the sun, but she was always forgetting her wide-brimmed straw hat. After seeing the way she hung around Will every moment she could, Patrick decided that she adored her big brother. On the whole, he thought she was jolly company, though when she remembered to act what her mother called ladylike, she became a pill.

What an odd thing to get a letter from her, though. He wouldn't have thought she had the spunk to do something so unconventional. And then to hint so casually that he write back via Will—in fact, start a clandestine correspondence with her—what on earth would Mrs. FitzHugh say if she discovered it! As he folded the letter and started upstairs, Patrick discovered that he didn't much care what Mrs. FitzHugh said. And he resolved to look into those games, badminton and—what was it?—yard tennis? He might enjoy a new interest, after all.

15

The New Departure policy has had almost two years to prove itself. I say it is a failure." Robert paused and looked around the table to assess the reaction to his speech. Degnan was fidgeting; eager to get downstairs to the bar, no doubt. Burke looked angry, and no wonder: he had been one of the strongest supporters of the New Departure among the inner circles of the Clan na Gael. McCafferty and Sheridan, however, seemed interested and Egan wore the look of a cat who has just been given a dish of cream.

"Yes," Robert continued, "a failure. Instead of Home Rule, we have been given a new Coercion Act as infamous as the Penal Codes of old. Parnell and the other Irish Party M.P.s have been ejected from the House of Commons. In a matter of weeks or months, we will see the Land League suppressed and its leaders—Parnell among them—in prison." Burke gave a snort of disbelief. "You may laugh now, but soon you'll laugh from the other side of your mouth! Unless we start to prepare now, all that we have built in the last two years will be swept away!"

"Suppose you are right, Curran? What then?" The questioner was Frank Doherty, an old Fenian who had returned to New York not long before, after a number of years as a miller in Kansas. "Do we go back to preparing a rising, which with God's help and great good luck will come to pass long after all of us are gray and doddering? I was out in '67, and I'd be loath to call out today's young men if their chances were no better than we had. To my eye they seem much worse."

"And to mine," Robert said swiftly. "I want no useless bloodshed, any more than the rest of you. But we must not let the foe think that we have abandoned our goal. We are pledged to see Ireland an independent Democratic Republic, and we all agree that the Saxon will not permit that unless it is won by force of arms. We are soldiers in the Army of the Gael, honorbound to strike the enemy when and as we may."

"I've heard that speech before," said Burke sourly. "I've even given it meself now and again."

Under the table Robert's hands clenched into fists. An acrid taste burned his throat, and he longed to throw himself across the table and wipe that condescending expression off Burke's face.

"What our young friend is forgetting," Burke continued, twisting the knife with each word, "is that we in this room are meant to be, not soldiers of the Gael, but generals. And before we sound the advance, we should discuss the direction we want our troops to go in."

"Forward!" Robert exclaimed before he could stop himself.

"To be sure, to be sure, but which way is forward? I say the New Departure is still working well and we should go ahead with it. As long as we are tugging at his left arm, Parnell will move toward us and bring many thousands along with him. The moment we let him go, he will begin to move in the other direction. He will be making a compact with Gladstone—and convincing those same thousands of its wisdom—before we know what is happening. He is a man of great gifts, but he is before all else a politician. He must have support, and if he does not find it from us, he will look elsewhere. It is that simple."

"Then we buy him at the cost of our principles! I call that bargain doubly corrupt!" Even as the words left his mouth, Robert was fighting to regain his self-control. He was the youngest and newest member of the Political Committee. He had to hold a delicate balance between goading the others into action and showing a proper respect for their greater experience. But tonight he was losing his balance completely.

"Call it what you like, young feller-me-lad," Burke snapped. Robert swallowed hard as he realized that he had unthinkingly made an enemy of the older man. "I call Charles Stewart Parnell a man made for Erin's needs at this time, and I say that our support gives him the strength he needs to resist the pressure put on him by our foe."

"But you admit that he will compromise," said Egan.

"Of course he will! If Parliament votes Home Rule tomorrow, I doubt if he'll even say hello to us in the street! But for now he is the sharp point at the tip of the spear, and until something blunts him, we must continue to work to push him home!"

"But isn't there a middle course? Suppose we. . . ."

Robert sat back and let the discussion flow around him. His outburst still disturbed him. When he chose the life of a professional revolutionary, he knew that it meant suppressing his individuality and judging every word and action by its contribution to the Cause. He could not allow himself to have a temper, never mind to lose it. His own life, the lives of others, even the life of the Organization and the Nation, might one day depend on his ability to govern his tongue. But tonight's performance suggested that he could not trust himself.

Maybe he needed a holiday. How would it be if he went home for a few days? His recent organizing tour had taken him all the way to California, and as soon as he got back to New York the Committee had sent him on a flying visit to London and Dublin. In all it had been at least six months since he last visited New-burgh. Though, now he thought of it, he hadn't much enjoyed that last visit. His mother was unhappy because she saw so little of him, and his father was un-happy because he somehow sensed what Robert was doing with his ilfe, and didn't like it at all.

Every time he thought about his father, he got con-fused. Sometimes he saw him as a typical member of his generation, who wore the Green on St. Patrick's Day and tried to forget they were Irish the rest of the year. But even in those moments he knew that was unfair. Liam O'Donnell had only contempt for those who changed their names to sound more "American" or took classes in losing their brogue, and he had great respect for those who carried on the age-old fight against Ireland's oppressors. But he did not want his eldest son to lead the life of a soldier of the Gael or to be a martyr to the Cause. Let some other man's son do it instead.

"Curran?" Sheridan, on his left, nudged him with an elbow. Robert sat up straighter. Had they called him more than once? He had never failed to respond to his nom-de-guerre before; maybe that holiday was more urgent than he thought.

"Curran," Dunne repeated, "we've agreed to set up a subcommittee to consider parallel courses of action, to consist of Burke, you, and Doherty. Are you willing to serve?"

Christ! Him and Burke on the same committee, with only Doherty to keep them from each other's throats! "Of course," he said calmly. "I'd be honored." The corner of Burke's mouth twitched, as though he was pleased at the correctness of some deduction. Robert gave him an expressionless glance, at which the older man smiled mysteriously.

The meeting ended, leaving Robert with the question of where to stay the night. There were many people in New York who would take him in gladly, but they knew him as Robert O'Donnell. Sooner or later they would wonder about his comings and goings, perhaps mention them to a neighbor or friend, and the secrecy of the Organization would be breached.

Doherty came over to where he stood. "I hear you need a place to doss down," he said without preamble. "You're welcome to come home with me if you like.

It's not very grand, but it's clean, warm, and dry."

"Thank you. I'd like that." There was something appealing about the old Fenian's simplicity, and it did not escape Robert that he would be wise to get Doherty on his side before the first subcommittee meeting with Burke.

Doherty had the subcommittee on his mind as well. As they were walking across town he said, "You're not to take Burke too much to heart, you know. Wasn't it meself heard him call John Mitchel terrible names once, for not agreeing to some daring plan or other? But Mitchel knew that boldness and rashness lie close together, and Burke will recall that too, when he comes to think about tonight's work. This is the house, we're four flights up."

He took the lead, shaming Robert by the ease with which he trotted up the stairs. Unlocking the door, he called out, "Mary *a cuisle*, I've brought a guest with me. Is there a kettle and a bite of something?"

A voice from the next room replied, "Half a minute, then; I'll put the kettle on and bring out the ham."

The girl who appeared in the doorway was perhaps twenty-one, tall and slender, with lustrous dark hair that fell to her shoulder in ringlets. She carried herself like a queen, thought Robert, for all that she bore before her a ham and a half-loaf of bread and not a casket of rare jewels. Her profile had a classic beauty, and her eye was fringed with long dark lashes that would give a magic to every glance.

She put the food down and started to turn away, perhaps to fetch the kettle. Doherty stopped her, saying, "Mary, this is Jim Curran. He'll be staying with us a few days."

She turned reluctantly and said, "I'm pleased to meet you, Mr. Curran."

Robert's words caught in his throat. The left side of the girl's face, from the forehead to the line of her jaw, was one terrible, disfiguring scar. In color it ranged from dead white to red to a bluish purple, and over it all was a shine like freshly polished brass. In the midst of the desolation a dark blue eye watched him with an expression that mingled shame and defiance and a challenge that was also a plea.

He had been thinking about self-control earlier; now was a time to put it to use. "The pleasure is mine, Miss Doherty," he said. There was no trace of shock, or pity, or revulsion in his voice, only the mild pleasure proper to a man meeting his host's daughter. She nodded in grave appreciation and went to fetch the tea.

Conversation was difficult at first. She was too much a Fenian's daughter to ask Robert about his background, or his work, or indeed anything that might suggest his identity or embarrass him into a lie, and that left little enough to talk about. Eventually, however, they discovered that they both admired Dickens' last novel, *Our Mutual Friend*, and spent the next half-hour comparing reactions to it.

Mary, perhaps inevitably, was drawn to the character of Lizzie Hexam, the motherless girl who fought to maintain her self-respect in spite of the stigma of her birth. Robert, just as inevitably, identified deeply with John Rokesmith, the "Man from Nowhere" whose own identity was almost lost in the maze of impersonations his situation forced on him. Robert quickly agreed that Lizzie was admirable in her strength and soon persuaded Mary that Rokesmith's apparent weakness was not a fault, but a necessary preparation for vigorous action.

On the larger implications, they disagreed. "Of course Dickens reveals the rot among the upper classes, but he also teaches us that there are people of good will who can overcome their backgrounds to work for a better world," said Mary at one point in the discussion. "The difficulty is to reach those people and show them the terrible things that are happening, and to give them something practical to do about it."

"What people?" Robert demanded. "An indolent lawyer like Wrayburn? A set of amiable half-wits like the Boffins? No, he shows us a society eaten away at the core, and the only solution he has is to shut himself away from it. In a diseased body there are no healthy parts. Every class in England, from the great lords to the common laborers, profits from the subjection of our country, and every class will resist our fight for freedom. They are all guilty."

"All?" Mary asked quietly. "Even the babe in arms? Even our poor countrymen who emigrated to Liverpool and Manchester instead of Boston and New York?"

Robert hesitated. Her question troubled him more than she could know. "Some bear greater guilt, of course. I don't hate all Englishmen simply because they are English, though they are quick enough to despise all Irishmen. But if they stand by while their rulers kill our leaders and allow our nation to starve, then they are accomplices. In a war like this, those who are not for us are against us and are liable to suffer the consequences. I'm not one of those who thinks that spilt blood purifies the earth; I hate the idea of bloodshed. But if it must be shed, let our enemies be the ones to shed it."

"And I suppose it must," she said sadly.

"I suppose so. Eight hundred years of history give me no grounds to hope otherwise."

As he changed the subject, asking her about her life in Kansas, Robert realized a surprising fact. During their discussion, he had time and again been drawn by the liveliness of her eyes, and he had quite forgotten to notice the ruin that surrounded them.

One day in November, Liam came home just at dusk to find Doctor Barrett coming down the stairs, bag in hand.

"Good evening, Doctor," he said. "What brings you? Is someone ill?"

"Good evening, Mister O'Donnell." He took Liam's arm and led him to a corner of the hall. "Please don't be alarmed. Your lady wife is in bed with a fever."

"Edith?" Liam frowned, trying to concentrate on the doctor's words and ignore the sudden tide of dismay sweeping through him.

"I don't think there's any great danger. I've left instructions with your older girl, and I'll call again tomorrow to see how she is progressing. Now you must excuse me, I have a confinement to attend halfway to Cornwall." He shook Liam's hand and was out the door before Liam could ask any of the questions that boiled up in his mind.

For a moment longer he stood, indecisive, in the hallway, then he took the stairs two at a time. Bridget heard him coming and stepped outside the bedroom, closing the door carefully behind her. "Mother's sleeping," she whispered. "She was talking very wild before, but the doctor said that's to be expected. Ronnie and I and Maggie are to take turns staying with her, he said."

"Ronnie's too young for such a task. I'll take her place."

Bridget looked at him doubtfully. "She's thirteen. And nursing's women's work; it's not fitting for you to do it."

"I've done it before. Don't argue, Biddy me lass, but tell me what I am to do. Did the doctor leave medicines?"

The hours stretched into days, and Edith's condition got neither worse nor better. She slept much of the time, and when she was awake she was not always in her senses. She muttered unintelligibly, tossed her head from side to side, and tried to throw off the blankets. Once Bridget fled the room in tears after listening to her cry piteously for Thomas, her wee lamb, her baby.

For Liam, the time spent sitting by his wife's sickbed brought him face to face with much that he had avoided looking at. Over twenty-five years of marriage, much came to be taken for granted. He had shared times of great joy with Edith, and they had helped each other through the sad times. Now he had to admit that that sharing might end at any moment. A crisis might carry her off before the next day's dawn. Would she go knowing how much she was a part of him? Or did she think that their marriage had become like so many others—merely the lot they had drawn in life, for them to make the best of? He hated that thought. He vowed that when she recovered he would make sure that she knew his feeling for her.

When he was not watching by Edith's head, he was in his study, looking out over the flowing river and playing the old tunes one after another. This too was a revelation, for he discovered that he remembered many but had forgotten more. Sometimes a few notes played at random called back a lost melody, but more often the tune lurked just beyond his grasp. Or a tune he had remembered just the day before eluded him again. In self-defense he started to keep a list of names, but many of the tunes he knew had more than one name, and many others had no name that he had ever heard. A few years before, when Bridget was learning the piano, he had taught himself the basics of music notation. Now, he realized, he was going to have to put that skill to use, for the only sure way to keep his store of melodies from vanishing forever was to write them out.

He had no notion, when he ordered a quire of music paper from the stationer in town, that he was starting a project that would come to rule his remaining years.

"You are going with Father, aren't you?" She sat on the edge of the bed with her back to him. Her black ringlets fell in lush profusion over the white cambric nightdress. "That's what you've come to tell me."

Robert stood in the doorway with his jacket half-on. He had meant to say nothing about his journey, to bid her goodnight and leave, but she had a strange power to drain away his strongest resolve.

"I know I shouldn't ask questions," she continued. He looked fixedly at the outline of her thin, tense shoulderblades. "I don't ask where you are going or why. But will you tell me when you return? I . . . I have a reason to know."

He bit his lip and fought the impulse to flee. She turned to look over her right shoulder, as if to see if he stood there still, and her eye glittered in the lamplight.

"I can't say," he stammered, fixed by that gaze. "I don't know at all. Mary—" He took a step toward her and she pulled back, turning to keep her left side from his view. After all that had been between them, she still tried to hide! He strode around the foot of the bed, angered by her lack of trust, angered at the careless fates that had so damaged her.

She shrank away from his approach, but he took her wrists and turned her toward him. She quickly bowed her head toward her lap, making of her hair a curtain before her face. Holding both her wrists in one hand, he grabbed a handful of hair and forced her head back. He knew he might be hurting her, but he was beyond caring. Through the strands that still clung to her face, she looked up at him with a new uncertainty. Slowly, deliberately, he bent over and pressed his lips to her scarred cheek. She tried to twist away, but he held her more firmly and moved down over her cheek to the line of her jaw, then up to nibble at her earlobe. She gasped. Pulling an arm free, she pushed at his chest, clawed at his ribs, pounded her fist on his back. His lips retraced their path across her cheek and found her tight-pressed mouth.

After a long breath-held moment, her defiance drained away. Suddenly she pulled him toward her as fiercely as she had pushed him away. He let her carry him down onto the bed and felt her knees part in welcome. Her small, firm breast fit his hand exactly; the heat of it seemed to burn through the thin cloth. She fought him when he pulled back to deal with his clothing, but then she understood and helped. As he bent over to remove his stockings, she dug her nails into the flesh of his buttock and laughed throatily at his startled yelp.

Later, much later, he got up to leave. Mary lay with her face turned away from him. Her lovely body was stiff with resentment at his desertion of her. When he finished dressing, he said, "I have to go now."

She made no response at all.

He looked down at her, baffled by her silence. Finally he reached to touch her hair. "Good-bye, Mary love," he said, "Bless you."

As his footsteps faded she sat up, looking wildly about as if she expected to see him still in the room with her. In the distance a door closed. Her mouth fell open to protest, to call out, to scream in rage and despair. She threw herself down onto the bed, burying her face in the pillow and sobbing uncontrollably.

Frank Doherty and Robert O'Donnell walked side by side along the promenade deck of the steamship *Virginia,* bound from New York to Southampton, and talked in a casual fashion. Their papers identified them as Dwight Johnson and William Benderby of the firm of Wilson & Weed, boatbuilders, but their conversation, if any fellow passenger had managed to get close enough to overhear, was not about yachts. Or rather, it was about one particular yacht.

"We're booked into a suite at the Globe in Cowes,"

Robert was saying. "It was a hell of a job to get, too. The place is full of silly upper-class twits next week."

"What if they check at Wilson & Weed, though, or try to reach us there?"

"A sympathizer who works in their office will intercept the message. And why should they, anyway? Our papers are in order. They'll suspect nothing. Who has a better reason to attend Cowes Week regatta than two yacht brokers?"

"And the equipment?"

Robert gestured impatiently. "It's all right, I tell you. What isn't waiting for us at Southampton is in my luggage. Stop fretting; it will all go like clockwork." An elderly couple turned to stare as he broke into loud peals of laughter.

A few days later, in the sitting room of their suite at Cowes, Doherty recalled and finally understood his comrade's strange mirth at the mention of clockwork.

Outside, the waters of the Solent gleamed in the early August sunlight. The harbor was full to overflowing with every variety of yacht, and offshore the iron-clad battleship *HMS Alexandra* rode easily at anchor. Like the yachts, she was decked with every scrap of bunting in her signal lockers. The whole scene was colorful and gay.

The atmosphere inside the room was very different. Robert was sprawled in a chair, gnawing gloomily at the cuticle of a nail, while Doherty examined the contents of the metal deed box on the sidetable. He clasped his hands behind his back and held his breath as he leaned over to peer at the strange assortment of items. There was a Waterbury alarm clock, of the sort found on bedside tables throughout America; a .22

caliber single-shot pocket pistol, almost as common as the clock; and forty small brick-like objects packed together. Across the front of one he read the words *Atlas Powder Co Phila Pa USA.*

"You understand the principle?" said Robert from behind him. Doherty jumped. "A wire leads from the winding-key of the alarm to the trigger of the pistol. Once the detonators are in place and the pistol is loaded and cocked, all we need to do is set the alarm."

"And get the device into position."

"Yes."

"That won't be easy."

"No. I'm beginning to see that." He crossed to the window, with Doherty close behind him. To the right they could see the mouth of the Medina River and the shipbuilding yards of East Cowes. Just up the river on the other side stood Osborne House, where the royal party always stayed during Regatta Week. The steam yacht *Victoria and Albert* was moored at the wharf at the foot of the gardens. Robert's casual stroll along the west bank of the Medina that morning had shown him that the extensive grounds and the riverbank itself were heavily patrolled.

"I think I've found a spot to enter the water," Robert continued. "It's a small cove on this side, a quarter of a mile or so downstream from the wharf."

"Isn't that a long swim?"

He shrugged. "I've done the Hudson often enough as a boy. All I need is a dark night and a little luck."

Doherty persisted. "How do we know the ould bitch will be aboard the next day?"

"We don't, and I don't much care. Her or her bloody yacht, what difference does it make? The gesture carries the same message either way—Home Rule or else!"

But the next night, and the night after that, were clear with a half-moon waxing to full. The two revolutionaries made a point of taking long evening walks along the Esplanade and then down the narrow streets of the old town along the Medina. In the moonlight the whole surface of the river glittered with a million fragments of light. When a small dinghy rowed up the center of the river, it was as apparent as if it had been a hundred-foot sternwheeler. Robert touched Doherty's arm and stopped, ostensibly to relight his cigar. A few moments later a four-oared craft shot out from the far bank and came alongside the dinghy. The beam of a darklantern flared and indistinct words reached them across the water. Then the dinghy went on its way and the police launch returned to its hiding place. Doherty grunted eloquently and the two men continued their stroll along the river.

Later that night the older man tried to persuade Robert to change the target. "It's too chancy, man. Not only the long swim in the dark, and the long swim back, but what if the box leaks and it all goes for naught? I could fix it against the wall of Cowes Castle tomorrow and demolish the Royal Yacht Squadron. Isn't that as good as the royal yacht any day?"

But the committee that had approved the new campaign had also put Robert in charge, and he was not moved by Doherty's pleas. He was determined to blow up the *H.M.S. Victoria and Albert*. If the fates smiled he meant to blow up its namesake as well: Victoria, Queen and Empress by the Grace of God, dead by the grace of the Clan na Gael and Alfred Nobel, the inventor of dynamite.

To Robert's despair, the next day dawned sunny and bright. Four fine days in a row, and Regatta Week drawing to an end! But after noon, the clouds began to drift in from the west, and by dusk the sky was a uniform gray. At supper the two men were subdued, each wrapped in his own thoughts. Robert ate nothing more than a bit of chicken and a custard, and took no wine.

Back in their suite, Robert stripped to the skin and donned a black bathing costume of lightweight wool that reached his ankles and wrists. His evening clothes went back on over it and he once more seemed an ordinary gentleman of means. Fetching a black leather satchel like a doctor's bag, he placed in it a Smith & Wesson .32 caliber Hammerless revolver wrapped in oilskin, a buckhorn-handled hunting knife in a sheath, a web belt, and two small jars.

"What are those?" asked Doherty, rubbing his left arm.

Robert smiled mirthlessly. "Blackface make-up, and cleansing creme to take it off. I'd best put in a towel too."

The last step was to arm the bomb. The fulminate detonators were in a jewel case, on a bed of cotton wool. He carefully inserted them into the cakes of dynamite, placed a cartridge in the pistol, and bent over to recheck the aim. For a moment his knees quivered, nearly pitching him headfirst onto the delicate mechanism, but he caught himself and stood up.

He held his right hand out at arm's length, fingers

splayed, and watched it for half a minute. Satisfied,
he bent over again to wind and set the clock and set
the alarm. He had decided that ten-thirty in the morning was as good a time for the fireworks as any. The
Queen was said to be an early riser, and he could not
set the alarm for much later than that anyway.

At last it was done. He wiped his hands and forehead, then closed and sealed the box. Back in New
York he had tested the seal to a depth of twenty feet
without a drop of water getting in, but it took care to
line up the two channels of the india-rubber seal with
the edges of box and lid. Doherty held the satchel
open while he lifted the box and placed it inside. It
fit perfectly, of course, he had picked the satchel for
the purpose. He snapped it shut and lifted it with a
jaunty motion that drew a half-protest from his partner.

At the door he noticed that Doherty's normally
ruddy face was white and beaded with sweat. "You're
fit, aren't you?" he asked. His concern was half for the
man and half for the mission.

"Of course I am." He was breathing heavily, but his
color seemed to be returning. "Let's get on with it."

They took their usual evening route and drew no
notice beyond a bright "Hallo, ducks!" from a street-
walker. Nearing the outskirts of the old town, Robert
glanced casually ahead and behind, then ducked down
a narrow, smelly passageway. The cove he had found
earlier lay at its far end. By the evidence of their
noses, it was a main outlet for the West Cowes sewer
system, but that very fact would help keep idle
passersby at a distance.

He quickly stripped off his evening suit and starched

shirt. Doherty folded them neatly while he rubbed blacking onto his face and hands and fastened the knife and revolver at his waist. Finally Doherty, sighing deeply, helped him into the harness that held the armed timebomb securely to his back.

Upriver and across the way, the lights of Osborne House glimmered, but no rays reached the secluded, noisome backwater. Robert turned toward Doherty, who was no more than a vague mass of deeper black. The moment demanded something. All he could think of were the words of the Fenian martyrs at Manchester fifteen years before. "God save Ireland!" he said softly.

"God save Ireland!" Doherty replied. His voice broke.

The water was chilly, but the exertion soon warmed him up. For all the practicing he had done in America, swimming back and forth across remote ponds with the weighted deed box on his back, the knowledge that he carried ten pounds of high-grade dynamite broke the steady rhythm of his breathing and made his movements awkward and tentative. Once his hand broke the surface with a splash that he was sure could be heard on both banks. He stopped in midstream, treading water, and listened for the first sounds of discovery and pursuit. There were none, and after a while he took a deep, silent breath and went on. The rising tide was helping him along, though he reminded himself that it would be against him on his return trip, when he would be more tired as well. Soon, sooner than he expected, he sensed the bulk of the great wooden-hulled yacht to his left. He turned to angle toward it, moving his arms and legs with infinite caution and submerging his head until only his nose and eyes were above the surface.

Suddenly his right hand struck a net that entangled his fingers. Somewhere on the bank a bell jangled. Before he took a deep breath and ducked underwater, he heard muttered curses and saw the flash of a bullseye lantern.

Swimming underwater, Robert retreated toward the middle of the stream and thought through his position. The make-shift alarm—for clearly that was what it was—probably sounded several times a day when the current carried planks, old casks, and other debris into the fishnet. His one contact with it was not likely to set off a full-scale alert. But if it rang again, a short time later—

That must not happen. His only course was to approach the net carefully and cut through it without ringing that damned bell. It would be tricky, but he was confident he could do it. Two minutes later he was hard at work, treading water and sawing through the vertical strands of the net two feet below the surface. The weight of the bottom part of the net would create the opening he needed without disturbing the floater line that led to the bell.

The exertion and the need to be utterly silent left him out of breath by the time he judged that the opening was large enough. He was about to risk the passage when he heard the quiet ripple of a cautious oar. Cursing to himself, he retreated once more and watched from midstream as the boat passed on its rounds, then approached the net again. It took forever to find the opening he had cut, but at last he took a deep breath, jackknifed, and glided forward.

He was partway through the net when he sensed the slight drag. The bomb was snagging on the uncut stretch of net. Forcing down a growing sense of urgency, he swept his cupped palms forward, arresting his forward motion, and felt the tension ease. Reaching over his shoulder, he explored the outlines of the metal deedbox with his fingers, hunting for the snag. He told himself—and it was true—that he had stayed underwater longer than this many times. He had known the pounding of the blood in his ears, the pressure behind his eyes, the strain of keeping the exhausted and useless air in his lungs, he had known them all before now and survived.

Suddenly a chill began at his feet and raced up toward his chest. His fingers touched one of the metal latches of the box and found it tangled in a thin, tough strand of the net. A film of red was descending over him, but he reached quickly for the knife at his waist and brought it up behind his head to slice blindly, frantically at the hempen cords. A glancing blow against the deed box knocked the knife from his nerveless fingers. He clawed at the net and sensed dimly that his left hand had found its way above the surface. But for him those few inches were as vast as the fathomless depths of the sea.

His overstrained lungs reached some ultimate limit. The air exploded from his open mouth and rose to the surface in a single large bubble while salty water rushed to replace it. A single reflexive choke, then his back arched tetanically. He flopped like a landed fish. The movement loosed the snared latch, and he slid backward through the opening in the net, drifting quietly to the bottom while the police searched the river for the cause of their alarm. When the tide turned, the scour rolled him over and over, springing open the burden he carried and gradually erasing all that was unique of him.

Frank Doherty waited an hour for Robert to return. The pain had spread from his arm to his chest now; he passed the time trying to rub it away. Then he heard distant shouts, and saw flashes of lantern light, from the direction of the royal yacht. Still he waited, breathing more quickly, hoping that his young friend had eluded the alert watchers and was making his way back to the western riverbank.

That hope faded slowly, but at last it was gone. A new thought came to him: Robert might be hiding somewhere along the bank, unable to reach the cove and unable to appear in a bathing costume and black-face. He grasped the valise and started up the street, softly whistling a tune he had often heard his companion hum.

"Good evening, sir." The unmistakable outline of a policeman's helmet loomed against the distant lights. "May I have a word with you?"

Instantly Doherty imagined himself explaining a satchel containing a complete set of another man's clothes. He cursed himself for not following Robert's example and carrying a revolver. He knew the clothes themselves bore no marks, and the constable could not have seen his face. Raising the valise in both hands, he flung it at the policeman's head and took off down the street at a run. A loud whistle sounded behind him.

He dodged left, away from the river, into the maze

of the old town. If only he could get well away, they would never find him among the thousand of Regatta Week visitors. He thought the running footsteps were fading behind him, but it was hard to hear over the roaring in his head. He pressed one hand to his side, trying to ease the pain, but instead it spread and grew like a flame consuming a crumpled newspaper. He gasped from the intensity of it, and at that moment his foot hit a badly-set paving stone. He fell full-length, spraining his knee and giving himself a deep gash across one cheek, but he was already beyond noticing such minor hurts. As his consciousness drained away, he repeated, "God save Ireland!"

Then he added, "God help my little girl!"

16

On September 4, Patrick O'Donnell married Margaret FitzHugh at St. Theresa's, Meadville, Pennsylvania. Michael Flynn was best man, and both Bridget and Veronica served as bridesmaids. The only member of the O'Donnell clan who did not attend was Robert, who as usual was off on one of his business trips. In the privacy of their bedroom, Liam and Edith agreed that Margaret was no great prize for their son, but she certainly was pretty, in a china-doll sort of way, and lively, and with luck she would not grow up to resemble her mother.

In his own way, Liam rather enjoyed Mrs. Fitz-Hugh. She was so predictable in her reactions, and so slow to realize that he was "taking the mickey" out of her. Around her, his brogue thickened until it was nearly unintelligible, he referred to everything and everyone as darlin', and he always called his newly married son Paddy me bhoy. He did everything but don a swallowtail coat and battered hat and smoke a broken-off clay pipe. But if the lady noticed his similarity to the characters played by Barney Williams, the great Irish comic, she gave no sign. Perhaps she thought that Williams was a master of realism and that all Irishmen *did* go about saying begorra and bedad and talking whimsically about the Little People. Her husband knew better, of course, and once or twice, when Liam's act became especially outrageous, Doctor FitzHugh gave him a satirical look, but he said nothing. His own way of living with a rather stupid, small-minded woman was to pass as much time as possible in his library and consulting room. Liam spent one quiet evening with him there, drinking brandy, smoking cigars, and exchanging stories about their lives.

After the ceremony, the newlyweds left for a wedding journey to the White Mountains of New Hampshire, and Edith and Liam took their brood back to Newburgh, stopping along the way to show Michael and the girls Niagara Falls.

A few days after their return home, Liam was in his study jotting down the notes of a Kerry slide he had recalled that morning when Peggy, the maid-of-all-work, tapped on the door. "Excuse me, Mr. O'Donnell, but there's someone to see you, a Mr. MacMahon."

"Really? Well, show him up!" He put away the music and waited at the door of the room. "Sean *a grá*, what a nice surprise! What brings you up—"

He broke off in mid-sentence. His old friend's ex-

277

pression told him that this was not a casual visit, nor a pleasant one. He dismissed Peggy and closed the door, then turned.

"Something is wrong. Is it Sheila?" Sean shook his head. "One of the children?"

"No. It's . . . I thought you should hear from an old friend, not from a stranger."

"Hear what? Spit it out, man! I'm no child!"

Sean closed his eyes and pinched the bridge of his nose, then looked up at Liam. "Very well," he said tiredly. "It's Robert. I'm afraid he is dead. I'm sorry."

For half a minute Liam stood perfectly still, as his mind fought to take in—or shut out—the terrible news. Then he said, "How did this happen?"

"I can't tell you."

"*When* did it happen?"

"I can't tell you," Sean repeated.

"Where is he now? Where is . . . the body?"

"I don't know. All I can tell you is that he died fighting for Ireland's glory. He died a hero's death."

"For Ireland's glory? For Ireland's glory? What is Ireland's glory to me? My first-born son is dead, though he was no more than a lad, and I am not to know even the day and the way of his passing! And you talk to me of heroes and Ireland's glory? For shame, Sean MacMahon, for shame!"

Sean looked away, and the lines were graven deep on his face. "I had rather not have brought such tidings," he said in a low voice. "I'm sorry for your troubles."

"Yes. Oh Jesus, I must tell Edith. This will kill her." He pressed his eyes, passed his hands down over his cheeks, and took a deep breath. "Will you take some refreshment after your journey? I'll send the girl up with tea, or would you rather a dropeen of whiskey?"

Without waiting for his friend's answer, Liam went to the cabinet and poured two stiff drinks. He drank one down and silently handed the other to Sean, then refilled his own glass. Sean watched with concern in his eyes.

"There's something more I must tell you."

Liam drained his glass and let it fall to the floor. "What then? I know where my other son is."

"There's a girl," Sean replied. "She is carrying your son's child."

"Is she, by God!" Liam said savagely. "Who is she then, some common drab who means to foist the bastard in her belly onto me?"

"She is not! Mary's a fine, upright girl, and Robert's widow in the eyes of God! And she is bearing up bravely under a double loss, for her father, rest his soul, was killed along with your son. She is alone in the world and nearly penniless, and in her condition."

Another cruel retort lay on Liam's tongue, but he bit it back. After a silence, he sighed. "I suppose we must provide for her and the child then. I'll not be heaping my wrath on the innocent. But you, Sean, and your men of blood—!"

"I knew nothing of this before," Sean said forcefully, "and it's little enough I know now, but this I know: your son chose to undertake a deed, knowing full well the risk he took and counting it worthwhile as a step toward a greater good. He was a man among men, a soldier of his people, and I honor his bravery."

"Words, all words," Liam said, but his tone was softened. "I know you mean well. I must go to Edith. She'll be wondering about your sudden visit. You'll stay on for the wake, won't you? Hey-day—one son married, the other dead, and a grandchild on the way. Life moves quickly for the old, Sean *a grá*."

"You're not old," Sean protested.

Liam walked heavily to the door, then turned. "After this day I am."

The woman in mourning dress stopped at the corner to consult a paper from her purse. A few heads turned incuriously to look at her, then turned away again. In a poor neighborhood like this one, mourning was commonplace. She studied the tall tenements crowded along each side of the trash-strewn street. She had passed through this area many times as a girl, twenty-five years before; but then it had been fields and orchards and an occasional cottage painted white.

Three grimy-faced urchins playing tag dodged around her shouting—at her or at each other, she couldn't tell. Slipping the paper into her purse, she picked her way down the sidewalk and turned in at a tenement no different from its neighbors. At each landing the odors grew denser, of stale cooking and old sewage and unwashed clothes and bodies. By the time she started to climb the fourth flight, she was aware of feeling faint. The thought of turning back, to return some other day, drew her, but she pushed it away. She was performing a sacred duty; her comfort was irrelevant.

Once more she checked the paper, then knocked at a door. As she waited, she lifted the black veil from her face.

Footsteps approached the other side of the door, which opened a crack, then more fully. She had been warned what to expect, but even so the sight shocked her. She swallowed and cleared her throat.

"Miss Doherty? I am Edith O'Donnell." The girl's expression did not change. "My dear, I am Robert's mother," she amplified. Was the girl deaf as well as disfigured?

For a long moment Mary Doherty's face remained wary and puzzled, then it collapsed in on itself. "God help me," she wailed, "but I never even knew his name! Oh whatever am I to do? Death has touched all who were near to me, and I feel the shadow of his hand over me and my fatherless child." As she began to sob, Edith reached out and held her as she would have held one of her own daughters. And indeed, she thought as she patted her back and crooned, she could almost think of the girl as her own child, so long as she did not have to look at that terrible face.

Later, after Mary had dabbed her eyes with cold water, straightened her hair, and brewed a pot of tea, she and Edith sat down in the tiny dining room. As Edith sipped her tea, she looked around unobtrusively. The building badly needed repairs, but the apartment itself was both orderly and clean. Her teacup, though chipped, was a tasteful pattern of porcelain, and the tea was a decent variety, well-brewed. The girl's dress, of dark blue silk, did not fit well, and there were signs that a light-colored bodice had recently been unstitched from it. Of course—the child could not afford to buy mourning.

"Tell me," she said gently, "how did you and Robert come to know each other?"

"My father brought him here, a year ago and more. They worked together, you know. I—" The color mounted in her right cheek. "You must think I am very silly, or very wanton. Jim—I mean Robert and I were not . . . In his position, there was no question of marriage. I knew that from the first, there was no deceit between us. If I must pay for my decision, I am willing. God knows the price is smaller than that he has paid."

Edith reached over and covered Mary's hand with her own. "I don't think you are silly or wanton, I think you are very brave. And I'm glad that my boy knew someone like you. One day, if you are willing, I would like to hear more. You saw a side of him that he kept hidden from us. I knew he was deep into something he would not speak of, and I suppose I knew what it must be, but I never pressed him. I wish now that I had. Maybe he would not have done whatever got him killed."

"Nothing would have stopped him," Mary said proudly. "Not you, nor I, nor all the armies of the Saxon queen!"

"Something stopped him, my dear. Something killed him. And they won't tell me what. Do you know?"

"No. My father's heart gave out, they say, but they say nothing about your son. *Och, mo bhrón! Ochón!* For they've left me both, and I am desolate! What am I to do?"

Edith refused to see the tears on the girl's face or to permit her own stored-up tears to flow. "This is what we must talk about," she said in a practical tone of voice. "We—Robert's father and I—want you to come live with us for a while."

"Until my child is born, you mean?"

"Yes, and until you have had time to think about the future. It's a big house, with plenty of room and plenty of help, so you will be more comfortable than you are here. That means something, especially in the later months. I know, I've borne six."

"I can manage here." Her voice was oddly flat.

Edith recognized her state of mind as if she were indeed her own child. "Of course you can," she said soothingly. "And so you shall, if that is your choice. And of course we shall give you whatever help we can. But won't you give it some thought? You would be doing us a favor by coming. We so much want to get to know you. And fresh air and sunlight must be better for you and the baby than dark, crowded streets."

Entangled somewhere in Mary's thoughts was the idea that the sacrifice of her father and her lover called for an equal sacrifice from her. When Edith had spoken of the comforts of her home, Mary's stomach had twisted as if she was suffering morning sickness again. She had no right to be comfortable; it would mock the martyred dead for her to live at ease. By staying in this slum and getting by however she could, she would be honoring their memory.

But then Edith changed the terms of the discussion. To go with her, to be coddled and cossetted, would be to do an injury to her own sensibilities. But if she did it for the sake of her baby, and to gratify these kind strangers from whom her lover had sprung—well, then, wasn't *that* a sacrifice of a sort?

* * *

Edith backed across the room and cocked her head to one side. After a long, considering silence, she called out, "A bit lower on the left, Peggy."

"Yes, mum." Balancing shakily on the top step of the ladder, Peggy shifted the long runner of evergreen branches.

"That's it! Tie it there, then we'll bring in the holly and mistletoe."

Peggy wrestled with the thin, slippery cord and cursed the branches for getting nasty, sticky pitch on her hands and her apron. A heathenish custom it was, hanging greenery about the house to celebrate the Lord's birthday, never mind the mistletoe and all the goings-on *that* led to! Still, it would be nice to hear some laughter and cheerful talk about the place again, if only for the holidays. Master Robert's death, and Master Patrick getting married and living across town, had sucked the spirit out of the family.

The master spent all his time at work or up in his room scraping at his fiddle, and the mistress crept off to Master Robert's old room to mope whenever she thought no one would notice. Miss Bridget was lively enough even now, but her fun was going to land her in the soup one of these days, and as for Miss Veronica, she was such a quiet, serious one that you never knew what she was thinking. And as for that Mary Doherty, Peggy was sorry for her troubles but wished she would walk with a louder step. It gave her such a fright to see that face suddenly appear in a doorway or just behind her in a room!

Still perched on her ladder with her arms over her head, the little maid stopped to let a smile cross her face and a faint shade of pink to invade her cheeks.

The year before, her first Christmas in service, she had missed her family sorely. Michael Flynn had found her in the hall with a tear in the corner of her eyes. He whirled her around as if they were waltzing, until she was smack under the mistletoe, then bussed her heartily. He meant nothing but kindness by it, of course, and he had never taken a liberty with her since, not that she would allow it. But oh! he was a handsome devil, with that hair dark as midnight and those eyes like the sky at Midsummer, and all the handsomer for not giving himself airs about it.

"Peggy! Come here, I need you!"

She started, and nearly fell from the ladder. A narrow escape: a few more moments, and she might have had something to confess on Saturday.

By late afternoon Edith was satisfied with her work. The parlor, hall, and dining room were gay with green branches and broad red ribbons and tall white candles. From the kitchen, the aromas of roasting and baking drifted out to fill the house. As if to cap the preparations, just at sunset a flurry of fat snowflakes started to float down. Edith took them as a sign that her campaign to bring a spirit of good cheer back to her family was going to succeed.

Christmas day was for the family, quiet and close, but more subdued than she would have liked. The next day, the feast of St. Stephan, was another matter entirely. They held open house all day, and in the evening the young people gathered in the parlor to play Charades and Forfeits and other currently popular games that Edith was less familiar with.

One of these, introduced by Bridget, was a variation of hide-and-seek, to be played with the greater part of the house in darkness. At first Edith was tempted to forbid this as being not quite proper, but then she reflected that all the guests were girls, friends of Bridget and Veronica from the convent school. Running around in the dark might seem terribly daring to them, but they could scarcely get up to any real mischief.

"Very well," she said, "but the third floor is out of bounds, and so are your father's study and my little sitting room. I'll be in there if you want me. And don't get in the way of Peggy or Cook!"

As she left the room, she passed Michael, who was watching the goings-on with a quizzical smile.

Bridget quickly explained the rules to the other girls and used some method Michael couldn't follow to decide that Barbara Kelley was "It" for the first game. Barbara went off to the kitchen to count to 200, and the others scattered through the house, turning off the gas lamps and blowing out candles as they went. Soon the entire lower floor, except for the kitchen and pantry, was in darkness. Michael was about to grope his way to the stairs and go to his room when a hand touched his arm and a voice whispered, "Come with me."

Amused, he allowed himself to be led away. He soon realized that his guide was taking him, with remarkable accuracy, to the storage closet under the front stairs. Aside from the slant of its ceiling, the only notable thing about this closet was that its door blended into the paneling. It was hard to find even in the light. A vague feeling of uneasiness began to grow in him. What deviltry was Bridget up to now?

The instant she had closed the door, she pressed up

against him and put her arms around his waist. Michael froze, trapped between his own strong inclinations and his equally strong sense of duty to Bridget's parents.

"Don't you like me any more, Mickey? Not even a little bit?"

"Don't be silly," he protested. "of course I do."

"I don't believe you," she pouted. "This year you didn't even kiss me under the mistletoe. You kissed Ronnie, though. Do you like her better than me?"

"Of course not!" To his horror, he felt a swelling in his groin. He tried to twist away so that Bridget would not sense it as well.

"Well then!" She put a hand behind his head and tried to pull his lips down to hers. He resisted at first, then decided that a ritual peck might satisfy her.

It didn't. With an impatient wriggle, she pressed her lips harder against his and probed delicately with her tongue. Michael gasped and pulled back.

"Stop that, Biddy, you don't know what you're doing! You're still a child!"

"A child am I," she replied grimly. She grabbed his hand and held it firmly against her breast. Through the thin gown he could feel the nipple harden against his palm. "Now tell me I am a child, Michael Flynn!"

Almost without his volition, his other arm encircled her and his thigh sought the meeting of hers. She made a noise between a sigh and a whimper and squirmed still closer to him. Her hand stroked his side and flank, sending waves of sensation through him that left him dizzy. His fingers closed over the breast so generously offered and squeezed, drawing another sigh from her, then his hand moved slowly, almost reluctantly, down over the smooth waist of her silk gown.

They froze, immobilized by the sound of footsteps in the hall outside. A treble voice called, "Bridget! Bridget! Come out, Bridget, it's time for another game!"

"Oh rats!" cried Bridget, and began to adjust her clothing.

In February Patrick came to Liam to tell him that he and Margaret were expecting a child in late summer. Margaret was with Edith, with the same news. Liam was delighted. He offered Patrick congratulations and a cigar, then said expansively, "You know, with Mary's child due in April and yours in the summer, I expect that 1883 will go down in my memory as the year of the grandchildren."

He was to remember those words ruefully.

A few weeks later, Michael knocked on the door to his study one evening after supper. Liam had noticed that the lad seemed distracted and moody, and expected that he had something to get off his chest. At that age it was almost certainly girl trouble of one sort or another.

Whatever it was, he had trouble getting it out. He cleared his throat twice, squeaked, and made three false starts, until Liam was moved to say, "Take your time, son. It can't be that bad, now can it?"

Michael swallowed, squared his shoulders, and said, "Sir, I've come to ask you for the hand of your daughter in marriage."

"What, Biddy?"

"Yes, sir."

Liam was dumbstruck. He thought of Michael so much as a son that the idea of him in connection with one of the girls had never crossed his mind. Even now, when he was forced to think of it, it had a faintly unwholesome flavor to it. He temporized. "She's still a child."

"She's seventeen. Patrick's wife was only a few months older when they wed."

"Yes, but . . . See here, Mick, you're like a son to me, and I've no objection in the world to you as a son-in-law. But you and Biddy are both young, too young maybe to know your own minds. I'd not have you tied in wedlock out of childish friendship, to learn later that it was a mistake. Come to me in a year or so, if you've still a mind to, and you'll have my blessing gladly."

He expected the boy to thank him and go. Instead he turned brick-red and started to stammer. A suspicion began to grow in Liam's mind. Michael confirmed it.

"I'm sorry, sir, but I don't think we should wait. We should wed as soon as possible."

Liam exploded. "You ungrateful gossoon! Have you no shame, to be seducing my daughter, her that you've played with since she was born? What viper have I been nursing at my bosom these many years? I should take a horsewhip to you, aye, and to her as well for making herself your doxy!"

Michael reddened further, and the veins stood out on his neck, but he held his ground. "You've a right to be angry, but you've no right to call Bridget names," he said firmly. "The fault is mine, if fault it is, for we love each other and want to marry."

"*Have* to marry, you mean!"

"That, yes, but the desire was first. If we anticipated the service, it's not the first time such a thing has happened, nor will it be the last, I'm sure."

Liam recalled certain episodes from his own past and was silent.

"I won't ask your blessing," Michael continued earnestly, "though we dearly want it, the both of us. But will you consent?"

"Is it a choice you're giving me?" said Liam bitterly. He regretted the words the moment he saw the hurt on the lad's face. He saw in it the faces of Tom, and of darling Maura, and of his own sweet Maíre, all inexpressibly dear to him, all gone forever. Would he now, through his own stiff-necked pride, drive their last living remnant away from him?

He pushed himself up out of his chair and crossed to where Michael sat. The boy tensed his body, not knowing what to expect, and flinched when Liam's hand closed on his shoulder. However hard he found it, he repeated his vow not to resist. He would not add that to his list of sins.

"Come, lad," Liam said, "accept my blessing and forget the hard words my anger spawned. You took me by surprise, that's all. I wish you joy. Now go, and bring Biddy to me."

Robert's posthumous son was born on the last day of March and was christened Kieran. Maggie, who had nursed his father as well, muttered that the babe was the image of Robert and just as fey. Most of the care of the child fell to her, for Mary Doherty was wan and weak from the delivery, and did not strengthen as the weeks went past.

Margaret's child was a boy as well. She and Patrick chose the names James Francis, which had the virtue, in Margaret's eyes, of sounding no more Irish than they had to. She had suggested George, but after seeing the look of disbelief on her husband's face she withdrew it and agreed to his choices.

Names turned out to be a source of difficulty for Bridget and Michael as well. Doubly so, for in late September Bridget gave birth to twins, a boy and a girl. She wanted to call the girl Delia, after the heroine of some novel she had loved, and Michael, who had no strong preferences in the matter, agreed. But for the boy, she insisted, with tears in her eyes, on Thomas. The name sent a superstitious shudder through Michael, but she claimed that it was after his father. He did not dare remind her of that more recent Thomas, her little brother who had drowned, and in the end he could not resist her pleas. She usually got her way with him, sooner or later.

IV

Then should music, stealing
All the soul of feeling,
To thy heart appealing,
Draw one tear from thee;
Then let mem'ry bring thee
Strains I used to play thee—
Oh! then remember me.

—Thomas Moore

17

O'DONNELL FOR CONGRESS, the banner read, and under it in smaller letters, *The People's Voice—The People's Choice*. Liam was rather proud of that, since he had thought up the slogan himself. He sat back in his seat and crossed his legs. Oliver Graves, the alderman who was giving the introduction, was a long-winded old so-and-so and wouldn't wind up for at least five minutes more. He was droning on now about Federal pensions, and he could be counted on to bring up President Harrison's support for the McKinley Tariff Act as well.

Liam glanced around and caught Margaret's eye. She smiled graciously and nodded. Anyone looking at her would think that Patrick was running for President instead of Congress and that he was a sure winner instead of a long shot. She condescended so beautifully to everyone, including Patrick's most important

supporters, that they forgot to be resentful until afterwards.

Still and all, she had given Patrick two fine sons.
They were sitting on either side of her, looking very
solemn and uncomfortable in short pants, velvet jack-
ets, and shirts with wide lace collars. James, at nine,
was taking an interest in everything—the elaborate
electric chandeliers that hung from the ceiling, the
statues of mythological heroes who contorted their
bodies to hold up the boxes along the sides of the
theater, even old Graves and his "few words" on the
subject of the tariff. Terence, the five-year-old, was
another matter. Margaret still refused to cut his hair,
which fell in dark red curls to his collar and framed
a face that was disturbingly beautiful on a little boy.
He knew it too. He accepted the cooing and petting of
all the ladies as calmly as a little duke. Those who did
not make much of him—and his grandfather was one
—he had no interest in. It was Liam's view that young
Terry had all the makings of a spoiled brat, in fact, but
he had sense enough to keep quiet on the subject when
Patrick or Margaret was around. Edith was the only
one he shared his opinion with.

He twisted his head. She was sitting two rows back
with Michael and Bridget. Delia and Kieran were with
them, whispering and giggling and paying no attention at all to the adult proceedings going on around
them. It was odd how much the two looked alike—
the same dark hair and dark blue eyes and small pert
nose in the middle of a roundish face. A stranger seeing them would take them for twins. Did Delia ever
think of poor Tommy? It was four years since he died,

half a lifetime for her. She had been inconsolable at the time, but green bones mend quickly.

The whole clan was there except Veronica. Liam shook his head in rueful amusement at the thought. He still did not quite believe that his quiet, serious little girl with the serious green eyes had gone off to get married to a wealthy young banker, the scion of a prominent New York family. Mrs. Robert Tyrone, she was now, and had vellum calling-cards engraved by Tiffany's to prove it. Robert was a decent fellow at heart, but he had all the stupid complacency and limited horizons of his class. Try as he would, Liam could not understand what Veronica saw in him. But then he had the same difficulty with Patrick's choice of a mate. According to Edith, parents rarely fathomed their children's marriages, because they knew them too well as children to understand them as adults.

Graves was finally running down. ". . . a native of our fair community, formed by its fertile fields and noble river; a man who has done his share, nay, more than his share, to build the arteries and veins that bring the golden stream of commerce to our stores and factories; a husband; a father; a stalwart and faithful Democrat: Ladies and gentlemen, our next Congressman, the Honorable Patrick O'Donnell!"

The applause was gratifyingly loud, though there were not many cheers. Patrick stepped to the podium and waved to the audience. To Liam he looked as though he would rather have been at home. As the applause died down, he took the text of his address from his pocket and spread it on the lectern.

"My friends—"

"GO HOME, YA MICK BASTARD!"

Half a dozen eggs sailed toward the platform. One struck Patrick on the shoulder and spattered yolk on his cheek. While the "honor guard," ten burly railway trackmen, escorted the most aggressive of the hecklers to the door, he took a handkerchief from his pocket and calmly wiped his cheek. "My friends—"

Loud boos from several places around the hall. An overripe tomato hit the back wall, leaving a blotch that reminded Liam of a wet Rhode Island hen. The honor guard split into three squads and elbowed through the crowd to the trouble spots. The disruption spread. Liam could see three fights between Patrick's supporters and the hecklers, and around each a circle of bystanders was shouting and trying to scramble away while the guards tried to force their way to the center. A rush to the exits could start at any moment, with a real danger of panic and injuries.

Patrick found a gavel and pounded it loudly on the podium. Those nearest the platform looked toward him. He motioned them to sit down. Surprisingly, most of them did. As he continued to bang the gavel, more and more of the audience resumed their seats. Soon the only sound was the grunting from three little knots of men that moved erratically toward the doors. As the last of the toughs was helped outside, Patrick raised his text over his head and ripped it in half.

"What just took place has given me more to say than I expected," he said. "Some people seem to think that I can be coerced into silence. They are mistaken. I will not be intimidated. One of the great gifts of the founding fathers is the freedom to speak our minds without fear or favor, and those who would try to rob us of that gift are un-American to the core. Those ruffians who just left us—with some assistance—think that they are acting because my father came to this land from Ireland. I despise them for that, but I pity them also. They do not know that they are merely puppets, dancing to the tune of the railway barons and the great trusts, but so it is. The combinations that are bleeding us white fear one thing more than any other: exposure. Once the American people see them for the leeches they are, they will rise up and say with one voice: No more!"

He continued in this vein, completely *ex tempore*, for another ten minutes, then sat down to enthusiastic applause. But Liam noticed that Alderman Graves looked like his name, and that a number of the more important men in the party were barely applauding.

Patrick noticed too, and spoke of it to him later that evening. "I'm afraid the fogies have decided that I am a Red," he said cheerfully, "and Father Coughlin as well. I thought that Ollie Graves would choke when I attacked the railway barons. He's Harriman's man, you know."

"I know," Liam replied, "but I wasn't sure that you did. Why then did you speak as you did?"

"I was mad. It's that simple. And I was right, you know. Those thugs were not acting on their own, they were organized."

"You do realize that without the party organization and the Church behind you, you haven't a chance?"

Patrick scowled. "I haven't a chance *with* them either. And I'll tell you, Da, tonight was the first fun I've had in a month or more. For the next three weeks I mean to do exactly as I said—speak my mind without fear or favor, and Devil take the hindmost!"

The increasingly radical flavor to Patrick's speeches hurt him with the more respectable elements of the community, but not nearly so much as a series of articles by Liam's old adversary, John Tyler Morton. Morton came out of retirement to write a history of Tammany corruption in his most sensational popular style. Every page was sprinkled liberally with Irish names, of course. Most damaging, Morton had somehow uncovered Liam's family ties, by way of the Flynns, with the late Tammany boss Pat Malone. He was careful to make no direct accusations, but he pounded away at the connection and pointed out every contract Liam's companies had ever had with any Democratic administration in New York or Albany. The implication was obvious to everyone.

By election day, Patrick's support had dwindled alarmingly, and he ran well behind the rest of the ticket. He pretended to take the loss philosophically. In a sense, he *was* undisturbed by it, for somewhere in the course of the campaign—perhaps on the night of the disrupted rally—he had realized that he disliked politics and had no desire to be in Congress. He had run because Margaret was ambitious for him, and because his father yearned to see an Irish-American triumph over the jokes and slights and intolerance he had suffered most of his life. Well, it hadn't been a triumph, but a defeat, and for Margaret's sake, and Liam's sake, he was sorry for it. For himself, there was still a week or two of good hunting left before winter set in.

Liam was bitter. He had given his adopted country

a chance to reward his loyalty and enterprise, and he had received a slap instead. Patrick's defeat swung his mind to an idea that he had been playing with for some time: to pay a visit to Ireland. The business was in good hands with Michael and Patrick, and he could afford the time and the expense. A trip would also be a perfect way to launch the project he had been working on in secret for years. This was nothing less than to gather and publish a compendium of the traditional music of Ireland. *All* the traditional music of Ireland.

He talked the idea over with Edith, of course, and was surprised to find that she liked it. He was further surprised when she made it clear that she did not intend to go along with him. "I've never liked traveling," she said, "and I don't want to be away from the grandchildren for so long a time."

Liam argued, and in truth the idea of being away from her for so long a time disturbed him, but a part of him saw her decision as fitting. Edith was the center of his life in America, but she had no share in that earlier life that was destroyed by the Famine. He was not sure what he was going in search of, but he knew instinctively that she would hold him back. Even something as simple as staying at a pub until closing time to collect tunes would be harder if he knew she was waiting alone in a nearby hotel.

Though he reached his decision in December, he did not carry it out until spring. He had heard too many tales about the North Atlantic in winter to dare it. The journey, aboard the American Line steamship *New York*, was both comfortable and quick. Before he could fully appreciate the ironic and awful contrast with his last voyage, the liner was entering the Mersey. Liam had no wish to see old sights in Liverpool, or to stay on English soil a second longer than he had to. He boarded the ferry to Dublin that evening.

Odd as it seemed, he had never seen Dublin before. The next morning he took a room for the night at the Royal Hibernian Hotel, then took a long walk along the Liffey, past the huge Guinness brewery, and across the river to Phoenix Park. After lunch, and a pint of draught Guinness, he strolled along Grafton Street and peered into the fashionable shops, then wandered through Trinity College. He was disappointed to find the library closed, for he had hoped to get a look at the famous Book of Kells. After gazing at a few of the Georgian mansions in the neighborhood of Merrion Square, he found his way back to the hotel.

He was surprised at how tired he was by his day of sightseeing but decided to blame it on the pints of stout he had taken in pubs along the way. Another surprise: in America his accent instantly marked him as Irish, but here they knew at once that he was from America. Apparently his adopted land had changed him in more ways than he knew. Everyone he spoke to had relatives in America and was astonished that he didn't know them, but he could understand that. He doubted if all of Dublin contained as many people as New York's Sixth Ward.

After supper he sought out a pub that was said to have fine music, but it was insipid stuff, molded for the ears of English tourists, and he went back to bed at an early hour.

In the morning he took an express train from Broadstone Station bound for Galway. For the first fifty miles the line ran along the banks of the Royal Canal through a green and fertile land like none he had ever seen, but at Mullingar he had to change to a local train that would carry him through Longford and Carrick to Sligo town. The route crossed the spine of the Iron Mountains before dropping down into Connacht, and what impressed him most was not the stern grandeur of the scenery, but the emptiness of the land. He had been to Carrick as a boy, and he recalled that every mountainside was divided into small plots of cultivation. Now only a few tumbledown stone walls remained to show where potato fields once flourished, and the sons and daughters of those who built the walls and tilled the fields were far away in Canada and America and Australia.

The same impression awaited him in Sligo. The Iron Man, a huge statue of a sailor, still stood on his rock in the bay, pointing to the safe channel, but little else was the same. The Ormsbys, or their successors, had turned thousands of acres into sheep runs. The cottage where Liam was born was gone, and the land changed so thoroughly that he could hardly tell where it had stood. He took a gloomy satisfaction in seeing that Cummen House, the Ormsby mansion, was also a roofless ruin. Its window holes stared blindly across the strand toward the bay, where crews were building a gravel road across the tidal flats to Coney Island. Liam studied their work with professional interest and decided that it would be buried beneath the sands in twenty years or less. He did not pass on this judgment.

Wherever he went he got into conversations, and

he never failed to ask after the best musicians in the area. In that way he met a good fiddler, and a fine piper, and several others who were not quite on the same level. He asked each of them to teach him their favorite tunes, which he then took down in notation. All were willing, even enthusiastic, but soon he found that all their time was spent learning traditional tunes from *him*. The Famine had not only killed a million people or more, it had all but destroyed an ancient culture. If he wanted to record his people's musical heritage, he would do as well or better going to Boston or Chicago as Donegal or Kerry.

He said as much to a dark, intense young man he encountered on the headland above the beach at Rosses Point.

"It may be so," the young man replied diffidently. "Sadly, I have no ear for music myself, but I know the old tales are passing from the minds of the people as well. How many now recall the story of Diarmaid and Gráinne, that ended not five miles from where we stand?"

"You are a scholar?" Liam said respectfully.

"In my way, perhaps," he laughed, "but not as the academy knows scholars. No, I am a poet, but a task I have set myself is to bring the legends of the Celt to the people of today. It is not the same as learning them at your mother's knee, but it is better than having them forgotten altogether."

"Wonderful! Has any of this been published yet?"

Two spots of pink appeared on the poet's swarthy cheeks. "Yes, a book of poems called *The Wanderings of Oisin,* and then last year a volume called *The Countess Cathleen.*" Liam took out his pocketbook to write down the titles, and his companion added, "My name is Yeats. Willie Yeats."

Liam looked up. "There was a Yeats at Drumcliff when I was a lad."

"My great-grandfather. You may have known my mother as well, Susan Pollexfen that was."

Liam chuckled. "Not I, but I sailed on one of her da's schooners as far as Liverpool, on my way to America. You might ask your mother if she knew my friend Willie Orne; he moved in such circles."

Yeats was inclined to take offense at the older man's offhand, almost disrespectful, way of referring to someone of the stature of his grandfather William Pollexfen. Then he recalled that he had spent most of his life in America. Americans, it was well known, were aggressively democratic in their speech. In any case, he was having difficulty placing his companion socially. Accent, so useful in dealing with the English, was no help at all. The man's vocabulary was extensive and well-chosen, reflecting both education and reading. As for his clothes, the fabrics were fine and costly, but the cut was outlandish. He might be one of those American millionaires one step away from the bog, but he might also be something more notable. His ambition to gather the melodies of the people had a certain grandeur to it; the poet found himself wishing once again that music were not a forbidden territory for him.

Liam sensed the withdrawal in the young man's silence. "I'll look for these books then," he said. "And I wish you success in saving the old tales. I once knew a grand poem of five hundred lines on Laeghaire McCrimthann's visit to the land of the sídhe, that I had from Sean McLynn, my old teacher. But I don't know that I could English it even if I recalled it all. Good day then, Mister Yeats, a pleasure to meet you."

As he strode off toward Sligo, the young men realized that he did not know his name or dwelling, and he wondered if a treasure had just sifted through his fingers.

From Sligo, Liam traveled north into Donegal, then south through Mayo and Galway to Limerick and Kerry. He saw some fine, stirring scenery, and he met some fine musicians and learned some fine new tunes. But as the end of his tour drew near, he realized that he still stood by the conclusion he had stated to the young poet at Rosses Point. The old culture of Ireland was dying.

Saddest of all was the fall of the ancient tongue. Before the Hunger, Gaelic had been the first language of half the people or more. Now it seemed confined to Connacht, and was dying even there. Liam knew from articles in the Irish papers of New York that the authorities had mounted a great campaign to make school children speak nothing but English, but he had never dreamed that their parents would go along with it. Yet more than one person he addressed in Gaelic refused to admit that they knew the language, though he saw in their faces that they understood him perfectly.

In Cork he came across a pamphlet of a speech by a young man named Douglas Hyde. The title was "The Necessity of De-Anglicizing Ireland," and the speaker was concerned by exactly the trends that had bothered Liam. Some of his suggestions—such as going back to homespun knee-breeches—sounded cranky, but the spirit of his protest was just what Liam felt the country needed. A few days later Liam read that Hyde was starting an organization to reawaken the Gaelic tongue. One of his last acts in Ireland, before going to Queenstown to board the steamer for New York, was to send a contribution to the newly formed Gaelic League.

18

Jim O'Donnell took a chair in the back room, near the corner of the room, and wiped his damp palms on the legs of his knickerbockers. He had been coming to the seisuins at Granddad's house since he started having them, after he came home from Ireland. Once a month—or oftener if somebody special, like the great piper Patsy Toohy, was passing through town—all the Irish musicians for miles around assembled at the O'Donnell house for a night of playing, drinking, and exchanging tunes. Those who were from out of town stayed the night, too, and sometimes a seisuin went on through a whole weekend.

Most months there were six or eight players and twice that number of listeners, enough to fill the big parlor without crowding it. Jim was one of the most faithful of the listeners. But tonight was different. Tonight he was changing sides. For a couple of years he had been joining in on bones or bodhrán now and then, but tonight he was really going to *play*. His fiddle was in its case, tucked under his seat. When the moment came, he would pick it up and play "Farewell to Ireland" with all the rolls and cranns and double-stops, and when he was done he would be one of them, one of the players. He would be a *musician*—unless his hands were too sweaty to play.

Liam had started teaching him to play three years before, when Jim was eleven. Liam happened to be walking by Patrick's house when he heard the strains of "Stack of Barley" coming from the backyard. Some of the notes were very unusual, but he couldn't mistake the basic tune. He strolled back to see where it was coming from and found Jim tootling away on a tin whistle. He stopped abruptly when he saw Liam.

"Well, gossoon, and who was it taught you that?" Liam demanded.

His grandson looked scared. "Nobody, sir. I asked Mister O'Rourke to lend me a whistle. He didn't mind, he said."

"And did he show you where the notes were and all?"

"Oh no, sir. I didn't want to bother him. I just found them, that's all. But some of them sound funny."

"And the tune? Where did that come from?"

"I don't know, out of my head I guess. Something isn't right about it, though. It's like my wind-up train: just when I think it's going well, it seems to jump the track."

Liam chuckled. "I've had the same happen to me in my day. But tell me, Seamus *á gra*, how would you like to come up to the house an afternoon or so to learn the ways of your instrument and maybe a few tunes in the bargain?"

The boy's eyes widened until they seemed to engulf his face. "*Could I?* Really? Oh boy! Can I learn to play fiddle too? Like you?"

"Not in one afternoon, you can't. But we can start you on it, to see if you like it. I'll speak to your parents, to tell them what we plan."

"Oh yes, please!" He flung himself at Liam, who tousled his fine sandy hair. "Thank you, Granddad! Can I start today? I can show you some other tunes too!"

Liam's mood as he walked slowly up the hill was mixed. He rejoiced, because he thought he saw in his grandson a kindred spirit, and he reproached himself because he had not seen it sooner. Liam himself had first held a fiddle when he was barely three, and here Jim was—what?—eleven or twelve? All those wasted years! How had it happened?

As he thought about it, he realized that he had been affected by the same tendencies he had seen and hated in Ireland. When his own children showed little interest in his music, he accepted that as normal. After all, the music was Irish, and they were Americans, why should they care that much? Even his great project was meant only to preserve the old music, to keep it from being lost forever. The idea that it could still *live*, that someone of his grandson's generation could love it just as he himself did, had not crossed his mind.

It was the same with the language. Each year he sent a check to the Gaelic League, but his own children and grandchildren knew hardly a word beyond a few endearments. He had simply assumed that they would not be interested. And indeed they might not have been, but he hadn't even tried them. He decided to raise the idea of lessons with Kieran and Jim; he knew that Hyde's organization was starting to publish simple readers and other materials that he could use with them.

And now, three years later, he was ready to sit back and enjoy the fruits of his labors. He loved to see the expressions on the faces of guests of his generation, when Jim or Kieran addressed them in their mother-tongue, and he was looking forward to the remarks tonight when Jim finished playing "Farewell to Ireland." The boy had a gift, no question about that. As the musicians and audience drifted into the parlor for the seisuin, Liam continued to turn over in his mind an idea that had recently come to him, a plan in which young Jim had an important role.

Margaret twisted a handkerchief in her hands and wished she had a small medicinal dose of brandy. "Are you sure that you don't mind wasting your summer this way?" she said to Jim. "I know your grandfather can be very stubborn when he gets an idea in his head."

"He's cracked!" Terence called from the next room.

"Don't be disrespectful of your elders," his mother said perfunctorily. "It's a lot to ask," she continued to her older son, "but he does want you along, and I'm not sure at his age he should be allowed to roam all over the country alone."

"Mother, you don't understand," said Jim, just managing to keep the exasperation out of his voice.

"I *want* to go! I can't think of anything in the world I'd rather do!"

"Well, there's no accounting for tastes, that's all. The idea of traveling around to spend time with a lot of low, ignorant old drunkards is beyond me. I know your grandfather was a poor immigrant himself, but I would have thought that the position and advantages he has won would have refined him more than they apparently have. In the end, breeding tells. I only hope that you don't catch his vulgar tastes from him."

Jim was wise enough to say nothing. The important thing was that his mother had agreed to let him go off with Granddad for a two-month tour of the United States. They were planning to go to every city where Irish immigrants had settled in large numbers, and seek out those musicians of the Famine generation who still survived. Jim had been practicing for months, taking down tunes as Liam played them. He still needed to hear a fast reel six or eight times through to get it, but most jigs and hornpipes he could transcribe in two or three repeats. Not the ornaments, of course, which usually changed from one repeat to the next anyway, but the bones of the tune.

In half a century, Liam had gotten to know a great many traditional musicians. Now he wrote to them, explaining what he was planning and asking their co-operation. The replies were prompt and enthusiastic. Everyone, it seemed, had been waiting and hoping for someone to gather the old music together. Liam and Jim spent hours with the stack of letters and a railway map of the United States, planning an itinerary that took them from Boston and Portland, Maine, west through Buffalo, Cleveland and Detroit to Chicago, then south through St. Louis all the way to New Orleans. Liam wanted to include the West Coast, but after studying the timetables they realized that it wasn't sensible if they wanted to spend any amount of time in each place.

In later years, Jim remembered that summer as a strange amalgam of smoky bars and parish halls, of tenement rooms and stuffy lace-curtained parlors and one or two sumptuous mansions. The thread that ran through all of it was the music. He heard fiddles and flutes and uillean pipes, tinwhistles, slidewhistles, accordeons, and concertinas, mandolins and banjos and guitars, and even an enormous walnut Chickering grand piano. By the time he and Liam returned to Newburgh, they had over four hundred new tunes and variants in their luggage. They had heard many times that number, of course, but most of them were already in Liam's collection.

Just as important, they had gotten to know each other in a way that even weekly lessons and daily contact had not provided. For Jim, his grandfather was a living link to a world that no longer existed—the world of old Erin, of Famine and coffin ships, of help-wanted signs that said "No Irish." And for Liam, the boy was his legacy to the future, his guarantee that the struggles and suffering of his generation would not be forgotten utterly. If observers found them a curious pair—the man of seventy and the boy of fourteen, each with a fiddle case in his hand, each as enthusiastic as the other—no one who saw them could overlook the love between them.

Ian Kavanaugh

* * *

"Liam O'Donnell, put down those papers and look at me! *Why* do you insist on going all the way to Cornwall in the middle of December? Have you no sense at all?"

"Faith, no," he said with a grin, "or I'd not have married a scold! And as to why I am going, Timothy O'Rourke is an old friend and it's his only granddaughter that is getting wed, and it's only a matter of five miles or so. And I've a fancy to play once more before the century ends."

"Some say it ended last January."

"Then I've a fancy to play once more in the first year of the new century. And Tim has promised that an old friend of his from Galway, who is living now in the wilds of Canada, will be there."

"Another fiddler, I suppose," said Edith in a resigned voice.

Liam looked abashed. "No, harper. It's been a long time since I've heard a decent harper."

"Will you be taking Jim with you?"

"I need no nursemaid."

"You need a keeper! For heaven's sake, Liam, you're over seventy and you mean to go out alone in the buggy on a dark winter night? I won't hear of it, that's all. Either you take Jim or you stay home!"

He knew that tone of voice. And in fact, he was not sorry to have his grandson's company on the drive. The Storm King Road was not easy in the best of weather, even though sections of it had been built by O'Donnell & Co.; and Fred, their bay horse, had been a bit skittish lately. On the trip down, though, he behaved himself like a gentleman.

O'Rourke's house was already full of guests, but he saw Liam and Jim arrive and came over with open arms. "I was after telling me niece, me sister Nora's girl, that the party would start when you were here, and here you are." He gestured across the room. "A dropeen to take the cold from your bones, and hot lemonade for the lad, eh, Jim? I tell me friends that you play as well as you do because I passed the spell along in lending you that whistle all those years ago! Liam hasn't an excuse like that, does he now? Then you must meet Dermot, he that I told you of. He's longing to hear you play."

"And I to hear him," Liam replied. "You mentioned a drop of something?"

As it turned out, O'Rourke's harper friend did not have a very large repertoire, but Liam was more than happy because it included two planxties by Turlough O'Carolan that he had never heard. He returned the favor by playing a couple of O'Carolan compositions that Dermot didn't know. A little later in the evening, O'Rourke cleared a space in the back parlor for dancing. Liam and Jim played together while the guests skipped through the evolutions of country reels and jigs or stood on the sidelines and clapped. The room grew uncomfortably warm, but the dancers mopped their brows and clamored for more. It was Jim who finally insisted that Liam stop playing. The hour was late, and Grandmother would be expecting them home.

He helped Liam into his fur driving coat and thick fur gauntlets. There was a buffalo laprobe in the buggy, and a rubber storm apron that fastened to the dash. As he was lighting the two sidelamps, he glanced up at the sky. The moon was in the west, glinting through high, fast-moving clouds. Jim shivered and climbed up onto the seat to take the reins.

Lulled by the clip-clop of Fred's hooves on the hard-packed road, Liam nodded off. Jim saw in the faint glow of the lamps that his face sagged with tiredness. He wished that he had insisted on leaving earlier, but he knew that the result would have been the same. His grandfather was accustomed to doing things his own way and was not easily led.

A gust of wind rocked the light buggy and sleet stung Jim's cheek. He shook the reins, but Fred would not be goaded into a faster pace. Granddad was murmuring in his sleep, but he couldn't make out the words.

They were nearly in town when a bolt of lightning turned the night blindingly white. Fred whinnied in terror and started to run. Jim pulled frantically on the reins, but the afterimage of the lightning still burned red on his retinas and he could not see the road. The buggy bounced from one side to the other, its motions multiplying the horse's panic. Liam was awake now, holding on grimly while his grandson fought to bring the carriage to a stop. Suddenly, with a stomach-churning lurch, the off rear wheel dropped into the ditch. Fred whinnied again and lunged against the increased drag. A moment later the traces snapped and the bay horse galloped away, leaving the buggy half-suspended over the ditch.

After a short, shaken silence, Liam said, "We'd best start walking, Seamus *a grá*. Will you carry the fiddles?"

The sleet was falling faster, mixed with freezing

rain that clung to their faces and coats and made each footstep treacherously slick. They trudged along in silence. After a few minutes Jim took his grandfather's arm. He was dismayed when Liam failed to protest.

Lanterns bobbed in the street ahead. Alarmed when the horse trotted home alone, Edith had sent Michael and the servants out with umbrellas and blankets to look for them. In a short while the two were sitting near the fire, wrapped up like Christmas parcels, sipping steaming cocoa. It was a measure of Edith's distress that she didn't once say "I told you so."

The next morning Liam's forehead was hot and he seemed to be having difficulty breathing. He insisted that all he needed was a day in bed, but when he was no better by evening, Edith sent for Doctor Barrett, who came around after supper. He examined Liam, joked with him, prescribed weak tea with a dash of whiskey in it, and promised to stop by the next day.

Edith could hardly sleep that night. Every breath Liam took rasped like a dull saw, and between breaths he muttered constantly. She finally turned the task of watching him over to one of the maids and went off to Bridget's old room to get some rest. Liam had always been hardy, surely he would throw off this cold in another day or so.

He was no better the next day. If anything, he seemed weaker. The fear she had been denying clutched Edith's heart tighter. The hours seemed endless until the doctor arrived and went upstairs, and the time he was gone lasted forever. When he returned, his face was grave.

"It's as I feared," he said, taking Edith's hand. "The inflammation has spread to his lungs."

She stared across the room. "Pneumonia, you mean?"

"Yes, I'm sorry."

"What can we do for him?"

"Keep him comfortable, that's all. If I were you, I would wire Veronica to come."

"I see." She struggled to keep her voice level. "Yes, I'll do that tonight. She can take a train in the morning. Is that . . . how long do you think. . . ."

"It's difficult to say. A day or two, perhaps. He may surprise us yet—he's survived a lot in his time."

In the town below, all the bells were ringing to welcome in the new year. Liam heard them, and wondered if they were one more fraud by his fever. His elbows and knees ached, and every breath felt as though it was less than he needed. It was hot under the blankets, but when he tried to toss them off, they were mysteriously replaced.

He opened his eyes. They were all in the room— Patrick, and Michael and Bridget, and Jim and Kieran, and even Veronica. When he saw her, he knew. He did not need to see Doctor Barrett's expression, or the two runnels of tears on Edith's face. They would not have fetched Ronnie up unless they expected the worst.

He reached for Edith's hand and patted it. "Don't cry, a *stóirín*," he murmured. "*Dá fhaid lá, tigeann oidhche.* However long the day, it ends with night." He tried to smile, but he was too tired. As he looked at her, he did not see an elderly lady who had given birth to six children and suffered the bitterness of outliving three of them. He saw a girl, almost a child, who clasped the railing before her while the sea breeze toyed with her blond curls, who listened with every fibre of her being as he played "The Trip to Sligo."

He could hear the melody still, if he closed his eyes.